"There is no doubt that Simon Maginn's books are disturbing and can be shocking. Sadly, there are no genres called 'disturbing' or 'shocking,' so his books will still have to be shelved under horror."
—WRITING MAGAZINE

"[one of] the bright young things of British horror fiction. It almost seems incorrect to label this a horror novel at all...massively unsettling...unusual and well-researched...this author is indeed one to watch."
—THE BIG ISSUE

"A simple scenario reveals complexities that touch on the myth of identity, loneliness, redemption and the purity of loving murder. The casual prose flips devastating stings, touching real nerves; the tale terrifies because we know that even if the resolution is upbeat, any show of joy will be merely laughter in the dark."
—TIME OUT

"a striking story of loneliness and not belonging...Not a book for the squeamish, and don't read it while eating your dinner."
—INSIGHT MAGAZINE

# VIRGINS and MARTYRS

a novel,

simon maginn.

| *virgins and martyrs* | *simon maginn* |
| *cover design & layout* | *larry s. friedman* |

*Virgins and Martyrs*
Copyright ©1995 by Simon Maginn.

Borealis is an imprint of White Wolf Publishing.

**PRINTED IN CANADA**

White Wolf Publishing
780 Park North Boulevard
Suite 100
Clarkston, GA 30021

*for my mother, Win,*
*and my late father, Jerome,*
*with love and affection*

WHITE WOLF PUBLISHING

BOREALIS

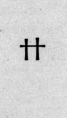

### *acknowledgments.*

All sorts of people have helped in all sorts of ways with this book, and I'd like to thank them. In no particular order they are: Michael Pompey, Sarah Jack, Jeanne Day, David Anderson, John Brendan O'Grady, Andrew Maginn, Daniel Livingstone, and Eileen Hughes. Thanks again to my editor Averil Ashfield for her endless patience. Particular thanks to Hugh Fisher for ideas and comments, for suggesting the word "cumbersomely," and for giving me the last line.

I need scarcely premise that the moral as well as the physical facts developed in the course of this enquiry are often exceedingly loathsome.

–"Interments in Towns,"
    Poor Law Commissioners Health Report
    Supplement,
    1843

The night before he moved into No. 8, Daniel had a dream.

He was looking at an orange that was on the table in front of him, in bright, flat light. As he watched a curious thing happened: the orange started to shrivel, to dry up. The skin, at first glossy and taut, became slacker, duller; the color faded; a region to the left-hand side took on a shadowy, unquiet quality, which turned into a bruise, the orange skin turning to brown, then black. There was a flattening of the shape, as if the orange were falling in on itself under its own weight. Finally the blackening skin split open along cracks like the pattern on an Easter egg, and from inside oozed out a vile white fluid, which crept over the surface of the hideous rotting thing.

He reached out his hand—

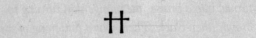

PART

# one

## THE DISSECTING-ROOM FEVER

### chapter one

The headline was so big it hurt his eyes: "Do you need a hand, Officer?" Below it was a picture of himself, a picture that had clearly been specially selected to make him look completely idiotic, and a caption: "Detective Inspector Outhwaite: 'There are no leads at present.'"

His phone had been ringing all morning; later in the day he was going to have to go upstairs "to discuss the progress of the case." He had been advised not to speak to the press, beyond repeating what he'd been saying since April, that the case was still open, that no one was currently being held, that inquiries were continuing.

He shoved the paper into a drawer and went over to the window, gazing out at the car park.

It was the same paper that had first given the case its name: "The Lady of the Lake." That was the fiercely independent local press for you. Give them a dismembered limb, and they turned it into Arthurian legend. Hardly surprising, considering what they were able to do with a mistreated cat (Find These Evil Tabby Torturers!) or even a young girl who could tap dance (Michelle Turns the Talent On Full!).

An arm had been found washed up on the beach. It belonged to a woman; it, or she, or in all likelihood both, had been dead for a considerable length of time; the arm had, however, suffered comparatively little water damage and could not have been in the sea for more than a day or two. It must, therefore, have been kept somewhere else for some time before being found.

Kept.

The palm of the hand had been pierced, possibly by a nail or something of the kind. There was also a ring, a plain gold wedding band, on the appropriate finger. From the lividity it was clear that the ring had been put on after death. The puncture mark and the ring had been withheld from the press, in the hope of discouraging the disturbed and the insane from coming forward with disturbed, insane confessions.

And that was that. No one knew anything. It was a singularity, an isolated episode in a world of broken connections. It didn't seem to mean anything, at least not in the way Outhwaite was used to seeing meanings.

It was, in truth, an impossible case to progress, Outhwaite reflected. No identification was possible; the best that he could hope for would be the rest of the unfortunate woman's remains being washed up, or a genuine confession provoked by the publicity. Nothing had transpired, though, and Outhwaite had been forced into the humiliating position of saying that the case was still open, but unsolved, and there were no leads. Baffling, frustrating, stupid.

VIRGINS and
MARTYRS

Outhwaite pulled down one of the sharp metal strips on the Venetian blinds to get a clearer view of the hot, dusty car park. The light was flat and heavy, uninformative.

Whoever the woman was, he was certain that when she was found there would be no one to claim her, no matter how much publicity they gave her. She was, he felt, one of the lost and lonely. He would be alone at her funeral. An MDB—minimum decent burial—and a single wreath, from him. If it was a member of the public who found her, perhaps they might come, surprising themselves by the responsibility they felt for simply having tripped over her ghastly, sad, violated remains. But those who die alone, by their own or others' hands, unnoticed, unremarked, he thought, have a special dread, a particular horror. There were few who wanted to know them, own them, after death, except for the professionals whose duty it was to give them the attentions they'd been denied while still living. There would be attempts to find relations, friends, just a neighbor, just a shopowner who treated them with respect and pitied their condition, protected as they were by an impenetrable wall of loneliness, like the veil of a bride. They had an almost ritual quality about them. But it was hard, very hard, to see what meaning the ritual had. If no one came forward, then a coroner's inquiry. Often just the legal technicality of the open verdict. Death caused by death, to a person unknown. Dead Body Number—whatever. The investigation would almost certainly just be a waste of everyone's time and patience. But the dead deserved to have a little time wasted on them, like the wasted flowers, wasted prayers. It was their right.

Outhwaite returned to the desk and the phone. He knew just what he needed to get the investigation up and running. He needed a miracle.

### chapter two

"Daniel? Call for you."

Daniel jumped at the sudden voice and the banging on the door—he'd been miles away.

"OK."

"I think it's your mum."

"Coming!"

It was Ian's voice. Ian was the least objectionable of the three louts he was living with.

He had to go through the kitchen to the lounge where the phone was. They were sitting round the table, smirking like idiots. Chris, as usual, was holding forth about something, something cretinous in all likelihood, Daniel thought. They glanced at him as he passed them. Ian called out "Hiya. Y'all right?" and Daniel smiled and grunted, and shut the lounge door behind. As he

VIR$GINS and MARTYRS

picked up the phone there was a burst of laughter, and Daniel flinched. They were so *loud.*

"Hello?"

"Daniel?"

"Yes."

"Daniel? Is that you sweetheart?"

"*Yes.*" He tried to keep the annoyance out of his voice. "Yes," he said more calmly. "Hi Mum."

"Are you all right darling? You sound funny, are you OK?"

"I'm fine. Of *course* I'm all right, is there any particular reason why I shouldn't be?" He tried to make it sound like a joke, but it wasn't and didn't, and he immediately regretted the attempt. There was another outbreak of *joie de vivre* from the three in the kitchen, and Daniel clenched the phone tighter.

"I just thought I'd ring to say hello, we haven't spoken for a week or two, so I thought it'd be nice to, you know, have a chat." As usual, he'd put her on the defensive. His own mother! Why did she feel she had to apologize just for ringing up? He couldn't possibly be busy all the time, could he? If she'd left it to him to ring they'd have spoken twice a year, maximum. In a *good* year.

"So. Everything OK?"

"Yeah. Fine." There was a pause; she could hear him breathing. She forced herself not to jump in and start blathering, as she so often did. She dragged deeply on her cigarette, held, exhaled. She would unnerve him. Serve him right for being so bloody bad-mannered.

"Yeah, everything's—everything's just great down this end."

"Good."

"How about you?" His voice conveyed only the chilliest caricature of real interest, but at least he was trying.

"Oh *I'm* OK. Rehearsing, you know. We go on in three weeks, and are we *ready*? We are *not*, darling."

He couldn't remember what it was she was rehearsing for, and couldn't very well ask, she must have told him often enough.

"Oh well," he said wittily and sighed.

"And how's your thing, your what-do-you-call-it?"

"Dissertation."

"Yes. That."

"It's OK."

"Have you finished it yet sweetheart?"

"No. Not exactly. But it's clearer in my mind now. It's just a matter of, you know—"

"Knocking it into shape?"

"Yeah. Basically."

It had been basically a matter of knocking it into shape for some time now. And she hated to say it, but it sounded so *boring*, something tedious about the Middle Ages.

VIRGINS *and*
MARTYRS

In fact, she hated to say it, but she couldn't help wishing that Daniel could be a little more—what?—well, a bit more *excitable*, perhaps. Not a maniac like his adopted father, and maybe not a neurotic worrier like his adopted *mother*, but just *something*.

"And how are those wicked boys you share with?" She thought they sounded like fun, despite what Daniel said.

"Huh," said Daniel. "They're about the same, overall. Actually," and he lowered his voice, wrapped himself more tightly round the phone, "actually it's possible I might be moving out soon."

"Are you darling?" She tried to sound enthusiastic, but his words made her heart sink. She knew he wasn't happy where he was, so a move might be good; but how she longed to hear him say that he was settled, happy, getting on. She longed to hear names, girls or boys, she didn't care, just people, people he *liked*.

"Yeah I'm going to have a look later on, there's a room going in a house not far from here, just sharing with one person. There was a card up in the common room."

"That sounds nice."

"Hope so. 'Cause it gets a bit noisy here sometimes, it's hard to work, you know."

As if work was all that mattered. What about *life*?

*simon maginn*

"But you like one of the boys there don't you, what's his name again?"

"Ian? Yeah he's all right I suppose."

All right. I suppose. He was so grudging, so unimpressed by the world. Her child, the baby she'd been so determined to have that she'd battled the adoption bureaucracy for more than eighteen months, fought and argued and finally *won* him! He was the second child she'd adopted, and she loved them both with ferocity, but Daniel was the only one of the two that she still felt needed her. He seemed so helpless, somehow, floating about out there in the world. Rudderless, compass and sextant lost. And he was hers in ways that no child born to her in the usual manner could ever be, because she'd had to look for him, find him, choose him, and then wrestle him away from the implacable adoption agency and their impossible obstacle courses. She adored him, then as now, with passion, with *heat*!

And now here he was, a young adult, seemingly drifting through life without forming strong attachments to anyone, doggedly pursuing his academic interests (if you could call such deeply boring things "interests"), head down, never stopping to admire the view. I wish you had a bit more spark, she wanted to shout, I wish you could be joyful and passionate and alive! Not this neutral, tepid, all-right-I-suppose thing.

VIRGINS and
MARTYRS

She dragged on her cigarette, flicked her ash into the opulent green glass ashtray on the padded leather arm of the chair.

"Still, you can stay in touch can't you, even if you're not living there anymore. Can't you?" Almost a plea.

Daniel shrugged.

"Maybe. We haven't really got a lot in common."

The brush off, so well-rehearsed. Daniel never seemed to have anything in common.

"Anyway Mum, I better get off the phone now. I've got to get on."

"All right darling. I'll ring again soon. And Daniel, if you do move, will you *please* make sure you give me your new number?" It had been three weeks after he'd moved into where he was now before he'd remembered to inform her of the change.

"Yeah."

"Promise?"

"*Yes.*"

"OK baby. I'll leave you alone. 'Bye."

He hung up. He could hear Chris's voice bellowing in the kitchen, and had to nerve himself to go back out there. They were just so *loud*. Still, not for much longer. He hugged the thought to himself, and returned to his room, smiling benignly at them as he passed.

*simon maginn*

## chapter three

Later that day, he stood outside the door of No. 8 Adelaide Street, watching a distorted figure approaching down the hall, distorted because of the fluted glass panels in the door.

A gust of air, like a last breath, as the door opened and a faint smell, like long-dead flowers.

"Daniel? Hello, come on in."

He'd got an immediate impression of a tightly coiled, tough-looking person, taller and fuller than himself. As he followed him up the stairs to the first-floor flat, Daniel found himself fascinated by the rhythm of the legs and hips. Skinhead crop, thick neck bulging out of a white T-shirt; Daniel noticed the veins and cords in the neck.

He had been ushered into the kitchen. The interview had been conducted with polite efficiency: what do you do? where are you from? the small change of acquaintance. One or two questions that Daniel had found unexpected: are your parents still living? any close family, friends in the area? Daniel had been ashamed, but "no" to all of the above. No parents, no family. No friends. His studies kept him pretty busy, he explained soberly, he hadn't really had the time for much of a social life. He found himself explaining, almost apologetically, that his friends from his first degree at Leeds had all scattered, he hadn't kept in touch with them. He was

VIRGINS and
MARTYRS

now in the second, final, year of a Master of Arts degree at the university. Medieval History, pretty dull stuff really, he muttered, and smiled awkwardly.

"Really? Do you think so? I always found the Middle Ages positively teeming with interest," the polite skinhead had said, and Daniel had searched for a note of irony or a raised eyebrow, anything to account for his feeling of being gently mocked; there was none.

"Well yes, yes they are actually. The deeper you go, you know, the more interesting it gets." Of course Daniel thought Medieval History was interesting, he would hardly have spent the last two years studying it if he didn't, but he was surprised that anyone else did. Very surprised.

"Wicked popes and pervy bishops and all," the skinhead added, leading him on.

"Yes but what's really interesting, or I should say what *I* find particularly, uh, interesting," Daniel said, aware of how his enthusiasm impoverished his vocabulary, "is the sudden growth of the economy, and the role of the foreign banks, particularly, of course, the Italian City State banks. You know, Verona, Venice."

The skinhead smiled and nodded, and Daniel faltered and looked at his shoes. His keenness was always making a fool of him. Why on earth should this person, who if things went well would be his new flatmate, want to know about the European

*simon maginn*

economy in the late Middle Ages? Of course he didn't, for God's sake!

"Well, you know—" he said, and tailed off.

"Yes. You must know Dr. Medway?" the skinhead asked, and Daniel, surprised again, said stupidly, "Yes, do you?"

"Oh yes, I know him quite well. Well, perhaps *knew* him would be more accurate. He was my supervisor for my doctorate."

"Really?" Daniel said, amazed that this thug could have such a degree.

"Yes. That was a few years ago now. I never finished the damn thing though."

"Oh? What was your subject?" Daniel asked politely.

"Church History," said the skinhead, and Daniel was once more ambushed by the unexpectedness of this person.

"He's a brilliant man," Daniel said, and the skinhead did now raise an eyebrow, a faintly incredulous expression lighting up his face.

"Do you think so? I have to say I always found him distinctly mediocre."

"Did you?" Daniel said, and, appalled by the inadequacy of his reply, stood up.

"Yes. Anyway, you look like you'll fit in nicely here. Care for a quick tour of the house?"

Daniel looked at him, frankly astonished now. Fit in? *Nicely?*

VIRGINS and
MARTYRS

"Yes. Yes I would."

It was a typical Brighton house (except that this was Hove Actually, he reminded himself), in that it was almost entirely vertical, all stairs. Starting on the first floor (the ground floor was a loan shark's office, and something much less clear-cut than that at the back) it rose up a further three narrow stories. First floor was a kitchen and a bedroom—"my room" the skinhead said briefly. Second floor, bathroom and another bedroom, apparently empty. Third floor, two further bedrooms. To Daniel it seemed to go up into the sky.

"Your room," said the skinhead, opening a door, and there it was again, a breath on his face, tickling his hair. He was so distracted that he could take nothing in; yes, he said, I see, it's perfect, yes.

A few minutes later, arrangements finalized, he was back on the doorstep, the rolling, distorted figure disappearing down the aquarium-rippling corridor behind the fluted glass. He could move in any time. He couldn't believe it.

An hour later Daniel found himself sitting in a padded swiveling chair, looking at the back of his head as a youth with a topknot swung the mirror round behind him.

"OK?"

Daniel smiled nervously at the reflection, and

*simon maginn*

at the back of his head. He didn't know why but he'd been abruptly consumed with the desire for a haircut. Though not perhaps, he reflected, this particular one. Surely he didn't really look like that from behind? It was ridiculous.

"Er—"

The youth with the top knot swung the mirror away again, dropping it expertly, casually, onto its hook on the wall, and loosened the black nylon cape.

"Could you just… hold on…." Daniel was loath to prolong the ordeal, but he couldn't really walk out looking like this, could he? People would surely laugh and point or at least turn to look at him after he'd passed.

"I'm not sure it's quite right at the back."

The youth considered him dubiously.

"I could square it off at the bottom."

"Square it off. Yes that could be it."

The youth refastened the cape and unleashed his cut-throat razor, brandishing it like an Elizabethan assassin. In fact Daniel's conviction was that his hair needed to be longer rather than shorter, but there was presumably no point in raising that. He avoided meeting the eyes in the mirror, which had taken on the trapped, pleading look he knew only too well.

The exquisitely cold razor scratched at his neck as the youth made tiny adjustments, exaggerating his actions so as to be seen to be willing.

VIRGINS *and*
MARTYRS

"OK?"

Another pass with the mirror. Daniel made himself look. It was worse. He shifted in the omnidirectional seat and noted the ache in his fingers where they were gripping the arm-rests.

"Well I don't know."

It was twenty to four, Thursday afternoon. The youth stroked the meat of his thumb with the razor and met the anxious, evasive eyes in the mirror. The kind of eyes any experienced haircutter comes to dread.

"You want me to take some more off the back?"

"No, no, it's not that, I just—I don't know—"

Daniel squirmed in his seat, regarding himself from all angles as the youth glanced behind him at the bench of waiting people. The stylist at the adjoining chair gave him a sympathetic shrug. Radio One dribbled out among the nests of cut hair and the sweet, high smell of hair gel. Oh Christ.

"I mean if you don't want it any *shorter*… 'cause if you want it *longer*, then we're really in trouble," he said, inviting Daniel to laugh with him. Daniel frowned, torn between his desire to look and his distaste for the peculiar, shorn individual who lived in the big, well-lit mirror, along with the cocky, impatient, topknotted haircutter and the three as-yet-unclipped heads behind him, waiting. One of them coughed. The middle one of the three was

*simon maginn*

apparently asleep, head lolling against the next one's shoulder.

Daniel sat on, miserable, defiant.

Tomorrow he was going to arrive at his new house, in a taxi, with his belongings in bags and boxes; he was going to ring the doorbell and be let in by the skinhead with the interest in Church history, and he was going to have to move into a strange house with someone he'd met only once, transport his whole difficult life to this new place; and he was going to have to do it with a ridiculous haircut. Brilliant.

Actually he was amazed that he'd got the room at all. The problems at his present address had become such that he was sure his desperation would be obvious, and damning. No one was going to give a room to a desperate person. He'd rung the bell with failure deadening his fingers, and his stomach had rolled appallingly as the figure loomed up in the fluted glass of the door. But the glow of his acceptance had lasted right up until the back of his head had appeared in the youth's mirror.

"Maybe you just need to get used to it," said the youth, but his client was miles away, unfocused.

"You look like you'll fit in nicely." If the skinhead had had a secret key to Daniel's secret heart and been able to read the inscription in it, he couldn't have said anything that Daniel wanted to hear more.

VIRGINS and
MARTYRS

Those three in Montpelier Road, they just weren't his kind of person. Daniel was no snob, but they just seemed to sit around all day with the telly on and talk crap, *loudly*. They all did the same course, something unspeakably dull to do with chemistry. Ian was OK but they were never going to be bosom buddies, and Daniel had quickly withdrawn; everyone was polite and they still ate together, but that was about it.

Then one day Daniel had woken up with the absolute certainty in his head that he was in the wrong house. The relief had been overwhelming. He could wash his hands of them and try again somewhere else. Freedom!

"You look like you'll fit in nicely."

And now here he was in the hands of this handsome grinning sadist with a razor and a topknot, and he had to find some way of getting out of this chair without getting into an argument. There was clearly no point in trying to salvage anything from the haircut; what was done was done.

"Yeah, I see what you mean actually," he began, and stared down the weirdo in the mirror, frowning appreciatively now.

"Yes I like it, it's great."

Everyone in the room seemed to breathe out simultaneously.

"You're sure?"

*simon maginn*

"Yeah, really," Daniel protested, fighting with the nylon cape and swinging halfway round, almost kicking the haircutter in his urgency.

"I mean, I could maybe just trim a bit more off round the ears…."

"No, no," Daniel said, and snatched at the tissue the youth was holding out. He went to the till.

"So, how much, er."

The youth named his price, inflated because of the extra time it had taken. Daniel was fumbling in his jeans pocket—and then it happened again.

"Oh!"

His hand jerked away, and he looked, startled, at the youth, who was watching him closely. Surely not more trouble.

"Anything wrong?"

"No no no," said Daniel, who had just felt the money in his pocket *writhe*. "Er," he said, and tried again, this time managing to pull out a collection of coins. He could see at a glance there was more than enough, and handed it all quickly to the youth, who began to sort through it.

"Don't bother about the change," Daniel called, grinning his way to the door. "Thanks very much. Really," he said, and left. The as-yet-unshaven watched him frankly now, as did the haircutter; he turned to them as Daniel pulled the door shut behind him, and spread open his arms.

"OK! Who's next please!"

# VIRGINS and MARTYRS

Get a grip get a grip get a grip—

Daniel strode away, pockets now mercifully empty. It had happened earlier that day; he'd been returning home from his (successful! successful!) interview at No. 8, and had walked past one of the innumerable homeless intoning their blank mantras about change. Feeling benevolent and philanthropic, buoyed up by the imminent change in his living conditions, Daniel had put his hand in pocket and been—well, unpleasantly surprised. Shocked even, like an electric shock. No, more like delving into a pocketful of slugs. He'd pulled his hand out and looked at it, almost expecting to see silvery trail marks, but of course there was nothing.

*Yes well hardly surprising*, said someone sensible and well-informed in Daniel's head, someone like his supervising tutor Dr. Medway. *High levels of anxiety and an up-coming life-change. Curious, bizarre, even psychotic manifestations are alas all too common in highly motivated, highly stressed individuals such as yourself*, said Dr. Medway. *Wouldn't be particularly surprised if you were to start barking at the moon, if you want my honest opinion.*

He had flung the money at the beggar, who had shouted something after him, to Daniel's buzzing mind it had sounded like "You're doomed!" He had all but run.

Anyway, here he was with a new haircut and a new

*simon maginn*

place to live. Things had to be looking up. He rubbed his hands on his jeans and aimed for home.

Ian and Chris were cooking something unpleasant when he got in, cooking with more vigor and enthusiasm than was usual. The television was on in the kitchen, and they had to raise their voices over the sound. Ian felt that whatever it was in the pan needed more water added to it, whereas Chris was of the opinion that you couldn't just chuck more sodding water on it, and a lively discussion ensued.

Daniel lay on his bed and listened, against his will. Why did they have to shout so much? Sometimes it felt as though they were carrying out experiments about acoustics and human endurance to extreme noise. How was he supposed to *think*?

He had been less than entirely honest with his mother about his dissertation. It wasn't nearly finished, and it needed a wee bit more than just knocking into shape.

The problems had set in a few weeks ago. He was reading in the library, just checking a fact, when his attention was drawn to the title of another essay in the volume. It dealt with the same period he was working on, the early decades of the fourteenth century, and he flicked casually to the page.

The article was quite short, but enough to make the sweat break out all over him.

He'd scanned it, tearing one of the pages in his urgency, and when he'd finished he read it again,

VIRGINS *and*
MARTYRS

slowly, taking a grim delight in its every word. It was a technical piece, about the money supply, but the most significant feature of it was that it completely blew his own thesis out of the water.

His eyes had widened almost comically as he'd sucked in the words that made toilet paper of his near-as-damn-it two years of plodding research and reading in this overheated bloody library.

He'd slammed the book shut, stood up and flung his things into his briefcase, banged out of the library. Damn it damn it damn it this was disaster.

His thesis was based on the contention that at periods when inflation was high and rising there had been the greatest numbers of executions of witches. That was what it was about. He had a marvelous case study, Sarah Hilyard, burned for a witch in 1336, and he'd found some (admittedly shaky) evidence that the 1330s were at the peak of an inflation cycle. It was all fitting together beautifully, right down to the fact that Sarah Hilyard had been accused, among much else, with false coining, or forgery. It was perfect.

And then some bloody medievalist from one of the those bequest-funded American Research Institutes (as they insisted on calling themselves) had come up with a new bloody theory about the fourteenth-century English bloody money supply.

Oh not just a theory, came the amused, tolerant voice of his tutor Dr. Medway. If it was just a theory you wouldn't be getting quite so excited about it would you? After all anyone can theorize, including yourself, am I right Daniel? No this is a paper with style *and* substance, yes? Brilliantly, meticulously researched from monastic accounts dug up in a muddy field in Worcestershire. War-sest-er-sheer, as even *clever* Yanks are inclined to say. Does rather tend to damage your own contention, wouldn't you say?

Dammit! He was nearly finished, and then some over-funded Ivy League daddy's boy from the Carter Ballard Carolingian bloody Center for Humanist Enlightenment (for Christ's sake!) called Buckley F. Tzasze comes up with "Some Observations on Discounting, Pricing and Credit in Fourteenth-Century England," and—pow!— you can throw your handsome smiling dissertation out of the window. What was the "F" for, Daniel wondered bitterly, as the bus sat ticking at some traffic lights, "Fuck-off"? How had Buckley got access to those papers anyway? They were unpublished, they were in a collection of newly discovered manuscripts in the care of the Bodleian Library at Oxford and they didn't let just anyone come and paw them. Daniel was fairly sure they wouldn't have let *him* at them, oh no, not some oik with an only moderately good degree from a 1960s provincial university and a dodgy theory. But Buckley Fuck-off Tzasze from the CBC bloody

VIRGINS *and* MARTYRS

C for HE, oh please walk right in Mr. Fuck-off, would you care for a glass of sherry?

(Plus the fact, of course, that the manuscripts were in Latin and Daniel had to admit that given the nature of his chosen specialization, his Latin was woefully inadequate. But whose fault was that? Buckley Fuck-off had probably had Classics shoved up his bloody arse with his enemas since he was two years old, whereas he, Daniel Nothing Blennerhassett, had been lucky to find an "O" Level class, which he'd had to pay for himself, *and* pay for additional private tuition when the course leader had made it clear that he was well on the way to an ignominious failure.)

Daniel, he imagined Dr. Medway saying, Daniel Daniel Daniel. Are you sure you're cut out for this? A Masters is one thing: but a doctorate? Because that's what would be next isn't it? A Ph.D. And you're going to need a little bit more than O-level Latin for that aren't you? The Buckley F. Tzaszes of this world aren't just going to go away you know. Academia, he would say, stroking his sleek black hair smugly, is not a game for gentleman players or amateurs of any stripe. Are you sure it's for you? Have you ever thought of schoolteaching?

Daniel grimaced furiously and shook his head. No dammit, he would *get* his masters, he would get a research fellowship somewhere, and he would take it from there; determination was what had propelled him as far as this, and he wasn't about to be beaten by some suave American.

He sat on the bus home fuming, and when it came wailing to a halt, the dust in its brakes sending out high, resonant cries, at Daniel's stop, he hurtled down the steps and swung himself off into the early evening air, oblivious to the scent of privet and buddleia, his mouth a hard, angry line. He strode down Montpelier Road and marched into his room, threw himself onto the bed. Ian popped his head round the door a few minutes later and got his head bitten off. Daniel had apologized afterward and in the course of explaining himself had produced such a torrent of fury at the blameless Buckley F. that Ian had been unable to help himself and had laughed, and so had Daniel.

But it wasn't funny, not really, and it was going to mean more extra work than he cared to think about. The dissertation was due to be delivered by 12 noon, October the third, not a minute later, all 15,000 words of it.

Still, now he had somewhere reasonable to live, somewhere quiet, he'd have a chance to really get to grips with it. It was bad, but it was manageable.

Yes yes yes! Everything was possible. Well maybe not *everything*. He lay on the bed and listened to the din of Ian and Chris cooking, and smiled.

VIRGINS *and* MARTYRS

## chapter four

She stood on the doorstep in the rain and could do nothing to stop the tears rolling down her face, was not even aware of them. He wasn't going to answer the bell, he's probably forgotten the appointment, gone out, and there was nothing she could do but stand there and cry in front of the door with the wobbly glass panels.

She wasn't surprised, she wasn't anything, as the February rain soaked into the fun-fur coat. She reached for the doorbell again, but her hand fell back. What was the point? If he was there he would have answered by now. Nobody took three minutes to open the door.

She remembered that other time she'd stood in the rain, on the side of the arterial leading out of Carlisle. A car had pulled up, slithering to a stop beside her, its tires whispering through the puddles in the gutters. The Driver had wound down the window.

"How far do you want to go?" he asked, intending no innuendo, nor did she understand any. Until he asked her she hadn't been aware that she wanted to go anywhere. She stood and looked at his face peering out from the near-side window. "I don't know," she thought of saying, or "Anywhere," but instead merely tilted her head on one side and made the smallest sound imaginable, the least possible communicative unit, almost nothing: "Uh," but less than that really, and smiled some parts of a smile.

"Love? Where do you want to go then?" he said, raising his voice.

She had been standing at the roadside, but her intention had been no grander than that she might cross over and look in a shop window. But now he'd said it, yes, maybe she might go somewhere.

"Where are you going?" she asked, craftily.

"Brighton. Can't go any further without getting your feet wet," he said.

"How far is it?"

"I don't know. Three hundred and sixty-odd miles I think. What difference does it make how far it is?"

Oh no difference, she thought, and then she thought: three hundred and sixty miles. One for every day of the year nearly. A year in miles would pass and then she'd be somewhere else: in Brighton. Also a full circle of miles, three hundred and sixty degrees. She would end up nearly back where she started. She was turning these ideas round in her head, which was still tilted to one side, when he decided to press her on the point.

"Maybe you'd like a couple of days to think it over. I'll just sit and wait here shall I?"

She opened the door and slid weightlessly onto the seat. He reached over her to pull the door shut.

"Belt," he said briefly, and she understood and pulled the belt on: he noted, without particularly wishing to, that hers, in contrast to his own, lay limply in her lap. His was a snug black constrictor digging a neat path into his paunch. He realized abruptly that she was awfully, dreadfully, terribly thin. He tried to smile reassuringly to her, and found that he couldn't.

VIRGINS and
MARTYRS

"All set?" he said, salesman-chirpy, and pulled out onto the shiny black road.

That had been before Christmas; now it was February and here she was waiting in the rain again. She found her concentration drifting, and was, more than anything, startled when the door opened. She stared at the figure in the doorway for a moment, unable to remember what she wanted to say to him.

He held the door open for her.

"Come on in," he said, and smiled.

### chapter five

The cooking was finished and the food was eaten. Adding more water had indeed been a mistake, and the result was something strange and souplike, but Daniel had politely finished it all up, and had even said that it was "very nice, very unusual."

There was often a lull in the house after the evening meal, as the three dispersed to try to digest whatever they'd just eaten. This was Daniel's favorite time of the day at Montpelier Road, and especially so today because the most beautiful thought had just floated up to him, like a scented soap bubble. He would have to start packing.

Daniel had no suitcase: instead he had a large roll-bag made of blue PVC. Anything that wouldn't go in there would have to be put in bin bags. Not that there was much. Clothes, most of them in an untidy spread in and around the wardrobe. One sheet, one pillowcase, one duvet. There was no box for the duvet so that would have to go in a bin bag. His academic books and paperwork, including the draft of his thesis. A radio. Some bits and pieces from the kitchen. He went to get them, feeling obscurely guilty, expecting at any minute to be challenged. Looking around he saw that he had some food left. The only thing worth having was a jar of coffee that was hardly used, and a large bottle of oil. The oil would probably leak all over everything unless he secured it somehow. He couldn't think how to do it, and a momentary wave of self-pity broke over him. He put the bottle back on the shelf. It could be a farewell present to the house.

When he'd got everything assembled on the floor of his room he was amazed to see how much it actually amounted to. A man of some substance, he thought, it would take at least three bin bags to pack himself into. Three-quarters of an hour later, sweating and pissed-off, he had filled the fourth and last bin bag and there was still material remaining. What about his towels and shampoo and razors? Soap powder. An opened box of soap powder, much remaining. Dammit, he couldn't afford to just leave all those things, they all cost money to replace. And he was out of bin bags. There was a drawer full of carrier bags in the kitchen. Asda. Designed for smil-

VIRGINS and
MARTYRS

ing, optimistic young families to bring home their scrupulously selected and beautifully balanced weekfuls of food, not for sweating, badly organized students to try and cram their whole damn *lives* into.

He grabbed a handful of the bags from the drawer and threw them onto his bed, then ran up to the bathroom to collect his personal grooming items. Even for someone who, he had to face the fact, looked like considerably less than a million dollars, there was an astonishing amount of it, tubes and bottles and sprays. He came downstairs with his arms full and dumped it all on the bed as well. Coat hangers. The two books he'd propped the wardrobe up with so that the door would stay shut. Forgotten, malodorous items of clothing on the top shelf, the arm of something sticking out from behind. And under the bed? Oh *there* was a surprise now! All sorts of booty, things stained and stiffened and with dust luxuriating in every fold, things wrinkled and discolored, things, to be candid, that looked like the items to be found discarded under the seats in launderettes. He crammed them all into the carrier bags, which began to look as if what they were carrying was some kind of communicable disease.

At last the room started to seem cleared, with a small mountain of bags in the middle of the carpet. One or two of the bags had torn, and odd corners of things could be seen sticking out naughtily. By the time he got them all down into a taxi they would have stretched and torn further, and he would be lucky if he ended up with a single one still intact at the other end of the journey. All this just to move a few streets west and a few houses up!

He sat on the denuded, bare-mattressed bed and for a moment the whole project seemed ludicrous. Why didn't he just stay where he was for God's sake? A room was a room, wasn't it? And people were, after all, people, however you looked at them. Could he really face the ordeal of trying to maneuver this shameful heap of tearing plastic in and out of taxis and up and down stairs? For what?

He lunged for the door as he heard heavy foot-falls on the stairs. They were on their way down. They mustn't see the stripped bed and the land-slide of plastic bags! He slammed the door shut just in time.

Ian tapped on the door a few seconds later and said, "You coming out for a drink Dan? We're going down the Grapes?" Daniel called out no, that he was busy. Work to do. He listened to their heavy foot-falls clumping through the hall, heard the door slam.

He lay on the bed, the naked, stained floral mattress rough under his body. The pillow, bereft of its cover, felt sleek and odd on his cheek. Now that he had the house to himself and was all packed and ready to go he was able to relax, properly, for the first time in God knew how long. He closed his eyes and pictured himself in front of Dr. Medway, who was leaning back, surprised.

"So you see the point *is*, Dr. Medway, that none of what Mr. Tzasze says really changes anything as far as my central tenet is concerned."

"Yes, yes," said Medway, nodding slowly. "Yes I see that now, Daniel. I must say, your thoroughness and attention to detail, and above all your imaginative grasp of this has impressed all of us here quite deeply. I was talking to an American colleague of mine, and she happened to mention a certain scholarship open to the most outstanding student of medieval history in any year. I would like to discuss it further with you, if you have no objection?"

"None," said Daniel, aloud. "None whatsoever. Fire away!"

When he awoke it was getting dark. His belongings were a shadowy heap in the middle of the floor. His pulse felt erratic and fluttery and his mouth and throat were dry and coarse. He sat in the semidarkness and his head sang with a sick headache. He swallowed and his saliva tasted of stale blood. He wondered idly what time it was: he guessed it must be about nine. His last night in this preposterous little room in this ugly house with these inane people! How best to celebrate?

It would be nice, he allowed himself to think, to invite some people round for a wee leaving party. Everyone could sit wittily on the unmade bed and say things like: God knows how you stuck it out here for so long, you're a braver man than I Charlie Brown. They could drink dry white out of corrugated plastic cups and eat samosas and potato latkas. (As to who these people might be, well...) That would be the kind of thing his mother would like to hear about, he knew. He could hardly fail to be conscious of her disappointment. He supposed he'd just have to improvise.

He stood and towered over his heap of belongings. Did he have any money? Remembering the strange, loathsome writhing of the coins in his pocket earlier, he cautiously rummaged in trouser pockets and astounded himself by finding a minutely folded fiver in the ticket pocket of a musty pair of jeans. He handled it warily, but it seemed OK. Of course it did! he assured himself valiantly, why shouldn't it? Enough money for a very modest bacchanal. Destiny! He beetled out into the warm twilight and returned with a bag, which he unpacked onto the floor: bottle wrapped in pale blue tissue paper, crisps, chocolate. The cork didn't come out cleanly, and there was a slightly mildewy odor from the neck of the bottle, and when he smelled the contents he found his lips pulling back and his teeth clamping shut at the peculiar thin, reedy smell—bouquet, he felt, was just not the word.

He took two glasses from the kitchen and returned to his room. He filled them both, drank one, leaving a little in the bottom, then drank the other. He grimaced and shuddered at the shock of the taste, then refilled the second glass and sat on the bed with his back against the wall. He sipped this one and his palate, prepared for the onslaught now, reacted less unfavorably. Serve well chilled said the label, and why was obvious enough, but it wasn't so bad once you'd got used to it. The others would be back sometime around 11:30. So, regrettably, Ladies and Gentlemen, it couldn't be a late party. No, by 11:00 he wanted to be tucked in, light off and ostensibly dead to the world. Couldn't risk them seeing a light and barging in—not that that was likely, though they might want to look for cups or glasses if they couldn't find enough in the kitchen.

No, let them return, he would be asleep. And come tomorrow, voom! No Daniel, no explanation and no four weeks' notice. He tried to feel guilty but just couldn't. This move was self-preservation, pure and simple, and he couldn't feel guilty about that.

He poured another glass. The alcohol, though it certainly wasn't going to win any awards, was doing its work and he lounged more easily on the bed, running through various versions of the future. At some point in all of them, he and skinhead gained each other's respect and the skinhead smiled his exciting smile at him. He was going to fit in nicely, of that there could be no doubt.

He polished off the bottle and decided to call it a night: and only then realized that he'd packed his duvet away in one of the bin bags. Getting it free of the stretched black plastic was not the smooth operation it should have been—would have been in normal conditions—and the bag ended up getting rather badly torn before the damn thing would let go of the duvet. Ah well, he'd think about that tomorrow. He opened the window an inch as he invariably did and wrapped himself up; he woke with a jolt shortly afterward thinking alarm clock, alarm clock. God alone knew where that was. He had two of the bin bags spread out over the floor before he recalled slipping it into one of the side pockets in the roll-bag. He set it for eight, though he was nearly always awake by 7:30 anyway. But better safe than sorry, he chided himself seriously, prosaically, drunkenly. Oh yes. Tomorrow was a big day. He cocooned himself in the duvet and, for the first time in years, dreamed of his mother. The second glass sat by the first, in mute, deceitful refutation of the act of drinking alone.

### chapter six

The alarm was pinging with its vile, electronic voice in his ear; he slapped at it and, cartoonlike, it evaded his grasp, falling to the carpet where it

VIRGINS *and*
MARTYRS

beeped on. He crawled after it and shut it off. Eight o'clock. His eyes buzzed and he had no spit. He caught sight of the crisps and chocolate and was simultaneously ravenous and nauseated. He sat on the bed, the duvet wrapped round his shoulders, and surveyed the room.

He tried to think what it looked like.

It certainly didn't look like the scene of an orderly move to another house. There was no neat stack of matched cases or sturdy trunk or even the efficient bundles that a refugee might have.

It was more, he reflected, like something he'd seen in a doorway recently. He'd been coming back late from the library and between the bus stop and the house he'd passed a charity shop that had just closed down. In the doorway there were ripped bin bags full of clothes, rejects from a community of rejects, the unwanted from a tribe of cast-offs. There was a damp, raw smell as of a recently turned grave coming from the bright pink and turquoise crocheted polyester and the ginger and cloacal-brown suit jackets. Daniel strode past, trying not to think that there might be a body in there among the abandoned remnants. And yet something very like this fetid assembly was what he was proposing to put in a taxi and take to his new house, his new life. If any taxi driver would have it.

Mercifully there were a good few hours before the louts upstairs crawled out of their pits. He ran out for more bin bags, forcing himself to handle the coins which seemed instinct with the potential for unpleasantness. He returned to the somnolent house, and by 9:30 there was something resembling order in his room. He rang for a taxi, an estate, though he was getting the feeling that a fleet of juggernauts was going to be required, and began to pile his bagged belongings in the hall. The taxi arrived and loaded up. Daniel was about to shut the front door for the last time, when a thought struck him. He ducked back inside and found the envelope from a phone bill reminder. He wrote his new address, and, after a few seconds' thought, the words: "You must come round some time! See you." He crept up to Ian's bedroom door and pushed the note underneath.

Another last thought: he took his keys off the keyring and left them on the kitchen table.

Then he left, pulling the door shut as quietly as he could manage. Ten minutes later he was standing on the doorstep of No. 8 in a black sea of plastic, ringing the bell.

Five minutes went by. He stood there, feeling ridiculous in the silent morning air; the buttermilk fascias and black window frames mutely condemned him in his slept-in clothes and his lamentable style of luggage. The move three streets west had put him—just—on the wrong side of the Hove border, and he imagined permed ladies and beady-eyed toy

VIRGINS *and*
MARTYRS

dogs glaring from every window as he stood, vulnerable, on the step of No. 8.

He realized with a jolt that there was no one home, he had no way of getting in, he was here forever with his moldy possessions, the permed ladies and the scratchy-toed dogs would come out and surround him, and they would shame him to death. He stood helplessly, and then saw a tiny brown envelope jammed in the crack of the door, with "Daniel" printed on it in childlike writing. Inside was a key. He closed his eyes in a prayer of relief and gratitude, and let himself and his unsavory cargo into his new house.

He dragged the bags into the hallway and went up the flight of narrow stairs to the first-floor kitchen. There was a note on the kitchen table in the same childlike hand:

"Daniel, sorry I couldn't be here, make yourself at home, there's plenty of hot water if you want a bath."

Then a scrawled name, which Daniel was unable to make out, and a scribbled PS:

"Good to have you on board!"

Daniel's room was right at the top, which meant two further flights of stairs. He went back down for his roll-bag and began the ascent.

## chapter seven

Strange, he thought, how even the smallest deviation from a simple cube shape could make a room attractive. The wall with the window, the front facing wall, sloped inward giving the room something of the appearance of a garret; that and the fact of it being three stories up lent it almost a sense of drama, as if one could be a poet and huddle meaningfully beside a candle here

*or sit on the bed with your towel underneath you, rocking to and fro*

He blinked the image away and surveyed the room. His new domain.

A bed, mattress on a box base. A chest of drawers, painted white, a knob missing from the top drawer. Large double wardrobe. Desk of stained wood and chair painted in yellow and bright cheerful green. A blue carpet that had literally worn away to nothing by the door and the window and by the bed, exposing hardboard underneath. Off-white walls, off-white ceiling. Woodwork and door a kind of very pale lavender that partook also of gray and blue. And everywhere the unmistakable look and feel of things done on the cheap, on a budget approximating to zero, with only the most cursory, vestigial of nods toward style or quality. Everywhere that stubborn, chipped, knocked-about, much overpainted look that spoke—or, more exactly he

VIRGINS and
MARTYRS

thought, muttered—of compromise, poverty and incompetence, together with the botched quality of jobs done in the full knowledge that they are temporary. Look, said the chair, I used to be scratched and rubbed bare of varnish, now I'm bright and shiny green! See, said the window, I should have been stripped back to the wood and filled and sanded, primed and undercoated; but what the hell, now I've got yet another sticky, lumpy gloss overcoat, and this time it's lovely lilac!

Yes but look said Wendy, and Daniel wheeled round to the door, the blood jolting to a stop in his veins, but there was of course no one there. Any visitor, he realized, would have to announce themselves by their feet on the innumerable stairs, some of which creaked, before they could arrive at the door. No chance of being taken by surprise here, unless someone decided to tiptoe his way up, creeping riser by riser, holding onto the wall for support, slowly and cautiously, moving stealthily through the darkened, silent house. Any why would anyone want to do that? Daniel went to the window: one of the panes was cracked and had had tape applied to it, clearly in an attempt to keep out the winter wind. There was a discolored patch on the ceiling where there'd been a leak.

Hard to imagine winter, he thought, as he gazed out into the warm, overcast day. He pushed the window open, the antiquated sash mechanism, to-

*simon maginn*

gether with the many overpaintings, making it jolt and jar on its way up. He leaned out and, twisting his head hard round to the left, he could see the heavy gray mass of the sea. A room with a view, he thought, as long as you were prepared to risk your life to see it. Seagulls edged about warily on the chimneys on the other side of the road.

He thought about the bags of belongings waiting obediently in the hall for him to go and collect them, drag them up three flights of stairs, and then unpack them all. The idea of it filled him with an inexpressible weariness. The air was still and thick, like leftover soup in a pan.

He stretched out on the bed. Soft. Very soft, in fact, with a noticeable sag in the middle. If he had any ideas of entertaining overnight guests (which, he had to admit, was not high on his list of priorities), then he and they would inevitably end up jammed together, like two tributaries finding union in a single valley.

Ah well, that wasn't likely to be a major or pressing worry, he reflected, and he locked his hands behind his head and gazed up at the ceiling

(*yes but look*)

and watched a fly rambling sedately round the room, tracing out an intricate and stately dance with the bare light bulb at the center. The buses on the main road at the top of the street rumbled and whined. There would be plenty of time for unpacking and

VIRGINS *and* MARTYRS

ordering things, but for now it was enough to lie on a soft bed, far away from any intrusion, high up in the warm sweet air, and take it easy. He felt over-poweringly drowsy and just had time to register the thought—really mustn't sleep through the day—before he fell away into oblivion.

Outside the heat gathered, stoking itself up under the stupefying white blanket of cloud, growing and blooming in dusty, parched gardens and breathing heavily on shop fronts and bus stops, as the invisible sun moved across the high white sky and the sea rolled sullenly over the pebbles, and began to express its filmy white wisps of heat mist.

He came to bit by bit and lay for a while, his eyes open but with no thought of any kind in his head—then he sat up with a jolt and looked for his alarm clock, which was nowhere in sight. His eyes were sore and grainy from sleeping in his contact lenses.

"Damn, what time is it?" he said aloud, and the room looked back at him with a bland, inexpressive sheen of light. It could be any time, it seemed to be saying, any time at all, but whatever time it is it's probably *too late*, and wouldn't that be just like you, Daniel, to be *too late*.

"Shit!"

He jumped up and went to the window, his legs and armpits feeling unpleasantly lubricated. And when did you last have a bath, Daniel, the room seemed to be saying, why not have one now? After all there's *plenty* of hot water.

He grabbed the roll-bag and thrust his hand inside, but the contents appeared to have congealed into something more unyielding than mere clothing, and he pulled the hand out again with disgust. You don't want to go poking around in heaps of old clothes, Daniel, you never know what you're going to come up with, do you?

Where was the damn *clock*?

He unzipped the side pockets and was rewarded with a bus timetable and various other documents, along with some socks and unused batteries. No clock. He wrenched the bag aloft and turned it upside down, the clothes inside falling in a single, unlovely tangle onto the carpet. He teased them apart, surprised and curiously disgusted that they could have massed together in this way, pulling shirt sleeves out from trouser legs and socks from trouser pockets, until they all lay, separately, on the carpet, each with its own integrity; and not among them, nor behind nor between them, not under and not inside them, was his clock.

His head pumped with the sudden exertion after his sleep in the hot room. He went to the window and again stuck out his head.

The sky was still uniformly white, still high and warm, but there was now a quality to it of distance, as if the ceiling of cloud had shifted away a few score miles and was still moving, inch by observable inch. A bus roared past, the sound muted by distance and the thickness of the air, emphasizing the otherwise silent world. There was no one around. He craned his neck, trying to increase his range of vision, but could see nothing. The dogs had all been walked, their tiny pointed claws clacking against the hot pavements. It had to be late afternoon. Damn! He could hardly afford the luxury of a whole day wasted. There was enough disruption with the move as it was, without compounding the waste. He had a thesis to rescue!

He broke away from the window, aware suddenly that the breeze from the sea was cool and damp; he could see ghosts of mist assembling themselves around the chimney stacks.

Which must mean late afternoon, he thought. Could he possibly have slept through to the afternoon?

He left the room, wading across the litter of clothes, and rattled down the two flights of stairs, dimly conscious of the shadows growing in the corners as the direction of the light shifted round. Some section of his brain was equipped to interpret this data about the angle of the light and the direction and the length of the shadows, though he wasn't conscious of it, and it was telling him in very clear terms that afternoon was long gone and that the evening was already slipping away.

*simon maginn*

His bags were brooding, deserted, in the hall by the front door, a mutinous company, disaffected and reproachful. He grabbed the nearest two and half dragged, half carried them up. Somewhere above the first landing the plastic in his left hand slid disloyally away, the bag tearing itself open. He tried to get his arm under it but the impossible thing was having none of it and resisted him, collapsing away back to the floor where it fell over sideways and tried to spill out its contents.

Coming apart you see said Wendy, but Daniel couldn't hear and, dropping the bag in his right hand, scooped up the recalcitrant left-hand bag with both arms and staggered up the remaining stairs, depositing it onto the shabby blue carpet.

By the time he had all seven bags in his room his arms were tingling and throbbing. All this effort to just get his horrible, rank belongings up to his room. He'd only have to get them all down again at some stage to wash them, then they'd have to come back *up* again. His mind reeled at the enormity of the task, at the pointlessness, the futility of this constant cycle of washing and soiling, of the unwinnable nature of the struggle. A very modern curse, this washing, he reflected: the medieval world was ripe with stink and filth and decay, and human flesh was not expected to be sweet and smooth and odorless, but was alive with smell and grime, richly informative.

VIRGINS *and*
MARTYRS

Ah well, that was then and this, he thought, his nostrils twitching, is now. Better have a bath.

There's something very odd about this bathroom.

He stood watching the gushing, spluttering taps, and the thought rose up to him with the steam. He dipped a finger into the water and adjusted the taps so there was more cold and less hot. As the water neared the right level he peeled off his clothes, letting them drop to the green lino floor. His body emerged, pallid and oddly sexless, as if it were merely another stage in the development cycle, a pupa perhaps?

He lowered his foot into the water, and immediately pulled it out again. More cold. He tried again with the other foot and this time the temperature was acceptable and he stepped in with both feet, crouching, then kneeling, finally lowering his backside, gradually, into the water. He sat upright, blinking as the steam floated around him, condensing on the taps and the window and

(odd)

preparing himself to lie back. The brief shock of the cold against his back and neck was always unwelcome and he delayed, observing the distorted shape of his legs and feet under the water. Then he lowered himself back until he was entirely immersed, just his head and neck protruding, his genitals floating and waving gently in the tiny currents.

*simon maginn*

He lay perfectly still and watched the steam curling round his head, beading the walls and ceiling, clouding the sink pedestal and toilet bowl, thickening the air as the water loosened the stickiness and grit from his flesh, opening his pores; his mind roamed freely, taking fully five minutes to tell him what was wrong, what the steam was trying to tell him.

There was no mirror.

No mirror in the bedroom either. Well at least it saved him from having to see that haircut sitting on his head like some kind of fancy-dress costume, turning him into a stranger to himself. He was pink and glowing now; he felt as if he'd sloughed off the skin that he'd been born with and here in his new room, in the new house, he had a new skin. He could start again.

He surveyed the domain. Surprisingly it hadn't been cleaned. It looked as if it had been empty and abandoned for months, after being hastily vacated. Dust was thick in the corners and over the furniture, and Daniel wondered why it had been left for so long. The light was fading fast, which put the time at about 8:30. He really ought to get on with it.

He was about to shove an armful of socks and boxer shorts into a drawer when he stopped short.

The drawer was full of paper, newsprint.

He picked a piece up: it was torn from a newspaper, with that brittle, powdery quality that newsprint develops over time. He scanned the page, the miracle cures for baldness, the phone sex lines.

Underneath these was part of an ad for a publication called *How to Handle those Little Hitlers* and Daniel was halfway down the column before a slight shudder of weirdness passed through him. He put the cutting back and closed the drawer. Then he opened the drawer again and lifted the whole pile out, taking it over to the window; he settled down to read it all.

The papers fell into three distinct categories; there were news cuttings, of murders and sexual offenses mostly, the everyday horrors that made up the fillers on the inside home news pages. Ugly, stupid, brutal events, the immemorial saga of human flesh being violated. The second category was, jarringly, composed of money-off coupons and yes-please-rush-me-my-free-introductory-gift slips, a motley array of too good to be true offers and insignificant discounts on products that were of dubious utility.

The third category was more disturbing: it consisted merely of shredded paper.

By the time he'd finished sorting through, the light had dulled down to a ghostly gray luminosity. He sat on the floor in the gloom with the cuttings—tearings more like—scattered around him, like a rat about to construct a nest. He suddenly felt very naked, and pulled on his jeans and the big black jumper. He flicked the light on and, returning to the window, scooped up the scattered fragments of paper and dumped them back in the drawer, slamming it shut again. Somehow the idea of simply throwing them out didn't occur to him, nor did it seem in any way perverse to return the papers to their original location. Daniel had spent much of his adult life in libraries, and his respect for written archives of any kind ran deep.

He was rummaging about on top of the wardrobe when he found the hair.

It was a good thick hank of hair, deep black, with a slight purplish sheen. Thick with dust. He backed away from the wardrobe, feeling dizzy, abruptly aware of how high up this room was and how far it would be to fall, how fragile the structure of a house could be, how easy it would be for the floor to simply give way and for him to sink sickeningly down in a rubble of plaster dust and broken glass. He sat on the bed and laid his palms flat on its surface. It felt as if it were trembling, and he took his hands away again. The whole house was quivering, vibrating in sympathy with the earthshaking motion of the buses on the main road. He considered the possibility of an earth tremor, then realized: it's me.

Someone had left their hair on top of the wardrobe, and he was trembling at the appalling, unexpected intimacy with this person, presumably whoever had had the room before him, presumably the compiler of the ghoulish clippings library. He went back to the wardrobe and touched the hair, felt its dry, dusty, scaly reality and its strange, alien deadness. He let it go and left it where it was. He couldn't bring himself to think what would be a suitable response to it. Throw it away? Burn it? *Bury* it?

No no no, no he would leave it where it was, that was the best thing, the only thing to do with it, just leave it where it was and not even think about it up there gathering dust. Yes.

Pushed to the back of the table, right in the corner, was a small plastic plant pot, half full of crumbling, parched soil and the shriveled remnants of what could once have been a house plant. He contemplated it for a moment; it was even more abandoned that he was, so he could be magnanimous. He brought it out of the corner and put it where it would get the most light, then ran down to the kitchen and got a mug of water and a saucer. He returned to his room. God it was a long way up and down in this house! Everything was vertical. He put the saucer under the plant pot and watered it. The water collected in the saucer, but maybe the soil would soak it up overnight. What it really needed was repotting with new compost, but it would just have to do its best. Sink or swim.

By the time he'd got most of his belongings more or less stowed away, or at least out of sight somewhere, he was good and tired. His clock still hadn't turned up, but he hadn't emptied all the bags out yet, it had to be somewhere. He guessed it must be about ten o'clock; the sky was completely dark in the window (there were no curtains) and there was neither moon nor stars. He still hadn't made up his bed: what ought really to happen was that everything he owned, particularly the bedding, should be put through the hot cycle before he used any of it again. If he was serious about a new start, it should surely include clean sheets. As a compromise he decided merely to lie on the mattress with the duvet but without sheets, pillow cases or duvet cover. He opened the window and put out the light; as he lay, attempting to sleep, his thoughts turned on tortured flesh and shredded paper and hair.

After what seemed like hours of this, he got up again and went in search of the phone, finding it in the room next door, a sort of upstairs lounge.

The phone rang eleven times before his mother picked it up.

"Hello?"

"Mum it's Daniel."

"Daniel?" She'd been asleep, and was perched in her nightdress on the arm of the big leather chair in the study. She was trying to reach the silver cigarette box on the desk, while still cradling the re-

VIRGINS *and*
MARTYRS

ceiver under her neck. It was all a bit gymnastic for the middle of the night.

"Sweetheart? Is everything all right?" She couldn't see the clock, but she was sure it must be late.

"Yeah. I was just ringing to give you my new number."

"What do you mean? Have you moved darling?"

"I told you, I said I was moving. Just yesterday." Accusation: you never listen to me.

"I thought you were only going to look, I didn't think…"

"Well I have, so I thought you'd better have the number. Just in case."

Just in case his own mother wanted to ring him up.

"Hold on a second." She gave up on the cigarette box and started to hunt for a pen; then she rested the receiver on the arm of the chair and walked round to the other side of the desk. Taking her time now, she picked a cigarette out of the box, lit, exhaled, and found a pen and a piece of notepaper. She returned to the phone, then had second thoughts and went in search of the ashtray, the nice solid glass one.

"OK darling. Fire away."

He read out the number and she read it back to him, just to be sure.

"So tell me about the new house, is it nice?"

He looked around him, struck by the unfamiliarity of it.

"Yeah. Seems OK."

"And who are you sharing with, sweetheart?"

"Don't know his name. He seems all right. He used to do history as well."

"Oh. So you've got something in common then."

"Suppose so. Not really the same thing though."

So nothing in common. Again.

"Oh well. Still, you'll be able to work better now, do you think?"

"Yes. Well I mostly work up at the library anyway, so it doesn't make any difference really."

*Infuriating.* Did he have *any idea* how infuriating he could be? he moved *out* of one house because he couldn't work there, then he says— She swallowed her annoyance.

"Well if there's anything you need, sweetheart, just you give me the word."

"Thanks. I think I'm OK though. I'm just really glad to be out of that other place."

Heavens, she thought, was that a *feeling* you just expressed?

"Are you darling?"

"Yes. Well these places can get you down somehow. You know?"

"Oh yes, abso*lute*ly." Actually she didn't really have the faintest idea what he meant. She'd gone

VIR**g**INS *and*
MART**y**Rs

straight from her father's house to Steven's house, and as her father was a barrister and Steven was a doctor in private practice, she'd never experienced the kind of place that Daniel described to her. Sharing. It sounded like great fun. All mucking in together. Attic rooms, midnight feasts, getting a pint of milk from the corner shop. She flicked her ash.

"So this looks like a nice place anyway. I think it'll be good, definitely," he said.

"Well, I'll have to come and visit, won't I?"

"There's not really much room…."

"Only kidding sweetheart. Mummy's only kidding." She had tried to get visiting rights so often that it was now just a joke. Not a good time, bit of a funny atmosphere, maybe when the evenings were a bit lighter, how about after Christmas.

"I wouldn't want to show you up in front of your friends."

"Ha ha." As close as he came to laughter, a mirthless, grim, close-lipped affair.

"Anyway Mum, I better get to sleep."

"And me. I've got bags round my eyes you could go to Port au Prince with."

"What, after you paid all that money to that nice plastic surgeon? You should demand a refund."

"I don't think they do refunds, sweetheart, I think you just have to have another operation."

"Bit late for that in your case, I'm afraid."

"Flatterer."

"Anyway Mum, better go now…."

"Nice to talk to you darling. We should talk more."

"Well I'm—"

"Busy. I know."

"Bye for now."

"Bye sweetheart. Don't be *too* good, will you?"

She put the phone down and sat back in the deeply padded chair. The cat climbed up onto her shoulder and stretched out a leg, and she scratched his belly. He closed his eyes and stretched out further, effortlessly sensuous.

### chapter eight

He woke in a panic, thrashing in the darkness. He'd dreamed of a hand reaching out to him from a doorway, catching hold of his leg, pulling him down among the stinking, piss-stained clothes.

"Don't leave it too long, Daniel," the owner of the hand was saying, as Daniel awoke.

"Daniel."

He froze, stopped breathing, stopped thinking. Someone had just spoken his name. The darkness in front of him and around him cleared little by little as his eyes adjusted. No one there. He lay back. Not the first time this had happened. Once on a long train journey. Once in the middle of the day as he was waiting to cross a road. Just some acoustical effect or self-hypnosis or something, Daniel assured himself anxiously.

It was an unnamable time of the night, three or four or some such hour. Daniel had an almost superstitious dread of being awake at night. To be awake at night meant to be asleep in the day, and that was just plain wickedness. Not to mention the fact that if you were asleep in the day you couldn't do any work, and if you didn't work then how were you going to get on in life?

Of his, admittedly tiny, circle from his first-degree days, he was the only one to go on to further academic work. One was "bumming" (whatever that might involve) round Australia, one was in some hideous management training program for one of the big chain stores, one was unemployed in London, hanging round the fringes of the Revolutionary Communist Party. Or at least that's what they'd been doing when last he'd heard from them, which had been some time ago. A BA in Medieval History from the University of Leeds, that ought to be a bond for life. And yet it quite patently wasn't. He alone had gone on to further research, even though his was not the best result in his year, far from it. A fairly good upper second, not a first. And what had made the difference was that he was determined: he'd worked the whole of the summer of the year he'd graduated on the bare bones of his thesis so that when it came to MA interviews he was able to present a clear-cut, well-articulated research project, with detailed plans of the sources to be studied and their availability. And he'd got a place, not through having the right accent or the right background or long eyelashes to flutter, but through determination and stubborn hard work. That was what got results.

And when the MA was finished he would condense it down and he would publish it. It would appear in the *Journal of Medieval Society* or even *History Quarterly*. It would be his passport to academia.

Daniel lay in the dark, calmer now, and tried to sleep.

A few minutes later his eyes batted open again. He had become convinced that there was someone else in the house. Not that he'd heard anything, nothing as definite as that, but some sense had picked up a change. Maybe the tiny detector cells in his skin had felt a change in air pressure from the front door opening. Or maybe his nose, or more properly the ancient, primitive rhinencephalon, the smell-brain, had caught a whiff of something, or someone.

Of course there was no reason why the skinhead shouldn't have returned, it was his house after all.

VIRGINS *and*
MARTYRS

It was terribly unlikely to be anyone else. The chances of a break-in on Daniel's first night were tiny, surely? You didn't just move in and get burgled did you? Not in Hove?

Nonsense nonsense nonsense, Daniel said to himself, then said it aloud:

"Nonsense."

There was no one. He would have heard the front door slam. Although that was the odd thing about being in a new house: you didn't know all of the sounds. In Montpelier Road Daniel had been able to plot the exact movements of everyone in the house, down to what drawer they were opening. Any unfamiliar tread he could spot instantly. If one of the boys brought someone back he would know straightaway what sex and the approximate weight. He would also know, whether he wanted to or not, whether the encounter was a sexual one and if so how successful (or at least how *long*).

But in this house he didn't know what he was hearing or not hearing. Perhaps people would be able to come in and out without Daniel hearing a sound. Somehow he didn't like that idea, though he couldn't say why. It became clear to him that he would have to go and have a look, unless he was prepared to lie motionless with his eyes open all night, listening. He'd already lost one complete day by falling asleep earlier on. He most definitely couldn't afford to lose another by lying awake all night.

*simon maginn*

He got up and put on his jeans and jumper, and fumbled his contact lenses into place. The air from the window was pleasingly cool and tranquil on his face, with the faintest suggestion of the heat of the day just gone and a promise of that to come. He thought he detected a curl of sea mist trailing through the window, but it was probably only an effect of the light, or lack of it.

He went to the door. He could hear nothing outside. He twisted the handle: the door was badly hung and made a harsh double crack as it opened. There was another room on this floor, unused. He crept past it and down the top flight of stairs. The floor below, the middle floor, had the bathroom and another room—Daniel didn't know what was in it. He stood by the bathroom door, but still could hear nothing. Down again, to the lowest of the three floors, the kitchen and the skinhead's own room. Nope. Nothing. He descended to the corridor that led to the street door, the front door, and found a door leading off that he hadn't noticed before.

*(look.)*

He opened it: a flight of stairs leading down into more darkness, deeper, more unknown. He followed the stairs down until he came into a large basement room, which appeared to occupy the entire length of the house. There was a window at the far end, heavily barred. The floor was concrete, and large objects stood in the corners, something that

VIRGINS *and*
MARTYRS

looked like a fruit machine, another that could have been the sort of wheeled dolly used for moving heavy equipment.

*(look.)*

Everything incredibly dusty, and outside the wind seemed to be getting up, he could feel a freshening, a movement against his cheek. A smell, strange but familiar. In the far corner, the shadowiest corner, he saw an opening in the wall, a doorway but with no door. He made for it, his footsteps muffled by the dust which rose up behind him, stirred by the breeze. Another staircase, going impossibly down, further, he steadied himself against the cool damp wall as the whole thing seemed to lurch horribly, drunkenly, and shudder. A great sound was beginning to insinuate itself, a sound that he knew he knew but couldn't place, and the stairwell doglegged, going deeper. It opened onto another room, smaller this time, bare boards, cracks between them. He could feel them vibrating, bouncing as he walked across them. The great sound was booming dully, mightily, and he came to a hatch in the floor with an iron hoop for a handle. He pulled it up: the hatch was stiff, warped, and the hinges were rusty, because of all the moisture, but he managed to lift it and below, not far below, but just under the level of the floor, was the sea, a touch choppy in the freshening breeze, too black and oh far too deep to contemplate for long.

*simon maginn*

You see? said Wendy. The house is over water. It's a house over the water. Do you see? Water below and above, oh horrible oh

Daniel dropped the hatch back and climbed up the stairs, up to the basement, up and up, until his legs were hot and heavy and he was in his room again, exhausted. He slammed the door shut, cra-*ack!* and got back into his bed, where he slept soundly. The sea mist caressed the window invisibly, and a stray wisp did indeed slip in through the inch-and-a-half opening, but Daniel didn't see it because he was asleep and dreaming.

### chapter nine

He woke in a panic, thrashing.

He'd dreamed he'd gone down to the basement of the house and pulled open a hatch, and there'd been water underneath. There'd been somebody talking to him. Come to think of it someone had been speaking to him the minute he set foot in the house, on the stairs, in the bathroom. He hadn't been able to hear, and yet he'd known. It was light outside, but he was horribly uncertain as to time of day. Also name of day. He tried to count back but was confused by the recollection of frequent wakings and sleepings.

He dressed quickly. He paused, fully dressed: something not done. Then he remembered: there was no mirror to check on before he went out. He had no accurate idea of how he looked. He smoothed his hair with his hand, convinced that there were bits sticking up at the back. Also he must need a shave, he certainly felt pretty rough.

He was staring at the oddly blank wall over the sink, brushing his teeth, when a little thought began to nudge at him, something to do with the toothpaste. And the curious thing was that the thought simply wouldn't come, it seemed a very long way away, though he was certain it was important, it *felt* important. He grappled with it for a while, but it eluded him. Something very simple, very important, to do with toothpaste: teeth, was that it? No, but that was related.

"Oh for Christ's sake," he spluttered, toothpaste foam spraying over the taps and sink, "so it's a *thought* and it's got to do with *teeth* has it? What is this, bloody charades?" Something that he hadn't done. Something that he'd left a very long time to do.

He shook his head in perplexity, and as he did so he became aware that the reason he couldn't think of this thought was that he was being prevented from thinking it, in exactly the same way that he'd been shown the sea under the house last night.

*(yes, don't think shhhh)*

Christ, he thought clearly, I'm finally going mad. Dr. Medway was right, I'm going to be barking at the moon before long. He decided that he needed to just get out and get to the library, he couldn't think properly in this house. Probably because his sleep kept getting messed up.

*(that's it yes, straight to the library)*

Now wait a minute, there was surely a line missing here. You didn't just go running out the minute you woke up. There was something else, something you did first wasn't there? You put in your contacts, you brushed your teeth, you combed your hair, you splashed your face, you shaved, and then you went downstairs and you—you—

*(shhhhh, shhh)*

He rinsed out his mouth and spat. He would think about it on the bus.


"In 1486—the year the Middle Ages finished..."

He leaned back in the chair, rotating his pen in his fingers. The table was divided into little enclosures with wooden partitions, and not surprisingly these walls provided a rich environment for graffiti, in a range of styles and colors. The content varied widely, from po-faced undergraduate academicism to the basest obscenity, thus "The Philosophical Investigations of Wittgenstein represent the triumph of words over language" nestled cozily alongside "My cock is a monster, enormous thou art." Daniel was not in the habit of reading these desk adornments, with their distracting mixture of the earnest and the hormonal, but today one of them had caught his eye:

VIRGINS *and*
MARTYRS

Q: What was Beethoven doing on his 57th birthday?

A: Decomposing.

It was very faint, up near the top of the wooden wall, and had been half obliterated by something else. Facile, irritating and meaningless, but Daniel found that it was jingling round his head like an advertising slogan.

The library was, of course, quiet, with that special additional quietness it seemed to achieve on weekday afternoons in vacations, a languorous, slumberous quality, out of time, with the dust settling gently, imperceptibly on the long, high walls of books, which stretched up and away in all directions. Daniel had been using this library for eighteen months, and he still found it confusing. It was on four floors; the ground plan for each seemed to have been devised by a capricious child with a devious mind, an unsteady hand and a big black crayon. Fire doors were everywhere, and the abrupt right-angle turn was the defining design point. It was a maze, with the difference that a maze has a center and a way out, whereas it sometimes seemed to Daniel that the library had neither. More than once he'd found himself turning a corner and facing a dead end, a blank brick wall, and had to beat a humiliating retreat.

He'd once quite literally got lost and been unable to find a way out: he'd circled round a section

of the second floor, repeatedly passing the same dili-
gent, bowed-over heads of working students, who
had glanced up at him each time, increasingly perplexed as he strode by, increasingly panicked. He'd
finally, quite accidentally, found a side door and a
flight of ill-lit concrete stairs, which had taken him
down to a peculiar sort of tradesman's entrance by
the enclosure for the bins.

"In 1486—the year the Middle Ages finished…"

He turned his face up to the ceiling and sighed.

He had to acknowledge it, the thesis was disintegrating. (Decomposing?)

Q: Do dyslexic insomniac agnostics like awake
at night worrying about the existence of dog? Q:
I'm into sadism, necrophilia and bestiality, am I flogging a dead horse? I hate you trendy lefty bastards,
queers off campus. Piss up a pole fuckstick. Your
mum's a good shag.

"In 1486…"

He stood up. He couldn't continue until he
knew where the bloody thing was going. There was
a very pertinent question to be asked, which was:
what was the damn thesis *about*? The title had been
agreed and registered, and there was no way of
changing that. Start from there.

He wrote the title down on the wooden parti-
tion, feeling a delicious thrill of law-breaking at the
tiny act of rebellion. He considered the words.

VIRGINS *and*
MARTYRS

To tell the truth (and shame the devil) he was bored to death with the whole thing. He'd been living with Sarah Hilyard (so to speak) for nearly two years now, ever since his final year at Leeds when he'd discovered her, been captivated by her. He needed a really fresh start, he needed to feel the drama of her trial again, feel the humanity of her and her predicament.

Grasp the nettle, he thought. Open with Buckley F.'s paper and work from there. It was the only way. He needed to go and have another look at the essay. It had appeared in the *Journal of Medieval Society*, and Daniel aimed himself in that direction. He could find that shelf in his sleep.

He turned a corner and found a fire door. He was fairly certain that he hadn't seen it before. They must have only recently put it in. That was another thing about the damn library, they were constantly working on it, redecorating, reshelving the books in new and unpredictable locations.

He pushed through. Shelves marched away in strict perspective, blocking his view. He turned right and went down a narrow passage with the wall on one side and rows of shelves on the other. The classmarks sailed past, PK, PL, PM. He glanced at one of the titles—it didn't appear to be in English. Russian? It had a beautifully decorated spine, with exquisite gold lettering. The lighting in this section was dimmer, the dust seemed to be thicker. He came to a kind of crossroads: the aisles between the shelves were wider and the perspectives longer. The stacks stood, one behind the other like dominoes laid out ready to be knocked over.

He turned right again. Long perspectives of racks, endless aisles with the towering, dusty shelves opening off them on both sides at regular intervals. He'd read in the university prospectus that the library housed over 50,000 items. It could easily have been 50,000,000 by the look of it.

Where was he?

He veered off down one of the subsidiary aisles, the books reaching up on both sides of him, close now, close enough to smell, that peculiarly intense smell of old paper and clothes, old dust, dry and feathery, tickling the back of his throat, desiccating his lungs. He picked out a book at random, it seemed to be something about art history, with grinning devils and gods with improbable limb arrangements. He put the book back and, as he did so, caught in the corner of his eye a figure standing at the far end of the aisle, half out of sight. Standing? He was struck by the oddness of the posture, unpleasantly struck, and moved on. PN. No PO, could be confused with P zero.

*(a little further)*

He went a little further on, though he was unquestionably lost now and was more inclined to

VIR&INS *and*
MARTyRS

go back.

*(no, no)*

No? But he'd seen enough, there was nothing to be achieved by going any further, this was completely the wrong area.

*(a little further)*

He turned a corner and came to classmark PR. PR? He'd never heard of it before. He reached up for a book and opened it at random.

"…instances of Disease caused by putrid Emanations from Human Remains after Death: It would appear that the stench arising therefrom, particularly where a grave happens to be opened during the summer months…"

*What?*

Daniel flicked the pages.

"…as an instance of the state of the cellars round the graveyard, it is stated that a workman engaged in one of them put his hand on the wet wall. He was warned that the moisture on the walls was poisonous, and was requested to wash the hand in vinegar. He merely dried his hand on his apron: at the end of three days the whole arm became numb, then the hand and lower arm swelled with great pain, blisters came out on the skin, and the epidermis came off."

Daniel blinked in astonishment.

"Amputation followed speedily but was alas found to be ineffective and the death was prolonged and agonizing."

*simon maginn*

What kind of book was this?

"In January 1837 a man named Clark, in George Gardens in this parish, having been kept a considerable length of time unburied (I was informed beyond a fortnight) I was directed to visit the case and I found the house consisted of two small rooms, wherein resided his wife and seven children. It was becoming very offensive."

He turned over a few pages.

"When you visit the room, in what condition do you find the corpse? How is it laid out?—Generally speaking, we find only one bed in the room, and that occupied by the corpse."

*Enough.* Christ Jesus what subject classification did *this* come under? He slammed the book shut, and the noise fell softly in the still air, choked by the immense volume of dry paper that was surrounding him, stretching up and over and around him. He paused, and the old academic habit prompted him, nudged him. He turned the cover of the book to the sheet stuck on the inside front which listed the dates of previous borrowings. The last one recorded was June 1968.

Twenty-four years ago. No one had borrowed this book for *twenty-four years*. Was that possible? He rubbed his hand against his jeans. There was a powdery trace, a sheen on his fingers.

"—when the remains are in an advanced state of decomposition, the liquid matter from the corpse

VIR$IN$S *and*
MARTyRS

frequently escapes from the coffin and runs down over their clothes—"

He couldn't help himself, he read on.

"In the years 1737 and 1746 the inhabitants of the houses round the churchyard of St. Innocens complained loudly of the revolting stench to which they were exposed. In the year 1755 the matter again came to notice: the inspector who was entrusted with the inquiry, himself saw the vapor rising from a large common grave, and convinced himself of the injurious effects of this vapor on the inhabitants of the neighbouring houses. 'Often,' says the author of a paper which we have before alluded to, 'the complexions of the young people who remain in this neighbourhood grow pale. Meat sooner becomes putrid there than elsewhere, and many persons cannot get accustomed to these houses.' In the year 1779, in a cemetery which yearly received from 2,000 to 3,000 corpses, they dug an immense common grave near to that part of the cemetery which touches upon the Rue de la Lingerie. The grave was 50 feet deep, and made to receive from 1500 to 1600 bodies. But in February 1780, the whole of the cellars in the street were no longer fit to use. Candles were extinguished by the air in these cellars; and those who only approached the apertures were immediately seized with the most alarming attacks. The evil was only diminished on the bodies being covered with half a foot of lime, and all further interments forbidden. But even that must have been found insufficient, as, after some years, the great work of disinterring the bodies from this churchyard was determined upon. This undertaking, according to Thouret's report, was carried on from December 1785 to May 1786; from December 1786 to…"

He flicked over the pages, glancing around nervously, obscurely guilty.

"…formerly in the school of anatomy which he attended, pupils were sometimes attacked with fever, which was called 'the dissecting-room fever,' which, since better regulations were adopted…"

The paper was brittle, dusty, the print tiny. Unconsciously he again rubbed his finger against his jeans.

"…a Dr. Chambon was required by the Dean of the Faculté de Médecine of Paris to demonstrate the liver and its appendages before the faculty on applying for his license. The decomposition of the subject given him for the demonstration was so far advanced, that Chambon drew the attention of the Dean to it, but he was required to go on. One of the four candidates, Corion, struck by the putrid emanations which escaped from the body as soon as it was opened, fainted, was carried home, and died in seventy hours; another, the celebrated Fourcroy, was attacked with a burning exanthematous eruption; and two others, Laguerenne and Dufresnoy, remained a long time feeble, and the latter never completely recovered…."

He coughed, the dust was getting into his throat, and the paper seemed to be disintegrating on his fingers. The book was bound in cloth-covered board, and the cloth was starting to tear along the spine. He really ought to go.

*(a little more)*

"…I cannot refrain from giving also the information which Fourcroy gained from the gravediggers of St. Innocens. Generally they did not seem to rate the danger of displacing the corpses very high: they remarked, however, that some days after the disinterment of the corpses the abdomen would swell, owing to the great development of gas; and that if an opening forced itself at the navel, or anywhere in the region of the belly, there issued forth the most horribly smelling liquid and a mephitic gas, and of the latter they had the greatest fear, as it produced sudden insensibility and faintings. Fourcroy wished much to make further researches into the nature of this gas, but he could not find any gravedigger who could be induced by an offered reward to assist him by finding a body which was in a fit state to produce the gas. They stated that at a certain distance, this gas only produced a slight giddiness, a feeling of nausea, languor and debility. These attacks lasted several hours, and were followed by loss of appetite, weakness and trembling…"

*simon maginn*

He felt as if the book were starting to attach itself to his hands, as if the paper were turning into a breathable dust which he was sucking up into his lungs. He wanted to drop the loathsome thing, the smell of it was becoming more than irritating, it was becoming—mephitic?

*(just a little more)*

"...the bursting of leaden coffins..."

No. For Christ's sake, that was enough.

"...bursting of leaden coffins in the vaults of cemeteries, unless they are watched and 'tapped' to allow the mephitic vapor to escape, appears to be not infrequent. In cases of rapid decomposition, such instances occur in private houses before the entombment. An undertaker of considerable experience states: 'I have known coffins to explode, like the report of a small gun, in the house. I was once called up at midnight by the people, who were in great alarm, and who stated that the coffin had burst in the night, as they described it, with "a report like the report of a cannon." On proceeding to the house I found in that case, which was one of dropsy, very rapid decomposition had occurred, and the lead was forced up...'"

He dropped the book and walked quickly away, glancing over his shoulder, but he found himself in another aisle with a book in his hand. It had last been borrowed in March 1952. Inexpertly bound, it fell open, cracking its spine completely. A clump of pages slipped to the floor.

*(you see?)*

"…to prevent putrefaction the soft organs are removed via a lateral incision from the sternum down to the pubis…"

Another one. January 1940. "…The Assyrian-Babylonian belief, to be left unburied was one of the greatest misfortunes which could befall one. The Gilgamesh Epic…"

He thought he could see the door, as the book disintegrated in his hands, tumbling to the dusty floor. The smell rose up, thick and choking, and he gagged.

*(look. look.)*

He came to a shelf; it had just a single book on it.

*(look.)*

He went to pull it down, and his fingers sank unpleasantly into it; he came away with a brittle husk of paper, fragments adhering to his fingers as he shook and rubbed it away, grimacing, disgusted.

He found the door and emerged into stronger, clearer light and the history of ideas, The Enlightenment. KL. He grabbed a volume and devoured the individual words: order, reason, experiment, rationality. Yes. Yes. He was shaking, uncontrollably, all over. The residue on his fingers wouldn't quite come away, the sheen, the slight glossy, powdery feeling remained. He had to wash his hands

*amputation followed speedily*

*simon maginn*

wash his damn *hands*, and then sit quietly somewhere for a while

*I was informed beyond a fortnight*

"No!" he said aloud, softly, but he was heard
and somewhere nearby someone whispered, answered by a giggle.

He made his way down to the toilets in the
basement. He was not altogether surprised to find
them closed for essential repairs.

He decided then and there to go and find
Dr. Medway, hand the thing over to him, ask frankly
and unambiguously for help. His dissertation, his
degree, was slipping away from him, he could feel
it. Two years' work.

He marched through the Arts block and found
Medway's secretary in her office, the sunlight pour-
ing through the window. She was deep in conversation with an extremely handsome Middle-East-
ern-looking man with a beautifully groomed mus-
tache, and glanced up at him as he came in.

"Would you give this to Dr. Medway?" he said,
and dumped the seedy bundle of papers onto her desk.
"And would you ask him for an appointment, after
he's had time to read it? It's really quite urgent."

The secretary took him in in a long look and
agreed that yes she would. It did indeed appear urgent. He walked out and the beautiful Middle-East-
ern student raised his glossy eyebrows at her and
she shrugged. Students.

VIRGINS *and*
MARTYRS

He sat on the top deck of the bus, and the thought that had eluded him a few hours earlier floated obediently into view: he hadn't eaten for more than forty-eight hours. He was starving.

(*shhh, shhhhh*)

### chapter ten

He woke the next day with a taste like shredded paper in his mouth, like a hangover. Like his first hangover.

"There's nothing, Elaine," said Moira, shuffling through a stack of letters and other papers. "Nothing." She shook her head, sorrowful but resigned, and despite herself grimly enjoying the hunt.

"You'd think she'd have kept those 'Congratulations on the birth of your first child' cards, you know, with storks and that on the front," said Elaine, opening and shutting drawers and peering underneath a cupboard. Nothing.

"But he's got to be, what, about eighteen months," Moira said, hands on broad hips, "wouldn't she have chucked them out by now?"

"You should meet my mum," Elaine said knowingly, "she'll show you a whole book full of them about me."

"Eh, maybe no one sent her any," said Moira,

and turned to look at the child who was playing gravely among the litter of papers and scattered belongings. He looked up at her and hiccuped, his head nodding on his doughy neck.

"Pissed as a fart," she said, and reached down for him; he stared owlishly at her with great bleary, unfocused eyes.

"You're pissed as a fart, arnchoo darlin'. *Arnchoo?*" she crooned as the child regarded her.

"Can't you tell us your name then?" she said. "What we going to call you? Eh?"

The situation was an unusual one. Alerted by the ceaseless uninterrupted crying, a neighbor had rung the police, who'd broken in. They'd found a woman, early twenties, lying in bed: she was dead, had clearly been dead for a number of days, three or four. Paracetamol and Jack Daniels, both in large quantities. And in the living room a young child, somewhere between one and two years old, asleep, with the whisky bottle clutched to him. He had slept through the noise of the police breaking in, and proved hard to rouse. When someone did succeed in waking him he blinked and hiccuped and allowed his head to fall to the thin nylon carpet, his body describing an inverted u, his bum sticking up in the air. He smelled heavily of whisky. He was drunk.

After the woman, whom a pile of unopened circulars identified as Kathy Blennerhassett, had been taken out, zipped up uncomplainingly, snugly, in a dark gray body bag, the Child Protection Officer and her assistant had been called in to collect the child's belongings and to take him off to his new life among social workers and foster parents and then (hopefully) an adopted family. But he had to have a name.

They gave up after an hour in the messy flat, and Elaine picked the child up and smiled at him.

"Well, little stranger. Eh?" she said. The now empty whisky bottle was on the floor near where he'd lain, hugging it after polishing off the contents. Jack Daniels.

"How about Daniel?" she said, and tapped him on the nose; he went briefly cross-eyed as he tried to look at the finger, then took hold if it in his silky little hand, his big brown eyes scanning her face seriously.

"Daniel," she said. "Daniel Blennerhassett. How about that?"

He could still taste that hangover, even at a distance of twenty-odd years. He had no memory of his mother alive, nor did he remember anything of the three days he'd spent in the quiet, untidy flat, with the curtains open day and night, lying awake, watching the moon as it sailed past, and his mother, cool and silent in her bed. He didn't know if he'd gone to her, touched her; he didn't know if he'd climbed into the bed with her, tried to rouse her. Did he remember the taste of the whisky that had given him his name?

As to what it was that had led her to unscrew the childproof lid of the little white pot, to pull the foil from the bottle of Jack Daniels (a reckless expenditure, but then she wasn't going to have to worry about money anymore, was she?); to finger the smooth white tablets, spreading them out over her palm; then, quickly, pile them onto her tongue and gulp mouthfuls of the rich, sweet liquid, forcing it all down, fighting the gag reflex, swallowing repeatedly; what enormity of desolation and blackness had made her ready to leave her little boy to whatever luck, good or ill, might befall him in her absence, Daniel didn't know. He'd heard that suicides occurred, not when a person was at the extremity of their despair, but afterward when they were once again able to see the reality of their position, and act on what they saw.

In his dreams, though, she moved about the flat quickly, quietly singing. She was getting him ready to go out, finding his woolly hat and tiny gloves. He was young, still young enough to be in his buggy, but he was also old enough to know that she was dreadfully unhappy, and that he had to help her before it was too late.

"Mum."

She turned and, her face breaking into an enormous smile, a joyful smile, she came to him, picked

VIRGINS *and*
MARTYRS

him up, hoisting him up on her hips, though he was really too old for that.

He wanted to say we'd better go, we're going to be late, miss the bus. But she rocked him about and made him laugh, poked her finger into his belly button, made him squeal and squirm about. He tried to talk, tried to say stop, it'll be too late, but was powerless, a giggling fool, in love.

He lay still with the hangover taste coating his tongue.

He was remembering the conversation with the woman he could no longer call his mother, who had ceased to be his mother with the words "Dan, it's time we had a little chat." She had given him his new identity, as an adopted child, the child of an unhappy woman who had committed suicide, and a father unknown. He had never entirely forgiven her for it. It was always between them.

That conversation had taken place in July of Daniel's eighteenth year. He was due to take up his place at Leeds in October. He left the house where the woman who wasn't his mother lived with the man who wasn't his real father, and arrived in a resort town where he worked for the rest of the summer in a hotel kitchen. His days were busy, crowded, but at night he found that he returned with obsessive regularity to the quiet room and the smell of the whisky, fabricating, elaborating. Sometimes he

*simon maginn*

thought he could remember the whiskering sound of the body-bag zip, or the sound of the lift door as the trolley was maneuvered in, the muted comments of the police. And sometimes, as he was lying in the dark after a day of loading and unloading the big steaming dishwasher, sometimes he would think he could remember his mother, his real mother, not the woman, the impostor, who had given him his new identity like a heavy awkward suitcase. His real mother, shaking him in the air, smiling, laughing into his solemn little pucker face. Before whatever it was that turned her in on herself, turned her dark and despairing, made her eat the pills and drink the whisky that had taken away his life in a body bag and given him his new name. But what had *she* called him? He would try out names, whispering them aloud in the dark. Luther, Charles. No, something more lighthearted than that, a bright, cheerful name, Mike or Col or Phil.

He'd gone to the university in the autumn, and his three years there had been a strange time, in which he found consolation in the far distant past; and one drizzly winter afternoon he'd found Sarah Hilyard and fallen in love.

She was born in 1321, the daughter of a respectable Norfolk farmer, the youngest of eight children. She was clearly quite a beauty, as well as having some considerable charm and no shortage of self-determination: she was engaged to the eldest son

VIRGINS *and*
MARTYRS

of a neighboring farmer, though there were three older sisters at home, all unmarried: engaged at the age of fourteen, due to marry at fifteen. But somehow she had come to the attention of the Church authorities, accusations had been made, and she had been sucked into the horrors of the Inquisition.

The trial had gone entirely by the book. She had made the tactical mistake of asking for trial by red-hot iron, which was taken as an indication of her guilt, since only someone who was being helped by the Devil would be able to survive the ordeal unscathed, and thus only a witch would propose it. It was agreed that the juices of certain herbs, known to the Devil, would prevent the hands from being burned. Such things were well-known and documented. Her request deepened the suspicions surrounding her. Witnesses swore to having seen her talking to devils; different witnesses stated that they had seen her in different places at the same time. The evidence, unanimous and damning, piled up on top of her. She protested her innocence. She was put to the question and subsequently tortured, as the procedure demanded. Still she maintained her innocence; by this stage her protestations were being taken as evidence of the Devil's stubborn residence within her. It was agreed that she could only withstand the torture with the Devil's assistance. She was found guilty and burned, in 1336, aged fifteen.

*simon maginn*

Daniel's fascination with the case came partly from the comparative rarity of an intact, thorough and (seemingly) reliable transcript of the proceedings. The witness statements, the prosecution charges, and her own initial statements and later defiant declarations, were all there, summarized in the curious legalistic style of the Inquisition. The documents had been collected and translated from the Latin in 1910. For Daniel this was the purest kind of historical pleasure: an unequivocal and self-contained source and a strong, simple story.

He had decided there and then, as the misty rain had trickled down the library windows, that he would write a research paper based on Sarah's case. Even through the double distortion of the official summary of her speeches into Latin, and then their translation back into English, Daniel could hear her voice. In a way she was a symbol for him of all the poor, guileless, victimized women who had fallen prey to the insane superstitions of the Church, and of the tempests of suspicion, envy, spite and sheer malice that the Inquisition seemed to whip up.

Daniel had spent many long hours pondering, and had slowly come to realize that Sarah was precisely the kind of woman he would like to know, to fall in love with, to marry. He had been for so much of his life on his own that the idea of meeting someone and, ultimately, marrying them, had taken on a somewhat idealized aspect. To fall in love, to marry: these would be great events, dignified and gracious. There would be a prolonged, ritualized courtship, hands would be held and declarations made and then there would be an engagement. The wedding would follow after a decently long interval. Sex was something that Daniel rarely thought of. It certainly had no place in his future marriage plans. No, his would be a union of well-matched intellects, of mutual respect and courtesy. He had yet to meet anyone who had impressed him as a possible partner.

But Sarah Hilyard, she was his own true love, he would champion her and keep her memory alive. He would protect her from the glib, sweet-talking Buckley F. Tzaszes, from the lecherous, cynical historians who could see only what she *meant* rather than who she *was*. He would write a beautiful thesis.

He was suddenly impatient to get to the library again. The—what to call it?—little incident, that peculiarly vivid *dream* that he'd had there yesterday, that was nothing to be concerned about. A mere brainstorm, a daydream. He had no time for such nonsense. Sarah was waiting for him, waiting for him to cow the wicked, faithless Buckley F.

He was assailed for a moment by a wave of giddiness, and his stomach filled with churning, molten metal. For God's sake, it said, it's been three days now, for God's sake get up and *eat*.

He had to acknowledge the demand: his body was weakened and trembling for lack of food, he was giddy, it was no wonder he couldn't seem to get going on the thesis.

He was halfway to the shop on the corner before he thought: damn.

No money.

He'd given the last of his change to the homeless person on his way back from the barber's, had in fact thrown it at him. He had simply not wanted it in his hand or on his person any longer. He literally didn't have a penny.

He patted his pockets and found his cashcard. It was for an account which, he knew, was already overdrawn, but he hadn't reached his agreed limit yet. It should be good for a terror. *Tenner*, he corrected himself immediately, a *tenner* not a terror (surely).

It was a Saturday afternoon. There was a queue for the cash machine, headed, as such queues seemed invariably to be, by someone who was incapable of using the machine with even the most rudimentary competence. Daniel resignedly took his place, and fell into a state of immobile impatience. The queue shuffled forward, like a time-lapse sequence on a nature documentary, with sudden bursts of movement separated by long still patches.

Daniel finally reached the machine and pushed in his card. He keyed in his number—and the ma-

VIRGINS *and*
MARTYRS

chine politely informed him that the code was incorrect. Did he wish to try again? Press "yes," the machine suggested insolently, or "no."

Bloody right he wanted to try again, but as there was no "bloody right!" button to press he made do with "yes" and again, this time more cautiously, tapped in the four digits.

Sorry, said the implacable, unreachably stupid machine. Do you wish to—

He pushed "yes" again. He glanced behind him: the person next in line was shuffling her feet and generally indicating impatience. He, Daniel, had become the person at the head of the queue, the one who was under no circumstances to be allowed to use even very simple machinery. He smiled apologetically, and she smiled back, but only just.

This time he keyed in the numbers with the kind of doggedness that a trained pigeon might display in pressing levers to get a food pellet in some laboratory. He knew the bloody number, he used the bloody thing often enough, it wasn't exactly challenging to remember a four digit sequence correctly. How he would have got it wrong twice already was completely beyond him. If only he could *think* straight.

The machine went into some kind of electronic trance for a moment, then said brightly:

"Please take card and WAIT FOR YOUR MONEY."

He took the card and the machine indicated

that he could now open the little hatch and get the money. He opened the hatch—

—and slammed it shut again. Oh dear God he didn't want to see anything like that again, oh dear God, whatever it had been.

He stared at the screen and, unconsciously, touched his forehead, as if saluting. His fingers touched chill sweat. He stepped back from the machine, unaware of the undivided attention he was now receiving from the queue. A young father in a shell suit toward the back took his little girl down from his shoulders and put her on the ground, as if he was preparing himself for some kind of action.

"Sorry?" Daniel said to no one in particular, in the tone of voice people use when they have not heard or not understood something; the woman behind him watched him with fear and annoyance equally balanced. He was still somewhere halfway between a nuisance and a menace.

He came forward again and tried the drawer, with what was clearly a strong effort of will. His face was narrowed, as if against the glare of a bright light only he could see. The drawer had locked— it was on a timer. He would have to go through it all again.

The card slid in the slot once more, sucked in by the hidden appetite of the machine. He keyed the numbers in. What amount did he want? It had to be a multiple of ten. Which meant multiples of

VIRGINS and
MARTYRS

that—that thing he'd seen in the drawer. He imagined the whatever-it-was multiplying, dividing, the drawer becoming full of them, and then when the hatch opened and his hand slid in—

He couldn't do it. He murmured an apology to the woman standing behind him and strode briskly away, staring straight ahead. He walked directly home.

### chapter eleven

The house was hot and silent when he opened the door, and the air had a slightly thickened quality to it, as if it had been so long undisturbed that it had begun to congeal.

He climbed up to his room and lay down on the bed, the heat applying itself to him, fitting him exactly.

He had to face it: there was something wrong with him. There had been something wrong ever since—well, he supposed really it had started the first time he entered the house. Not eating, sleeping at all hours of the day and night, seeing things (they were no dreams, he admitted, not the incident in the basement and not the terrible books in the library)

no not dreams

and now this money thing, this

(terror?)

no, this *problem* he seemed to be experiencing with handling money. These things, he told himself soberly, were not within normal limits. He seemed to be in the grip of something like an illness,

*"which was called 'the dissecting-room fever'"*
some kind of illness

*"a feeling of nausea, languor and debility"*
no

*"followed by loss of appetite, weakness and trembling"*

(Surely, though, you could only get a dissecting-room fever if you were in a dissecting-room, not an ordinary suburban bedroom, the kind of room where people sat and drank tea and

rocked back and forth, your towel spread beneath you, as you tore the paper, pushed it into your mouth)

He jolted upright, suddenly alarmed by the stillness of his body. He went to the window and watched. Every so often he twitched violently, as if trying to shake off some creeping paralysis, to demonstrate that he could still move. The acids in his stomach trickled and burned. He considered the fate of the unlucky Corion, who fainted, was carried home, and died in seventy hours.

*many persons cannot get accustomed to these houses*

There was a faint buzzing sound, coming from down

VIRGINS and
MARTYRS

below in the house somewhere; Daniel realized that
it must be the doorbell. It could hardly be anyone
for him, but maybe he should answer it anyway. It
might be urgent, like—well like something urgent.
And in any case, you couldn't just *not* answer the
door, could you?

He descended, flight by flight, still feeling like
a complete impostor, ready to be challenged at any
moment, and saw a shape through the glass door.

He pulled it open a few inches and peered
round, squinting. It was Ian.

"Hi Daniel. How ya doing?"

Daniel opened the door fully and gestured to
Ian to come in.

"I just thought I'd look in on you. Have a look
at your new place. Hope I'm not disturbing you?"

"No. No I was just…"

He led the way up to the kitchen.

The kettle and cups were easy enough, but the tea
bags were proving elusive. Ian watched him, be-
mused, as he blundered around the kitchen, opening and shutting cupboards, which all seemed to be
pretty bare.

"Settled in all right then I see?"

Daniel grunted.

"Looks like a good place anyway. Bit more room
than Montpelier Road."

"Yeah. It's pretty quiet. So far, anyway."

"Not like us lot eh?"

Daniel shrugged, wrenching open an airtight jar and finally finding tea bags. He sniffed them. Old.

"Well I've got to get this dissertation finished, you know, and I need somewhere quiet to work. I can't concentrate with a lot of noise around me, I find it very jangling," he said, not looking at Ian.

"Yes. I suppose we can be pretty rowdy sometimes."

Daniel poured water into the cups. He knew that Ian was trying to apologize for driving him away. He knew he should try to rise to the occasion.

"Yeah. Well."

He opened the fridge. There was half a lemon, dried and wrinkled, a wedge of what could once have been cheese, something green and liquescent at the bottom. He shut it quickly.

"It'll have to be black, I'm afraid," he said, and put the cup down in front of Ian.

"Have you got someone else to move in?" he asked, giving Ian an opportunity to bring up the matter of his four weeks' notice, which was what he assumed had brought him here.

"Oh yeah, mate of Chris's took it, right piss-head. He comes in late and puts on these horrible old records, Led Zeppelin and that, starts singing along. You thought it was bad when *you* were there, you should try it now!"

There was either unspoken approbation for all this bedlam or maybe, just maybe, an implied complaint and a wish for Daniel to come back. Daniel's mood almost allowed him to believe the latter. They were sorry he'd left! He felt a sudden urge of unexpected affection for this Ian, and blurted out:

"Sorry I couldn't give you a bit more warning, but this place came up suddenly and…"

"Nah, don't worry 'bout it. I don't know how long I'm going to be there myself. Chris is really pissing me off actually."

"Is he?" Daniel had assumed they were all joined at the hip. He sat forward, and Ian launched into a foul-mouthed description of Chris's manifold short-comings as a human being, moral, intellectual and hygienic, and Daniel thought: he's *confiding* in me. He nodded sympathetically, frowned, smiled, and all the time glowed with the physical warmth of vindication.

Ian stood to leave ten minutes later, and as Daniel ushered him to the door he was surprised by how sorry he was to see him go.

"Well. Stay in touch," Ian said, and Daniel assured him that he definitely would. He watched Ian disappear up the street and shut the door. The house seemed to close in on him again.

He felt oddly drained, and the walk up to his room emptied his legs of their remaining strength. He lay on his bed and was asleep in minutes.
When he awoke it was growing dark, and the phone was ringing.

*simon maginn*

The sound was coming from the room next to his. He went in: the curtains were drawn and there was a restful, diffused light, as if at the bottom of a coral reef. The phone sat on the arm of an armchair, purring gently but insistently. He picked it up.

"Hello?"

"Is Wendy there?" It was a woman's voice, as harsh and croaky as his own, a little slurred, as if she might be drunk.

"What?" he said, still in the grip of a kind of numbness, a suspension.

"Is Wendy there? Who's this?"

He put the phone down, returned to his room.

Must be early Sunday morning, he thought, though he was aware that such niceties as day and time were presently beyond him. It was daylight, certainly. He had been asleep, fully dressed, now he was awake. Had something woken him? He couldn't be sure, until he found that he was kneading his stomach with both fists. Jesus Christ, he hadn't realized that hunger could be actually *painful*, but it was. His stomach was a hard little ball which was currently shooting jets of acid down into his groin and up to his chest, his breathing felt oddly restricted, as if there was a weight on top of him, a boulder or a heavy door perhaps. The nausea seemed to have passed, but he was fairly certain it hadn't gone far. There was an excited, buzzing sensation

VIRGINS and
MARTYRS

below his ribcage, a low-voltage electrical fizzing. His throat was swollen from the acids he was having to swallow, there was a raw, coarse feeling running down his gullet.

He wandered into the room next door, where along with the telephone there was a television and video, both of fairly primitive design. He put the television on, hoping for a clue as to time and date. No such luck however. The readout on the video said simply 00:00, no time, no day. But that surely couldn't be correct. The pictures when they came made no sense to him: a serious balding man speaking very quickly, a woman and child getting onto a bus, dogs running through a field in slow motion. A woman and a man sitting by a large plate-glass window: a plane took off behind them, but they were ignoring it, they went on talking. Their words sounded strange, then type appeared at the bottom of the screen. Subtitles. It must be a foreign film. Daniel tried to follow the words but was having difficulty focusing. He gazed at the screen for a while, but nothing much seemed to happen: the two people looked uneasy—the woman rummaged in her handbag. Daniel moved around the room, glancing periodically at the screen, opening drawers. All empty.

Then he opened a drawer and found a small stack of videos, half a dozen. They were all the same brand, all unmarked.

He took the top one out of the drawer and turned it over in his hands, like an archaeologist fingering an ax-head. He took it over to the television—the woman was crying, the man was putting on an odd-looking hat, though that was surely not the cause of her distress.

He inserted the video and pushed "play." The machine whirred and clunked as if it was steam-driven, then the man in the distressing hat and the woman and the apparently irrelevant airplanes vanished, and a bland-faced man took their place.

He was holding a microphone, talking in a very serious voice. Daniel sat on the floor and watched, absently rubbing his left arm.

A pretty woman was standing in a tent, holding something very small and dark: it was a child, an incredibly tiny creature with a head that was slightly too big and an expression a little too old. She was injecting the child, who was twisting away from her in distress, screwing up its face. Another woman came into view and took the child from the pretty doctor. This woman was unbelievably thin, she had sticks instead of arms and curiously bowed legs. Her breasts hung flat against her chest, and the child clung to her, pushing its face into her.

"These people are starving," Daniel said aloud, appalled. The camera swept over a bare, rocky field of dust: everywhere there were people sitting and lying. They looked up at the camera, or ignored it.

VIRGINS and
MARTYRS

Someone in a white jacket was holding up a child; the child couldn't stand, its body had ceased to be of any use to it, it dangled grotesquely as if it were trying to dance. Again the head too big, the expression too old.

He ejected the tape, and the airport people returned like old friends, still messing about with hats and handbags, crying, leaving and so on.

He tried another of the tapes: this time the people were queuing for something, a tinful of some kind of liquid; the queue seemed to stretch into the infinite distance. The people wore brightly colored clothes, but you could see that they too were starving, their faces were hard and bony, their eyes seeming to bulge out from their faces: flies buzzed round them and crawled over them, round their mouths, into their eyes. The people flicked them away, but without any conviction or feeling, and the flies returned.

Another. People in striped uniforms, shuffling forward, with men in black uniforms prodding them with guns. Shaved heads. They were shuffling into a vast compound ringed with barbed wire. Bone-thin.

Daniel carefully put the videos back into their sleeves and replaced them in the drawer. He sat on the floor again and gazed at the foreign people in the foreign airport, who seemed to be unable to come to any kind of conclusion.

*simon maginn*

He changed the channel and found a local news item, about a human arm that had been discovered washed up on the beach. A good-looking, heavily built policeman was saying something, and his name came up underneath him: Det. Ins. Outhwaite. He looked sorrowful, and Daniel thought how unusual it was to see such an expression on a policeman.

The news moved on among a flurry of computer graphics. Daniel sat in front of the screen.

He found that he was wondering, quite calmly, how long it would take to die from starvation. He hadn't eaten now for three days. The phrase "forty days and forty nights" floated into his head, and a voice crying in the wilderness, though that could have applied to something else, he wasn't sure.

The thought formed itself: carry on like this, and you're going to find out the hard way.

And then something rose up in him, the spirit that had propelled him through his three years at Leeds and his constant battle to get through without any parental contribution. He was hardly the kind of person who just lay down and *died* now, was he?

He left the room: he felt the need to move, to be in motion. He descended the innumerable stairs and slammed the front door shut behind him. The air outside was cooler, and he breathed it in, trying to clear his head which seemed to be full of
    shredded paper
no, not exactly, it was more like—like—

VIRGINS and
    MARTYRS

"For Christ's sake!" he said aloud, thumping the wall with frustration. What did it matter what exactly his head felt as if it was full of? This was the problem. He was just not thinking properly. That bloody woman kept on distracting him, twisting his thoughts around, confusing him....

He came to an abrupt halt outside a bookshop. Bloody woman?

And what bloody woman would that be, exactly, Daniel? Hm?

Christ, was he really going mad then? Because he was now certain, suddenly, that the voice he'd been half-conscious of since he first walked through the door of that house was that of a woman, and that she was deliberately interfering with his thoughts, more than that: showing him things. She'd shown him the hatch that opened, impossibly, insanely, onto the sea. The library shelves full of crumbling books about decomposition, the dead unburied. Those clippings in the drawer, they were hers. The hair. The shredded paper.

She was the previous occupant of his room.

The certainty swept over him and he stood, amazed, gawping sightlessly at the window full of true crime and Royal Sensations.

So was it she who had made the coins squirm in his pocket, like maggots in carrion, made the cashpoint deliver up that thing, that hideous, repugnant thing in the drawer, that terror? Why would

*simon maginn*

she do that? The books in the window stared at him, full of all kinds of information and ideas, and he stared back, absently rubbing at his left arm.

Well just consider it for a moment, Daniel, said Dr. Medway in his coolest, let's-think-this-through-together voice. What has been the consequence of your recent inability to tender Her Majesty's coin? Apart from not being able to determine who should bat first at a cricket match, and having a temporary incapacity to win negligible amounts on fruit machines like the one in the basement, or was it the subbasement, but that wasn't what she meant, was it?

There, it had happened again. He backtracked, staring at the cover of a book about astrology, a complicated mandala covered in squiggling signs and symbols.

Where were we? Yes, Dr. Medway was exploring all the things that you couldn't do if you weren't prepared to soil your hands with filthy lucre. Dr. Medway?

Well let's just get right down to it, he said, what you can't do is *eat*, because you can't buy food. That's why you're starving, and that's why you're unable to think coherently. Hence the visions, hence the feelings of unreality, hence the fear. Simple. Eat.

So why did she want to starve him?

No, the question was why did she want to starve herself?

VIRGINS and
MARTYRS

(rocking on the bed, towel beneath her, stuffing the shredded paper into her mouth, she's already thin, perhaps just a touch more than that, perhaps "thin" doesn't really cover it.)

There was something missing here, something he wasn't understanding. A thick, warm rain began to fall, and he stood in the doorway of the bookshop. A smartly dressed middle-aged woman, taking him for a homeless person, and caught unawares by a sudden feeling of human sympathy in this respectable street in the saddening rain, reached into her purse and, finding some coppers, dropped them gently at his feet.

"No!"

She backed away, startled, as he kicked the coins away and pushed past her. Her charity lay, despised, on the wet pavement, and she watched him go, dismayed by the kind of person you encountered on the street these days. He ran, his left arm held awkwardly to his side, ran through the wet, empty, featureless streets of Hove, past a floral clock where all the flowers were dead and the clock had stopped, past squares with no pigeons and no dogs and no people. He came to a bank and some shops, the fag end of a commercial district, occupied by down-at-heel newsagents and fast-food outlets, many of the shop fronts boarded up or merely empty, the dusty interiors gazing out at the eternally passing trade, the letters and circulars and mailshots forming small, neglected avalanches under the letterboxes. Ghosts of the mercantile world, empty spaces; no longer trading. The doorways to these watchful properties were the occasional residences now of an amorphous tribe, the ones who were casually designated as homeless. Dispossessed—or rather newly possessed of a limitless variety of abodes that they built as they went, wherever they stood or lay for a few hours.

A baby-clothes shop, Ba-baa Boutique, the Akash Tandoori, a deserted hardware shop, Chas H. Madden, Trade and Retail. At a bus stop a woman struggling with a pushchair and a little girl, aged about seven, followed him with their eyes. The woman forgot the cussed pushchair for a moment as she took in his haunted eyes, the rigid arms, the abstracted determination of his gait. The little girl subjected him to a look of complete candor.

He knew he had to go back. There was something he wasn't understanding, something more she had to tell him.

He retraced his steps, grimly, determinedly, as if walking up the steps of a gallows. He opened the door,

*(Daniel, quickly, oh)*

and her voice was immediately with him. He mounted the stairs, flight after flight, up through the warm, fetid air, until he opened his door, her door, and lay on the bed, her bed, folded his arms across his chest, waited.

VIRGINS *and*
MARTYRS

It was like trying to sleep when you weren't tired, he decided after what felt like a year and a half had crawled by. You just couldn't do it. His arm had gone to sleep though, his left arm.

(yes!)

He tried to shake it but it was a plank of wood, he rubbed it with his right hand and couldn't feel anything, not even tingling. Nothing. His eyes were still closed, and he was abruptly certain that he didn't want to open them. His right hand tactfully withdrew from the weirdly, intolerably absent other arm. "Other" was the right word. Oh Christ.

He opened his eyes. Pulled off his jumper. Took off his shirt. Get a grip, get a grip now.

His left arm was little more than bones covered in loose, sagging skin, whiter than human skin had any business being, and oh God, much colder, also wet.

(the hand, Daniel, look)

He clamped his eyes shut again. It would go away, all her nasty little shows had disappeared pretty swiftly so far, and this one would do *exactly* the same, *exactly* the same, *exactly*

(Look. Look.)

The hand was lying open, palm up, on the duvet, dead, bony, cold. And through the palm, a neat round hole, blue-tinged.

It was then that he pulled his jumper back on,

with some difficulty, and walked the short distance to Hove police station.

"I would like to speak to Mr. Outhwaite," he said to the duty officer, and refused to be drawn any further.

PART

*two*

FLOWERS

### chapter twelve

The Linden was a place distinguished solely by its anonymity: you went down a short flight of concrete steps and rang a bell. A stout man in a navy blue blazer opened the door and nodded you in if he knew your face. If not, the exchange of a small sum of money conferred membership onto you like a moth-eaten graduation robe. The blinds were always down and the overhead lights on, even on the brightest day; and only at certain times of day and year did natural light winkle its way in between the slats, picking out the pugnacious faces and gleaming bodies of the boxers whose pictures covered the walls, and creating patches of shiny brown and green on the vinyl upholstery. Mid afternoon in mid-February, however, was not such a time, and the overheads cast a dull luminosity through surprising amounts of cigarette smoke, surprising because the place was almost empty.

Wendy sat against the wall in her fun-fur, looking away at the floor, at nothing. An older woman sat on the other side of the table, a woman with short, square-cut, gray hair. Dogs scrabbled on the floor under the table. Dachshunds: Loulie, Patti and Maddie. Loulie was heavily pregnant, her teats dragging over the dusty floor. She was tired and droopy in the stuffy room. The older woman bred dachshunds, not really for profit though she had cups and trophies on her back-room mantelpiece, and called herself a viscountess though she was in truth the second daughter of an incredibly ancient woman presently languishing malevolently in a geriatric ward, refusing to die: *she* had been divorced a long time ago by the son of an unimportant viscount. In the Linden, though, they called her "Dowager," and handled her gently when they put her in the taxi home, though she frequently had no money to pay for it and was currently bound over for nonpayment of a fare and disorderly conduct.

Wendy signed, and the Dowager glanced up at her.

"Hadn't you better be off?" she said, and looked around for a clock. "Quarter-past three wasn't it? Must be nearly three now. Has anyone got the time?" she called in the direction of the bar, and the girl moodily drying glasses called back, "Ten to."

"Don't want to be late. They don't like it if you're late. They always think you're up to something."

Wendy tilted her head to one side, and sighed again. She had drunk very little of her lager.

"Best be off, eh?" said the Dowager once more, and Wendy stood, shoulders drawn up, and crept away.

Half an hour later she sat in front of a person whose title was "Claimant Adviser," and whose function

VIR$\varsigma$INS *and* MARTyRS

was the routine harassment of people in receipt of the amusingly small amounts of benefit they were entitled to. She was a few years older than Wendy's twenty-five, and much better dressed. Her name was Sue Polk. Her make-up was flawless and restrained, and her hair perfectly unobjectionable. She smelled strongly of fabric softener and deodorizing body spray, with a faint almondy note from her hair conditioner, and a little dab of Obsession thrown in for balance. Wendy found her nasal hairs tickling from the heady concoction and was fiddling absently with her nose. Ms. Polk, needless to say, was getting nowhere.

"Now when you sign on, Miss Bishop, you are in fact signing a declaration that you are still entitled to the benefits you're claiming: that you have done no work, paid or voluntary in the preceding two weeks, and that you are actively seeking work."

Wendy made a very small sound, somewhere between a cough and a "Hm." Sue Polk glanced briefly at her, and continued.

"So one of the reasons I asked you to come in today was to discuss with you whether you need any help in looking for jobs, and how best I can assist you in getting back to work."

Wendy frowned, demonstrating concentration. She nodded slowly, though to Sue Polk it wasn't wholly clear what she was agreeing with, or to.

"For instance, there may be avenues you haven't thought of trying. Something that a great many people find beneficial is the Job Club. Have you ever thought of attending one?"

Wendy nodded again. Yes? No? Anything at all? *Hello?*

"You see Miss Bishop I have to be satisfied that you are acting in compliance with our requirements," said Sue Polk, realizing that her language was growing denser, more opaque, as Wendy became stiller, and seemingly paler, shadowier. She felt a gust of irritation: really, she shouldn't have to be interviewing this sort of claimant, there was absolutely no point. Polk had come to distinguish sharply between the respectable unemployed (of any class), those who had genuinely fallen on hard times and were resolved to improve their situation: and the Other Lot. Wendy was patently of the second tribe, her fellows the truculent, tattooed and inappropriately dressed army of the dispossessed, ill-disciplined and unreachably marginalized. Perhaps not entirely, in her case, but mostly. She raised an eyebrow and took a look at Wendy Bishop.

There wasn't anything obviously wrong with her appearance, Polk decided. Her hair was, in fact, nicely cut, a tidy bob, if perhaps a fraction too long in front. It hung well, framing her face. Or at least that had clearly been her stylist's intention, and it was hardly his fault that his work had been derailed, thwarted, by the almost complete absence of anything you would wish to dignify with the word

VIRGINS *and*
MARTYRS

"face." Features certainly, but a face? Pinched, expressionless; a mask. And thin, not so thin that you'd necessarily notice immediately, but a shade more than model-girl thin, just a shade.

The fun-fur was brown, the clothes underneath only to be guessed at. Black tights, flat black shoes, showed below the knees. Polk guessed at the dress: little black number? Possibly, but she doubted that Wendy wanted to draw attention to the body that accompanied the slightly-more-than-thin face. None of this was her field really. Her one-day courses had not equipped her to empathize or intuit, and her Obsession marked her off too decisively from this slight, shadowy creature for her to pick up any really useful clues: it drowned out Wendy's faint, pale, papery scent.

"Is there anything you'd like to ask me?" she offered, a subdued patience overtaking her earlier annoyance. After all, what was there to be annoyed by?

Wendy tilted her head, looked a little sad, could think of nothing.

"OK, Miss Bishop, we'll be inviting you back in three months' time to review your progress. Do please get in touch if you should think of anything we can do for you, or if you'd like any information." She smiled and closed the file. Wendy seemed uncertain what to do, and Sue Polk felt a chill on her neck as she for the first time sensed

simon maginn

the depth of Wendy's depression.

"Thanks for coming in Miss Bishop. Please feel free to leave now." Wendy stood up and turned to the door. She makes no sound, Polk thought, without wishing to. Wendy twisted the door handle very slowly, very carefully, as if this were an operation requiring great skill and deliberation, like neurosurgery. She opened the door just enough to slide through sideways: the low pile of her fun-fur rustled statically against the gray gloss paint. The door was pulled shut as silently as the mechanism allowed.

Sue Polk sat in the adjustable chair and almost slumped back. It seemed very hot in the tiny cubicle-office, her flesh was slightly clammy, and the potpourri of her body spray was complemented by the musk of her sweat. She glanced at her watch: the interview had lasted little more than ten minutes. She reached for her shoulder bag under the table and took out a tube of sugar-free mints, unpeeled one and put it in her mouth. The most innocuous of crutches, she knew, but felt a tinge of guilt anyway. Wendy had unsettled her. Too thin, too quiet, and a bit too damn close for comfort.

Wendy had said she'd meet Keith after her interview, in the Woolworth's café, or Coffee Shop as it had recently become. She arrived before him; her interview had been shorter than she'd anticipated. She pushed her tray along the counter and asked

VIRGINS and
MARTYRS

for a cup of tea. Milk and sugar were separate, in a molded plastic container. She of course needed neither and, waiting at the till, poked about in her black purse, pushing the coins around.

By the time Keith arrived at her table the tea was practically cold in front of her.

"Hiya," he said, brisk and smiling, "been here long? Do you want another one?"

Wendy nodded, and he cupped his hand behind his ear, frowning.

"Sorry? Didn't quite catch that."

"Yes. Please," she said, and he kissed her, quickly, on the cheek before going off to the counter.

The first thing Wendy had noticed about him was that his hairline was rather low and that he had "love" and "hate" tattooed on his knuckles. And his head, she thought, was a bit of a funny shape. They'd been in the same queue for inquiries at the Housing Benefit Office at the town hall. He was animated and chirpy, but somehow not too irritating. He'd waited for her and walked her back to town. Almost immediately, it seemed, he had decided that they should be going out, and so they did. A short series of exquisitely restrained and inexpensive meetings followed, he ribald and courtly by turns, refusing to be put off by her muteness, her abstraction. After one of these budget rave-ups in a town center pub, he'd walked her home and kissed

*simon maginn*

her at length in the front garden of the house she was staying in (she was sharing a room, so anything else was out of the question). She had allowed him to and had even gone to the extent of putting her hand on the back of his neck. He'd gone home happy. He thought she was lovely, just a bit shy.

"Aren't you having anything to eat?" he said, returning with the tea and his own cup of coffee. She shook her head.

"Haven't you got any money? You only got your giro on Friday. You must have a bit left. What do you do with it all? Eh?" he mocked her, gently, courteously, playfully, and she smiled and shook her head, murmuring something. He again cupped his ear.

"Not very hungry," she said, just loud enough to hear, no louder.

"Wendy you've got to eat," he said. "Shall I get you something? Cake or something?" but she refused, stoically. She wouldn't eat.

Someone, Keith surmised, had said something to her. He knew how she could be. Once he'd said to her, *jokingly* obviously, why don't you ever wear anything except black, what are you a vampire or something, and hours later she'd started to cry, silently (of course), but definitely cry, and just would not say what was the matter. It had taken him days to get it out of her. He'd been astonished: aston-

VIRGINS *and*
MARTYRS

ished at how alike they were. He'd spent days brooding over all sorts of slights and snubs, real and imagined. Things could take you that way: once he'd thought the woman in the paper shop was trying to get at him in the manner in which she gave him his change. He'd turned it over and over in his mind, trying to find some cause for her attitude, something he'd done. Mercifully he was only like that occasionally—he guessed that Wendy was like it pretty much all of the time.

And somebody (and he could guess who) must have said something to her about her figure, though what exactly he couldn't quite imagine—nobody in their right mind could accuse her of being overweight, and why else would she be starving herself again?

"How's himself then?" he asked, and Wendy shrugged minimally. Himself was Wendy's new flatmate and landlord, the owner of the house she'd moved into. Keith had met him once and been shaken by the hand. Somehow it had been made clear that Keith was not welcome in the house, and in the three weeks since she'd been there it had for one reason or another happened that he hadn't been back.

His experience of people was wide rather than deep, and Wendy's new landlord had fitted into none of the categories that Keith was used to operating. Skinhead haircut, but he was no skin, though he had the thrust and some of the swagger. By Wendy's account he was rarely there, she had no idea what he did in these absences, though she'd mentioned once that he'd come in late, and his feet were wet, he'd left the imprint of his boots on the stairs and the kitchen floor. Very illuminating, said Keith, so he's a scuba-diver? Wendy had shrugged. She didn't know. Don't know much, do you? he'd teased her, and she'd shrugged again with half her face and one shoulder.

Keith had spent nine weeks, earlier on in his career, in an institution for young offenders. He'd worn dark blue trousers and jacket and pale blue nylon shirt. The shirt had stains under the arms, rings, permanent reminders of whoever had worn it prior to him. He was there because he'd been stopped on a motorway with no lights, and was unable to produce license or registration document or insurance. Or anything. The car was a new model sports hatchback, and it was immediately clear to everyone present that the probability of it belonging to the fifteen-year-old with the low hairline behind the wheel was slight. It soon became clear also that his first offense was a long-distant childhood memory.

In this institution—which the inmates referred to as a Borstal though it went by a more decorous name among the probation officers, social workers and clinical psychologists who had cause to visit

VIRGINS *and* MARTYRS

it—Keith first encountered the people who were to shape his world view for good. It was there that he was given the love/hate tattoo, done with a sharpened length of wire from the machine shop and ink teased out of a ball-point pen; the pain had been unlike anything he'd ever known, and had squeezed water from his eyes as he lay in his bunk that night, his cell-mate breathing quietly below him. The tattoo had cost him the equivalent of a week's wages and had rendered both hands almost useless for more than four days. Fortunately for him the phrase "blood-poisoning" was not a part of his vocabulary, as the days of crawling, aching misery in his knuckles would have been supplemented by nights of sleepless anxiety.

Along with the tattoo came the sudden need to judge people quickly and accurately, to be able to look at someone and know instantly if they were bad news or harmless, friend or foe. With the need, very soon, came the ability, and Keith had negotiated himself through his nine weeks with no fights and no real trouble. Once only had he looked at someone and registered nothing: the person in question had a glaze of something over the habitual bellicosity that the inmates wore like someone else's nylon shirt. A glaze that Keith couldn't see through. He'd found out, much later, that this person, Carl by name, had gone on to perform a quite stupefyingly ugly series of rapes and molestations.

*simon maginn*

And, shaking hands with this skinhead who wasn't a skinhead, this new landlord of Wendy's, Keith had felt again the faintly brittle, abrasive quality of the nylon under the armpits, the itchiness of the thick trousers and had again fetched up to no clear impression, a veil.

"You wanna watch that one, Wendy," said Keith, wise, in Woolworth's born-again Coffee Shop, and Wendy took a sip of her tepid black tea, saying nothing.

"You look like you're going to fit in nicely."

She sat on her bed and gazed at the flowers Keith had bought her as a moving-in present. Some of them were carnations, she wasn't sure about the others. She'd put them in a wide-necked glass vase she'd found in a cupboard in the kitchen: they drooped and leaned all over the place. They'd clearly been on their last legs when Keith had acquired them, though he had probably not known. They were fading fast now, growing brittle, the various colors toning down to a brown compromise, the heavy heads falling further.

He'd also bought food from the Chinese as a first-night celebration, representing a huge, extravagant tranche of his giro. They'd eaten it on her bed, straight out of the cartons. She'd picked fastidiously at noodles. The scent of the flowers had floated round the room, strong in the cold air.

VIRGINS *and*
MARTYRS

She'd tidied up the foil cartons and sticky cardboard lids, had stood up to throw them in the bin, and he'd grabbed her round the waist and toppled her onto the bed. She made no resistance, though she didn't really help much either. Ten minutes later she pulled away and Keith fell back on the bed, frustrated beyond belief. She got up, reassembling the food containers as if there had been no interruption. Despite a great many hints, suggestions and outright demands since then, she hadn't thought it proper to allow any recurrence. She was lucky, said Keith, that he had the patience of a bloody *saint*. No sooner had he got her out of her shared room in that slummy bed and breakfast and into a single room where they could have some privacy, than she'd developed some peculiar notion about propriety or something, she didn't feel right about it.

Well, she couldn't explain it.

"You look like you're going to fit in nicely."

But he hadn't said anything about Keith, and she'd picked up the clear message (somehow) that Keith was not included in this nice fitting-in.

Going to, he'd said, not do, already do. The fitting-in was to come. And by some means, again she was quite unable to say how, she'd got the message: *when you've dropped a couple of pounds*. It had been in the way he'd looked at her, sized her up, she felt, literally. She had to agree: no matter what anyone said, she'd been steadily gaining lately. Ever since she'd left Carlisle, in fact, she'd been gaining, she could feel it. Living in the bed and breakfast, without a kitchen and no cooking allowed in the rooms, not even a kettle for cup-a-soups, she'd been forced into the whole high fat/low fiber thing, and even if she fasted every other day to compensate, it still all piled up on her hips and the backs of her legs, she could grab fistfuls of it and squeeze. She could see it all hanging there in the mirror. How did she expect to fit in with her fat hips all over the place?

For the first week at No. 8, she fasted two days on, one day off. Sunday she'd had crackers and low-calorie soup. The second week she'd fasted Monday, Tuesday, Wednesday and Thursday. On Friday she'd binged on Swiss rolls and meat pies and tinned ravioli. She'd thrown it all up again almost at once, most of it undigested.

In Carlisle, her doctor had referred her to a self-help group for "women like herself," as he'd put it, but they'd all been bulimics, and Wendy had been, frankly, repelled and disgusted by them. One had told of how she bought frozen food and ate it, frozen; another of eating a whole box of dry breakfast cereal in one sitting. One woman, who to Wendy's clear eyes was all too obviously on the way down, had sat up very straight and described throwing up undigested food and going back to it later. Wendy

VIRGINS and
MARTYRS

had held herself tightly and had forborne to speak to these creatures. How could anyone think she was like them? If she did sometimes lapse and get sick later, well, that was innocent enough, a simple miscalculation. She certainly never made herself sick, not like these *creatures* with their fingers down their throats in locked bathrooms.

Wendy shuddered. No, she watched what she ate, and if she sometimes got it wrong she always made up for it afterward. More than made up for it. What she'd hated, despised, about the women sitting in that overheated basement room was that they were having it both ways. They ate as much as they wanted (more, to be exact) and they didn't even pay the price in flabby bellies and thighs rubbing together: they erased their crime and then did it again. They didn't even have the courage of their convictions, thought Wendy, screwing a little drop of bitter comfort out of being better, nobler, purer than those other ones.

She sat on her towel on the bed, watching Keith's flowers die. She had a Sunday color supplement open on her knees, and began idly filling in the return coupons. Catalogues and recipe cards and free seed samples. She invented names: Gail Elliman, Julie Park, Denise T. Montgomery. It was so long since she'd used her own name she sometimes had difficulty remembering what it was. Some of the coupons were Freepost, some not. She tore out the Freepost ones and put them in envelopes. Silently, furtively, she stepped out of the house and over the road to the postbox. On her way back she thought, oh dear, this probably wasn't fitting-in-nicely behavior, was it? She wished she'd thought of that before. Oh well, too late. She'd get up early and make sure she was the first downstairs to collect the morning post.

Back in her room she saw a small pile of torn paper from her activities. She picked it all up and looked round for a bin—then she remembered, there wasn't one. The room was filling up slowly with rubbish. The Chinese-food containers were still in a corner somewhere, and various other bits and pieces on the floor and under the drawers and bed. She sat on the bed, shredded the leftover paper and, piece by piece, ate it.

"You look like you've lost a couple of pounds there Wendy," he said, encountering her one day on the stairs (she slid past, her face half averted, in a gesture somewhere between deference and terror), and she felt a completely unaccustomed burst of pleasure, was not at first able to identify it, so rare it was.

"Looks good on you," he called after her, and she crept away, eyebrows raised, and flushed, prey to a delight she could neither name nor accommodate. Her nostrils curled involuntarily at a scent, a smell really, that he trailed behind him, but it didn't register.

She was now in her third week at No. 8. She rose at six-thirty and crept—noiselessly, stealthily—through the still house, down to the front door where she waited for the post, which generally came at seven. She took the whole lot back up to her room, where she sorted out the catalogues and packages addressed to her under her numerous pseudonyms, plus anything for her landlord that took her fancy. These would be hidden in a drawer beneath her black tights. She'd slink back down and replace the remainder, if any, under the letterbox. Then upstairs again to read what she'd hidden. When the house was empty, which was most of the time, she would walk, silently, up and down the stairs until she was exhausted. She sipped a cup of hot water when the pangs in her stomach got too much.

She'd lost more weight in the last ten days, not at all surprising since she'd stopped eating completely. But that wasn't the real reason, she knew. In the first trimester it was usual to lose rather than gain weight as the body adjusted to its new condition.

She sat on her bed, hugged herself, rocking back and forth. Oh yes! It was true.

She was pregnant.

## *chapter thirteen*

The one thing Terence Outhwaite had never encountered, in either his professional or his private life, was an authenticated incident of the supernatural. The evils he met with, overwhelmingly the wholly mundane ones of theft and assault, were invariably explicable in terms of human actions and motives.

Someone stole a car, because he was greedy and stupid. Someone burgled a house: he was interrupted and knocked the elderly owner over, injuring him, because he was stupid and frightened. Someone abused his children and wife, subjecting them to years of fear and petty humiliations, and often more serious injuries, because he was vicious and stupid, simply because he could. For Outhwaite the question "why" was less important than the question "who," and the punishment of them. He had few illusions about reform and rehabilitation. He saw the justice system as a simple retributive equation: you do this, we catch you, we punish you.

Like many policemen, Outhwaite privately believed that the best deterrent was a public flogging, the best prevention of serious crime the execution of criminals. If a rapist found that his actions led him to a police surgeon and the removal of his testicles, surely he would think carefully about committing his crime. If a thug went out on a burglary

VIRGINS and
MARTYRS

with a gun and knew that if he, accidentally or otherwise, shot someone then he too would die—would he ever leave his house so equipped?

Outhwaite had devoted his whole working life to administering the criminal justice system and he did so scrupulously and without any compromise. But that system sometimes now seemed so overwhelmingly loaded in favor of the perpetrators of the crime that flooded into the police station every day, every hour, that he occasionally despaired. Magistrates could be unbelievably capricious, social workers could apparently find exonerating circumstances for a concentration-camp torturer, and juries sometimes seemed to delight in bringing in the most inappropriate verdict they could contrive.

And that was if you could get your man as far as an appearance in front of a magistrate. Not only did the scummiest, nastiest hooligan have a right to say nothing at all, and for that to be interpreted, not as one might imagine as evidence of guilt, but as mere caution; not only were the police hedged about with a jungle of procedural requirements, the breaching of any one of which could lead to an entire case being disallowed; but now it wasn't just juries who routinely disbelieved the evidence given by police officers—it was magistrates. Even, he permitted himself the thought with a sour little grin, in Hove.

*simon maginn*

There had been a case a few years back, a simple enough matter of gross indecency in a public toilet. Two plain-clothes men had gone in, and observed a man "in an excited condition" standing at the stall. This man, apparently well able to discern the true identity of the two policemen, had immediately moved away from the man he was standing next to, and had "put himself away and attempted to leave." He had been apprehended and charged.

Unfortunately for the case, he had contacted an organization of solicitors who specialized in defending men in precisely these circumstances. The solicitor had convinced his client to plead not guilty, itself a rarity in indecency cases where the shame and remorse involved usually provoked an immediate plea of guilty. But not this time.

The case had gone to a magistrate, and after the plain-clothes men had given their evidence, the defense solicitor had introduced an expert witness, a doctor.

This doctor had shown the magistrates photographs, the kind that in any ordinary circumstances would themselves have been the subject of a criminal prosecution. They showed the defendant's manhood, at its fullest extension, and alongside this impressive organ was a tape measure. The dimensions of the organ were duly noted by their honors. Then they were shown a photo of the defendant's trousers, with measurements of the

VIRGINS and
MARTYRS

zip aperture. The two measurements were compared, and it was immediately clear that the first item could not conceivably have been inserted into the second without injury: the first was simply much too big. The sequence of events described by the plain-clothes men was physiologically impossible. At this moment, the presiding magistrate had raised his gaze from the photographs and met the eyes of the police. Since then, Outhwaite had noticed a much higher incidence of acquittals from the bench, even in what were apparently the most unambiguous cases, and not only that but an increasing skepticism about the police cases which had been almost wholly absent before. Oh yeah? they seemed to be saying, *prove it.*

Life, Outhwaite thought, was difficult enough. Allow the supernatural in and—well, you might as well throw the towel in and go and hand out soup to derelicts, as one of his burned-out colleagues had recently done.

Daniel Blennerhassett had come to see him, to tell him something.

Funny, he'd thought, observing the young man, that "hunted" and "haunted" should be such similar words. Daniel looked both things. He had sat very still, his left arm held rigidly at his side. He'd produced his story, mostly incoherent, but embedded within it had been the fact that Daniel had known about the mark on the palm of the Lady of

*simon maginn*

the Lake's hand, the puncture wound. Outhwaite tried hard not to think of it as a stigmatum.

There were, Outhwaite considered, precisely three ways he could know this. Daniel had made the mark himself, and was thus the person being sought by police. He knew, or knew of, the person who made the mark, and thus would lead the police to the person being sought. Or it was a lucky guess.

Daniel's explanation was, frankly, in the category of "inadmissible." He'd had a series of visions, culminating in seeing his own arm becoming the arm that had been found washed up. Oh yes. That would certainly look good in front of a judge. Similarly the lucky guess explanation. No innocent person had any business having guesses that lucky.

But neither was it at all likely that Daniel was the person responsible for making the mark, and, presumably, murdering the woman. Because if he was guilty, then why did he come forward and give his statement, thus bringing himself to the attention of the police, and not confess? And why did he not mention the ring?

It could only mean that Daniel knew something.

For Outhwaite this presented the problem of how to respond to what Daniel was, obliquely, telling him. The obvious point of departure was to search the house, and see what turned up. After that, well, Daniel could perhaps be encouraged to remember other things. He might, for instance, have a few more visions up his sleeve—a vision of the guilty party's face would be nice. Perhaps a vision of an address, a name. Daniel seemed very willing to oblige—in fact he'd seemed grateful for Outhwaite just to listen to him. It was a tragedy that there wasn't enough to hold him on, he'd probably be grateful for that as well.

Lonely, needy, haunted. He'd reminded Outhwaite of nothing as much as a grieving child, wailing in the night, but internally, silently. A few times in the course of his curious statement he'd looked up at Outhwaite, and Outhwaite had for a moment thought he was about to show him a bruised knee or a broken Action Man. Whatever Daniel knew, he would sooner or later tell Outhwaite, that was certain. In the meantime, the house must be searched.

A uniformed constable was given the enviable responsibility of going through the ground-floor bedroom and kitchen, including the bin. Outhwaite, accompanied by the skinhead, made a more general inspection of the premises.

"How many people live here?" Outhwaite asked, walking round the second completely abandoned bedroom; he ran his fingers over a dusty cupboard top.

"Just one."

"Daniel Blennerhassett?"

"That's right. He's not in any trouble I hope?"

"Oh no. Nothing like that."

Outhwaite turned and smiled, gesturing widely. Nothing to worry about.

"No no. We're just following something up. Please don't worry."

"If you say so Mr....?"

"Detective Inspector Outhwaite." Outhwaite was used to having to repeat his name—he'd already introduced himself at the front door.

"How do you do, Detective?" To Outhwaite's surprise he found that he was being offered a hand to shake. He took it gravely, and the young man said, "Pleased to meet you."

Outhwaite found himself growing tense before this courteous skinhead. He was having trouble placing the accent. He was having trouble placing anything.

He'd searched, in all probability, several hundred houses with and without good cause and proper paperwork. A house could tell you an immense amount about its owner or occupant. Quite apart from physical evidence of the kind you could show a magistrate, or wave in front of a witness, there were all the tiny, subtle, inexpressible things that your suspect was busy trying not to tell you in the interviews. His tastes, his habits, values and aspirations. In short, what Outhwaite tried hard not to think of as his *kind*. A dangerous lazy concept that, but one that he couldn't help himself using. What *kind* are you?

In this case, though, he found that he was developing no picture at all of Daniel's landlord. Polite. He was polite the way other people were diabetics or Muslims: it was a defining characteristic. Caucasian male, twenty-eight to thirty years old, five foot eleven, cropped hair, well-built, polite.

Outhwaite let go the hand, resisting an impulse to rub his own hand against his jacket.

"So you don't live here?"

"Yeah, I do. I rent out the other rooms."

"Really?" Outhwaite gestured round at the disused room, the empty flat.

The skinhead laughed.

"Well people come and go. You know."

"How long has Mr. Blennerhassett been living here?"

"A few days, he moved in, let me think—" he frowned, calculating, "—Tuesday and today, er…"

"Friday."

"Really?"

Outhwaite assented gravely.

"Well then that'd make it four days."

"Is he a friend of yours?"

"No. No actually I put ads up round the university common rooms."

"I see." Outhwaite nodded.

"Shall we?" he added, as the skinhead showed no signs of moving.

"Please." The skinhead gestured with his arm: after *you*.

"Perhaps it would be better if you led the way," said Outhwaite, "since it's your house."

"Oh. Of course."

Outhwaite followed him ponderously up the stairs. The staircarpet was neutral and very dusty. Outhwaite coughed and was aware of an irritation in his nostrils. Not just the dust. Something.

They were at the top now. The skinhead opened a door to a small room. Outhwaite peered in. Dust. A settled, fixed look to it. He shrugged. The door was shut again and they passed down the short corridor to the next room. The last one. Top floor front.

"This is Daniel's room," he said, and pulled the door open.

Here at last was evidence of recent occupancy. Bags of what he initially took for rubbish in the middle of the floor.

"He apparently hasn't found the wardrobe yet," Outhwaite said, and the skinhead laughed with him.

"Well you know students, Detective."

Outhwaite snorted; yes.

"He must be a very busy student. He's certainly not at home pushing the hoover around. Is he?"

His landlord curled his lip.

VIRGINS *and*
MARTyRS

"It would seem not, no. I wouldn't know really. I'm not here very much."

So where exactly are you then, Outhwaite thought but didn't ask. He entered the room with exaggerated caution, stepping elaborately round the scattered detritus on the floor.

"I shouldn't say this, but I've been to scenes of crimes that were prettier than this." He sniffed, making a big production out of it. "This must be where he keeps the bodies," he said, and met the skinhead's steady, uninformative gaze. He was reminded for a moment of the expressions he saw on the faces of teenage thugs released with a caution on their twentieth offense. He went to the table by the window.

"Definitely a student," he said, "unmistakably," and waited until the skinhead made an inquiring sound, then added:

"No books. No paper. No pens. Has to be a student."

"I think he mostly works up at the university library."

"What exactly is it he's studying? How to be a total pig?"

The skinhead smiled, politely acknowledging the joke.

"It's an MA. Master of Arts—"

"I know what an MA is."

"—in medieval history. This is his second year, final year. He's trying to finish his dissertation."

*simon maginn*

Outhwaite nudged open the wardrobe.

"Well he's clearly not trying to finish tidying the place up," he said, laboriously, and the skinhead sighed.

"I hate to disappoint you Detective but being an untidy bastard isn't an offense. Not that I'm aware of anyway."

"Detective Inspector," Outhwaite said, noting the change in tone.

"Sorry. A—a policeman's a policeman to me I'm afraid." Outhwaite sensed that "policeman" had been substituted for another, less neutral word in that sentence at the last minute.

Outhwaite raised himself onto the balls of his feet to check on top of the wardrobe, and was momentarily disgusted at what his fingers found.

"Shit!"

He recoiled, then, watched minutely by the skinhead, reached up again and brought down something that he was unable for a second to identify. Outhwaite held it in front of him, and raised his eyebrows: anything to do with you?

"Oh that," he said, and felt something blocking his throat, raising the color in his face.

"This is yours?" Outhwaite asked, and he nodded.

"Certainly is."

"Not Mr. Blennerhasset's?"

"No. No, it's mine."

VIRGINS and MARTYRS

"Sir, you're not under investigation here, but I would be enormously grateful to you if you'd tell me what exactly this is?" He held the long tail of hair by one end; it hung, lifeless, like a suicide from a rope.

"It's my hair."

"You mean hair that belongs to you?"

"I used to be a bit of a hippy, you see. Then, when I was seeking training, I had it all shaved off, and I kept it. Don't ask me why, just a souvenir I suppose. Not that I really missed having it, it took such a lot of looking after. Still it was quite an image change, as I'm sure you can imagine." He smiled.

Outhwaite held the hair, studying it. Something, something…

"And so you kept it as a…"

"Souvenir."

"Or a relic?"

"If you like. I must have just chucked it up there one day and forgotten about it."

"This used to be your room?"

"Used to be, yes, though not for a while now."

"Been up there for years, that's why it's so dusty?" He waved the hair vaguely.

"Must be. Yes."

"Who was in this room before Mr. Blennerhassett moved in?"

"Well. Let me see…"

"Was it vacant very long before Mr. Blennerhasset moved in?"

"No, no just a few weeks: before Daniel it was occupied by a Ms. Bishop, Wendy Bishop."

Outhwaite was stroking the hair as if it were a pet rabbit. The skinhead couldn't take his eyes off it.

"You said training. You were seeking training."

"Yes, you know, Holy Orders."

"Really? You trained as a priest?"

"No I didn't, not in the end, there was a question about my vocation."

"Do you know where she went to?"

"What?"

"Ms. Bishop."

"No, I'm afraid not, she didn't leave a forwarding…"

"Do you know why she left?"

"No, she, we didn't discuss…"

"Do you know where she is now?"

"Detective, I…"

"Detective Inspector," Outhwaite said, and smiled. The skinhead took a breath.

"No. I don't," he said and slid his hands into his pockets.

Outhwaite shrugged, and held out the hair to him—he took it and looked round for somewhere to put it, but there was nowhere. So he just held it. It felt dusty, rough, almost scaly. Something a reptile might shed.

VIRGINS *and* MARTYRS

"Right. Thank you very much sir, you've been very helpful. I hope I won't have to bother you again."

"Not at all, Detective. Detective *Inspector*. It was no bother." He was terribly aware of how much this was the wrong thing to say. He might as well have added, "The pleasure was all mine. Do please drop by any time."

He accompanied Outhwaite down to the front door.

He closed the door behind him, resting his weight against it for a moment, and went up to the bathroom. He still hadn't found anywhere to put the hair so he shoved it into the breast pocket of his white shirt.

He turned on the hot tap and put in the plug, and his lips began to move.

"*Judica me Deus et discerne causam meam*": judge me O God, and distinguish my cause.

The old words, useless now, but a powerful habit. He reached into the cupboard for the bottle of Dettol, and watched as the water clouded, swirled, thickened, becoming like milk. He plunged his hand in, forcing himself to withstand the heat of the water for the length of the line:

"*Quia Tu es Deus fortitudo mea, quare me repulisti?*": For Thou O God art my strength, why hast thou cast me off?

*simon maginn*

*Repulisti*—cast off, repulsed: rejected.

His hands were red and stinging. He went to the bath and rinsed them under the cold tap, then picked up the nailbrush and turned back to the sink.

"*Quare tristis es, anima mea?*: why art thou sorrowful, O my soul?

He plunged his hands back into the scalding water, held them there, rinsed them again at the bath. If he timed it right he would reach the *Confiteor Deo*, the Confession, by the end of this second rinsing. He speeded up, the words a thick, unmodulated murmur.

"*Adjutorium nostrum in nomine Domine*": our help is in the name of the Lord. The final dip in the Dettol, hold, the final rinse. He reached for his towel.

Bang-on. "*Confiteor Deo.*" I confess. His hands throbbed.

At the age of seventeen, while trying to decide whether to seek training as a priest, he had undertaken a four-week retreat in a drafty monastery in Yorkshire and had, alongside thirty other intense, troubled young men, performed St. Ignatius Loyola's Spiritual Exercises precisely as indicated.

The purpose was to subdue the appetite, to focus the mind and body exclusively on the glory of Christ and the unworthiness of the sinner, to induce a state of humility so intense that the peni-

VIRGINS *and*
MARTYRS

tent could truly appreciate the greatness of God in comparison. Loyola had designed the exercises to take place over a four-week period, and had indicated exactly what meditations, prayers, thoughts etc. were to be entertained at what time of what day. There were also general instructions concerning penance, prayer, sleep and food ("the better to control any irregularity in his appetite or any temptation from the enemy, he should eat less when he is tempted to eat more"). By the end of the second week, eight of the original thirty had withdrawn from the retreat, defiantly or miserably or with relief, according to their natures, and only eighteen young men emerged into the damp gloom of an October Friday night at the end of the fourth week. Several of them had had experiences that they were as yet unable or unwilling to discuss with each other, hugging them to themselves.

The skinhead had, however, admitted to his confessor, a distant, distracted Jesuit of forty, that he had experienced "something" while lying on his bed contemplating the mystery of the Assumption of the Virgin. His confessor had cautioned him against chasing after miracles and chimeras, and had advised prolonged prayer and meditation in which he might discern God's purpose for him. Vocation, stated the measured, bland voice of the Jesuit, was as likely to come gradually and stealthily, like a secret lover, as in visions and voices. A "something" experienced on a retreat could signify many things, but by no means did it necessarily indicate a miraculous intervention into someone's life. He had come away angry, disappointed, and with his confessor's warnings against pride ringing tinnily in his ears.

Now of course, at the distance of fifteen years, he was more inclined to attribute his "something" to the effects of prolonged isolation, silence, discomfort and, perhaps most importantly, hunger. Loyola's warnings about appetite had been very vigorously observed at the retreat, and he had found himself becoming increasingly light-headed as week succeeded week on a diet composed largely of potatoes, fish and bread and margarine, and not very much of it at that. Hunger then was a novel experience, as new and astonishing as the perpetual tiredness brought on by the endless round of services and prayers; his head had felt full of a thick buzzing light, and it was this light that had finally focused itself before his bloodshot eyes in that scrupulously miserable cell, had become a cloudy, shifting image, had taken on a face and an arm, a hand that had shown him—something.

Sleep deprivation, starvation, ritual intoning of prayers and exercises such as the one he had just performed, in which prayer and breathing were synchronized; isolation, and a species of studied cheerlessness. Put this together with a constant exposure to the details of Christ's martyrdom in pictures, statues, prayer cards, readings from the Bible—not to mention the literally omnipresent form of the crucifix—and even in people less suggestible than he, these were circumstances in which one might see just about anything.

Since then he had seen maybe half a dozen other "somethings," in a variety of circumstances. On more than one occasion he had seen that hand stretching out to him again, and the whatever-it-was that it was holding had been a little clearer each time, though never close enough to see. He had had visions of such paralyzing beauty that he had been afraid. He had seen a procession of state barges, decked out in scarlet and gold, and on the last of them a throne; they had swept past, a blur of brilliant Renaissance colors, vermilion, saffron, green, the oarsmen in slashed tunics. Over the throne there had been a fringed canopy, and he hadn't been able to see who occupied it, he had just had a glance of a bowed figure in a brown cloak. He'd seen a shower of fire coming out of the sky and falling into the sea.

But the thing he had never seen, clearly, unambiguously, was the evidence for the existence of God. He had never heard his voice. Not even when he was agonizing night and day over the reality of his vocation. On his knees for as much as three hours a day, arguing, debating, occasionally plead-

ing. Silently. And in all that time the Man Upstairs had kept his counsel, apparently indifferent
to the undignified, unequal struggle going endlessly
on beneath him. The skinhead had begun to picture him as a television magician holding up the
queen of spades and refusing, *refusing* to explain how
you do it, shaking his head, smiling. In a glitter suit.

This time, he had been sure all that was about
to change, had been certain that this time the grinning television fake would have to break his intol-
erable, bullying silence and make himself known.
However as day followed day it was looking increasingly unlikely, and he had to admit that his optimism was becoming more and more stubborn and
mechanical. If not this time, then certainly next,
definitely next. The idea was forming itself bit by
bit, and this time it would be perfect.

Driving back along the seafront that evening, the
sun a hot pink blur against the Shoreham B power
station behind him, Outhwaite found the word he'd
been looking for.

He'd been hunting for it all day, his tongue working round a loose filling, the word that would describe what was wrong with that house, those rooms.
It had refused to come, but now it came, accompanied by premonition tickling the hairs on his neck.
Shrine. The house was like a shrine. And sure
enough, in the room occupied by that troubled, trou-

VIRGINS *and*
MARTYRS

bling, haunted young man who had known things he couldn't possibly know (unless…) there was what you would expect to find in a shrine: a relic.

He drove back to the neat, quiet house in Peacehaven, hours late, for the third time that week, back to Sean and Grant and Karen.

He opened the front doors and chaos greeted him, grabbed him by the lapel and dragged him into the kitchen.

A familiar scene: Grant yelling something at his mother and Sean sitting at the table, his head down, his lips moving. Counting.

Outhwaite ducked over to kiss Karen, but she pulled away from him, chasing after Grant, who was still yelling.

"Hey hey hey," said Outhwaite, but no one took any notice and he sat at the table with Sean. He put his arm around him, but Sean kept on doing what he was doing.

He was counting the frozen chips on the oven dish, pushing them around with his finger, checking them off, one by one.

"Did you have a good day?" Outhwaite asked, but Sean just shook his head slowly, his lips still moving as he counted. Outhwaite sighed and went to look for Karen and Grant, Sean's mother and little brother respectively.

He found Grant in the lounge, staring at the television, a look on his face of such ferocity that

Outhwaite felt helpless and angry and exhausted by it.

"What was all that about then?" he asked after a short, loaded pause; Grant, twelve years old and furious, grimaced bitterly and twisted his mouth up into a kind of snarl.

"Why don't you ask her?" he said, and Outhwaite was immediately enraged.

"I'm asking *you*, that's why," he said, and was sadly conscious, even through the rage, of what a lame, stock-parental thing it was to say.

He knew it wasn't easy for Grant. It was hard to be twelve years old and to have an elder brother who was, in the common, brutal speech of the schoolyard, a retard, a spas, a drooling, muttering cretin. He knew that Grant got into trouble in the playground because of his brother, got into fights, and consequently felt picked on by the teachers, bunked off, got caught…. He was having a hard time. Outhwaite tried hard to do better than the stock-parental.

"Something to do with Sean?" he asked, as gently as his mood allowed, and Grant twisted his face up again into that horrible grimace.

"Could be."

"What. What was it."

Grant spat out the story, how his mum had been about to put the oven chips in when Sean had appeared and demanded that he be allowed to count them. Which would, of course, hold everything up for some time because he counted very slowly and often had to have many recounts until he got a number he liked, a number he could work with. So Grant had said for Christ's sake, just put them in the oven, except he hadn't said "oven" he'd said "fucking oven," and Karen had yelled at him, and he'd yelled back, and Sean had sat hunched over the table, counting.

Outhwaite sighed. He went over to Grant and, regardless of his son's considerable size and inauspicious demeanor, grabbed hold of him and picked him up.

"Get out of that, then!" he said, and he and Grant fell sideways on to the sofa and Grant laughed. Outhwaite ruffled his hair, and promised to have a word with Karen.

Later, as he lay beside his wife who was sleeping the sleep of the chemically assisted, he slept also, and in short, bright dreams he revisited the house on Adelaide Street, went from room to room, and everywhere he went he could feel the presence of something that was hidden from him, just out of sight.

### chapter fourteen

In the days following his interview with Outhwaite, Daniel began to feel much better. True his arm was still numb and stiff, and he was having to find ways of getting along without using it or looking at it, but he was managing better than he'd thought he would. Thoughts of food came at him from time to time, but his fast seemed to have developed its own logic now and his fantasies about eating were tinged with nausea. He was, however, nerving himself up for another attempt, and was ready to face the kitchen.

He went down and surveyed it.

Kitchens, in Daniel's experience, were dark, disorderly places, crammed full of battered chairs and ranked masses of unwashed dishes, arranged chronologically like geological strata. Thursday—curry; Wednesday—spaghetti hoops and sausage; Tuesday—the remains of a pie and chips with brown sauce smears. The oldest dish was nearest the sink. *In* the sink, generally speaking, he expected to find a bowl full of cold, rank water and sediment with pans arranged in it. Pieces of fried egg, interestingly enough, always seemed to figure prominently in these compositions.

So he was surprised that the kitchen here was more like one of those television kitchens, clean, clear surfaces and orderly cupboards. In fact it was so clear it was hardly like a kitchen at all. For one thing, there didn't seem to be any food. He investigated the cupboards but there was almost nothing, not even the packets of raspberry jelly and dried lasagna that he'd imagined were always to be found. He finally disinterred a bag of spaghetti quills, about two dozen or so remaining. That would do. Probably wise, if he really was going to eat, to start small. Work up to the steak and chips and onion rings gradually.

He was continually surprised by how difficult it was to do things using only one hand. The cupboard doors were springier than he'd anticipated, for one thing, and he found his forearm and foot coming into play more than once. The sink was a little narrow, and there was unexpected awkwardness in taking the pan of water out of it; he ended up spilling most of it, and found that more kept tipping out of either side on the way to the cooker. It was somewhat like trying to cook after five pints of beer, where exaggerated compensations for motor clumsiness led to surprising and unfortunate results.

He had the pan on the ring, he had the ring heating up, he needed just to wait for the water to boil.

He sat at the clean, scrubbed table. Very scrubbed. He felt guilty but defiant at his filching of the spaghetti quills. Should anyone come in and challenge him, he, Daniel, would simply declare, with dignity but some force, that he was sorry, that he would of course replace them, but that he simply *had* to have them. There was no room for argument. He became aware that he was prepared to argue, to dispute, even to *fight* for them. His body

*simon maginn*

was screaming for nutrients. Simple carbohydrates particularly. Not sugars or vitamins, certainly not vitamins, but starch. Pasta and rice and potatoes and bread. *Bread!* He was on his feet again, opening cupboards, looking for bread. Not a crumb.

The question burst into his head: where was everyone? Surely it was peculiar, to say the least, for a whole house to be just left empty like this. All those rooms, fully furnished, quiet, vacant, dusty. His landlord claimed to use one of them: Daniel had yet to see him. Bathroom, kitchen, spare rooms, all of them maintained like museum exhibits of late twentieth-century domiciliary units, correct in their detail but totally, horribly wrong in essence. They were empty, dead, quietly accumulating dust that was suffered to settle completely unopposed by the slightest stirring of breath or movement. He breathed in silence.

*Hiss.*

The chair fell over behind him as he swung to his feet, alarmed beyond all reason. He called out, a sound like "whoh!" or "who," his eyes hunting furiously for the origin of the sound, as it came again, *hissss!*

His eyes found the cooker; the water in the pan was boiling, splashing onto the ring, hissing. That was all. Get a grip now.

He tipped the sharp little pasta tubes into the water, their shape reminding him of an instrument

VIRGINS *and* MARTYRS

used by embalmers called a trocar. He shook his head: the thought puzzled him, because he had to the best of his knowledge never seen or even heard of an embalmer's trocar. The memory didn't seem to belong to him at all. He was considering the oddness of this when a clump of the pasta quills fell out of the bag, stuck together by damp. He jerked his hand back as his wrist was splashed with drops of scalding water, his sleeve catching the handle of the pan.

He danced back, but the idiot water flung itself at him, onto his hand and arm.

He regarded his red, scalded hand, in the second or two before pain flooded his consciousness, and laughed.

### chapter fifteen

Dr. Medway stood courteously as Daniel entered, inclined his head, and indicated a chair. His tutorial room had the stylized impersonality of most of the rooms in the university: lifetimes of endeavor, struggle, deadly competition and occasional despair were spent in these little studies with the neutral-colored journals stacked in floppy heaps on the shelves and the coordinated carpets and stretch covers. Generations of earnest young men, defiant young women, dilettantes, oafs, empty-headed poseurs and (infrequently) able, gifted and sometimes even brilliant people had sat in these rooms, talking talking, talking. The study stank of stale controversy.

And behind his functional, tidy desk presided Dr. Medway, tall, shrewd, not quite malicious, not exactly amused; indulgent. He would listen, gazing at the phone or the light switch, while someone offered an interpretation or an opinion, and when they'd finished he'd smile:

"Yes…"

The student would sit back, pleased.

"…but of course, as you know…" Medway would continue, frowning now, and chuck a bomb on it. Boom! The student's idea would lie, charred and smoking, on the low-pile neutral carpet tiles, and Medway would contemplate it, sadly, pityingly. A shame, his face would say, such a shame.

It was with such a face that he admitted Daniel into his study. He took in the clumsily bandaged hand, the other arm held stiffly down, the untidy hair. He picked up Daniel's dissertation from his desk.

"*First*," he said, as Daniel settled himself in the low-slung chair, "thank you for letting me see this. I'm glad I had an opportunity to read it. And thank you for coming to see me." He smiled, graciously.

"*Actually*, I'm not supposed to be here at all," he continued confidingly, "I'm *really* supposed to be at a bash in Milan, for my sins. Carl Schonberg, a symposium on his eightieth birthday. You know the kind of thing, *sincere* tributes from former students (I, regrettably, among them) and even the dubious promise of a paper from the man himself. *If* he's still capable of connected speech. *Venerable* is simply not the word. I mean really. I cried off," he said leaning forward conspiratorially, "claiming domestic problems. Marvelous phrase! I always think of middle-aged homosexuals of a certain sort staging suicide bids whenever I hear it. Nothing so interesting in my case, I regret to assure you!" and he laughed, a big stage laugh, practiced over many years in the company of tongue-tied undergraduates and anxious junior lecturers.

He sat back again.

"Ah well, you're going to tell me what's bothering you sooner or later. I rather doubt there's anything I can do or say to stop you." He smiled a patient smile. Daniel opened his mouth.

"Before you *do*, however," Medway said, smoothing his hair, "I would just say this: please do not imagine that my title of Personal Tutor confers on me any kind of ability to intervene meaningfully in any difficulty you may be experiencing of a *personal* kind. Students have, on occasion, addressed problems to me in a manner which I could only characterize as *devastatingly frank*. Embarrassing on all sides, of course, since an avuncular display of feigned interest is really the extent of my abilities in that direction, I am all too sorry to say."

Daniel again opened his mouth to protest, even got as far as the "oh" in "oh no nothing like that," but was again interrupted.

"The other thing I really ought to say before any kind of agonized unburdening gets under way *is*, that as far as your thesis, your dissertation, is concerned I am really not at liberty to discuss it at any level of detail with you. At this time. I have read your draft," he indicated the sheaf of papers on his desk, "with great interest, and beyond that I really wouldn't feel it proper to comment. I would not, for instance, feel able to tell you whether, in my *opinion*, you are likely to be called for a viva-voce examination, though, as you are certainly aware, it is unusual for Masters students to be called unless there is a risk of the student failing. However, it would not *necessarily* mean, *were* you to be invited to such a discussion, that you were in any danger of failing. Borderline is an ugly word. You are well advised, however, as I surely don't have to tell you, to keep October free of any engagements that would prevent you from attending a viva. *Were* you to be called."

Medway smiled and shrugged, as if disassociating himself from this farrago of double talk and indirection, but the bureaucrat in him was loose, banishing the urbane, high-minded freethinker and

VIRGINS *and*
MARTYRS

replacing him with a book of university regulations. Daniel sat, cowed by this sudden conversion and by the calculated intimidation of words like "Milan" and "symposium," and by Medway's restrictions on what he could and couldn't say. He felt a little crunch of anger, a spurt of self-pity. If the roles were reversed, he thought passionately, I would be kind, so much kinder.

"Really, I wish I could be more helpful. A worrying time, I know," Medway said, perhaps sensing Daniel's dissatisfaction, perhaps remembering his own gawky shamefaced student days.

"Look, permit me the impudence of a suggestion: there's a simply *marvelous* paper in, I *think*, the *History Review* of Spring '88. Don't quote me on that. It's called "The Relic, the Icon and the Company of Saints." I'm modest enough to hesitate to mention that its author is a former student of mine. I lost contact with him, unfortunately, and I don't believe he ever completed his degree. Probably the best thing in his case though, best for everyone concerned."

Medway stood up: the interview was over.

"Read it. The author has some remarkable comments to make and I think you'll find them, shall we say, *germane*? I think in the light of them you may want to *reconsider* one or two points in here." Medway raised an arm in a gesture that irresistibly suggested the direction of the door and with the other hand held out the bundle of paper, Daniel's dissertation.

"Why?"

Medway's poise trembled on the brink of annoyance for a moment.

"Why what?"

"Why best for everyone concerned?"

"Daniel my dear fellow you have me at a disadvantage. Why best for everyone concerned *what?*"

"Your former student, why did you say it would be best…"

"Ah that. Yes I suppose I did say that didn't I. Well, all I really meant is that there's a certain kind of mind that can become its own worst enemy, *turn* on itself. There's a sort of rigor of thought that can become troublesome to its owner, can become terminal. Thought can so easily become obsession, possession, can *devour*—"

Medway looked at Daniel, whose hand was still on the door handle, the door partly open.

"It is possible to imagine the mind as a predatory animal. Animals have many sides to their natures, many *aspects*: they are capable of exquisite, adaptive behaviors, extraordinary athleticism and skill, leaping, flying, all manner of showy and delightful things. And these same dazzling little beings simply gobble each other up in the most *bestial* manner at the merest drop of a hat. You've seen the wildlife documentaries I have no doubt. Quite shocking really. Something ought to be done. So with certain minds: they flash and glitter and pirouette, cavorting in treetops and diving into rivers and so forth, and then one turns round and catches them with a mouthful of something wriggling and gory. Only with the *mind*, one finds that, all too often, the gory, wriggling item in question is—well, is *itself*, is the mind."

Medway grinned hugely.

"My dear, you look quite *mesmerized*! Off you go now and read read read. Icon, Relic, Company of Saints. Do you far more good than all the Buckley F. Tzaszes put together, and heaven knows how they do multiply!"

Daniel found it exactly where Medway had described. He pulled it off the shelf with some difficulty and took it to a table.

The book, although only four years old, had already about it the hopelessly abandoned quality that so many of the publications in the library seemed to develop, more or less immediately. They rolled, fresh and fascinating and controversial, off the presses and into libraries such as this where they were dutifully catalogued and shelved, and left. As if intimidated, humbled by the colossal weight of their fellows on all sides of them, they fell into a kind of inapproachability, a kind of silent rage.

Daniel checked the index and found the page. "Although specifically outlawed by St. Gregory the Great in his Letter to Constantine, the practice of dividing up the corpses of the saints continued late into the eighteenth century. The demand, from pilgrims and miracle-seekers alike, for relics was such that competition for these body parts was fierce, and the practices employed to obtain them often profoundly dubious. Monasteries, cathedrals and wealthy princes, even popes, were all involved in what amounted to an international market for dead human flesh."

Daniel closed his eyes and sighed. It seemed that he couldn't pick up a book in this damn library without encountering the dead and their attendants and admirers. He scratched absently at his left palm, and his eyes flew open— someone was watching him. He stared around, head jerking like a chicken. Everywhere the faintly hostile presence of the books. Were they too the children of a suicide? The rage felt familiar. (If they were to *fall*…) He cast round anxiously, and caught movement in the corner of his eye, a sly dragging movement. Shit. He stood up, and his breathing was hard, labored. He gripped the desk with his right hand, and the bandage slid over the shiny wood. His fingertips were slippy with sweat. He rubbed them on his jacket.

*(Daniel)*

VIRGINS *and*
MARTYRS

Shit shit *shit*; he flung himself around, desperately scanned the racks, the big heavy volumes like rocks poised for a landslide that could be triggered by the slightest thing, a scream for instance, or a sly creature dragging itself around, undermining the stacks, pulling, pushing,

(ƒind me)

or merely leaning too hard, leaning up against the books,

(ƒind me)

get a grip now, get a grip now

He forced himself to sit, to breathe, to meditate on good things, calm things, tranquil rivers flowing through flower-strewn meadows.

What kind of flowers?

Oh daisies and, you know, buttercups probably, dandelions and so on. It didn't matter did it? He put his hand to his chest and breathed slowly, deeply. He picked the flowers, slowly, with the hot sun on his back. That's it. Pick the flowers.

When the blood had receded a little from his skin, and the spit had come back onto his tongue, he cautiously opened his eyes and tried again.

"Where genuine relics, which is to say human remains, of the saint were to be had, the most extraordinary scenes were witnessed. A sixth-century observer at a shrine commented thus:

'She shuddered at the sight of so many marvelous happenings. For there she was met by the noise of demons roaring in various torments, and, before the tomb of the saint, she saw men howling like wolves, barking like dogs, roaring like lions, hissing like snakes, bellowing like bulls; some twisted their heads to touch the earth by arching their bodies backward; women hung upside down in midair, yet their skirts did not fall down over their heads.'

"These scenes are of course highly reminiscent of the behavior of those possessed by demons, and it is clear that divine healing and demonic possession were, to some degree, interchangeable signs. These *laetitiae*, or feasts held at the shrines of saints and martyrs, share a great deal also with the reports of the nocturnal meetings of witches.

"Perhaps more significantly, though, the distinction between the saint and his or her image, or icon, became increasingly blurred. The icon could, itself, have miraculous properties of healing or divination. Thus the gloriously vivid, and often appallingly violent, pictures of the deaths of the saints and martyrs, were to be regarded as holy in exactly the same way as the saint or martyr himself. The Company of Saints was not an abstraction, a mere list of names of the long dead to be chanted in litanies, but was a real, physical presence in the lives of those who sought their help: literally, company…"

Yes but what kind of flowers?

He blinked the thought away, turned the page.

VIRGINS *and*
MARTYRS

"To the modern mind, the details of the lives of the saints can seem perverse, even repugnant:

"St. Catherine of Alexandria, who courted illness to the extent that she drank a cupful of the pus of a diseased beggar.

"Blessed Beatrice of Ornacieu, Virgin, who was in the habit of driving a nail through the palms of her hands, which then, miraculously, bled not blood but pure water, and which healed immediately.

"Blessed Julia of Certaldo, Virgin, who lived for more than thirty years walled up beside a church.

"Innumerable saints, often no more than young girls, flogging themselves to exhaustion, regularly; denying themselves food to the point of death; inventing novel torments for their bruised, emaciated bodies. Taking vows of the most extreme austerity. In one case, keeping the eyes shut *for the whole of her life* in order to avoid temptation.

"To us, such stories are insane, sick, even disgusting. But to the medieval mind such behavior indicated the highest form of blessing, and upon their deaths the physical remains of those strange, tortured individuals, and even merely pictures of them, could bring about miraculous events in the lives of the faithful."

What are you doing with the flowers? Are you going courting?

Daniel again tried to push the thought away, tried to concentrate.

*simon maginn*

"They also, of course, represented material wealth of a negotiable kind, and became part of the treasuries of the great cathedrals. The *Inventories of Christchurch, Canterbury* list the contents of one 'chest of ivory with a crucifix' as follows:

*three fingers and two teeth of St. Alban, the Protomartyr of England;*

*some dust of St. Pancras, martyr—*"

Are you taking them somewhere? Are they for someone?

"*some of the beard and vestments of St. Cuthbert, bishop and confessor.*"

He held the flowers tightly; the sun was hot on his neck and back, and the grass grew thick by the side of the stream. On the other side of the stream there was a wire fence, and then trees. He jumped the stream, easily, it was no distance at all, and climbed over the fence.

The air was cooler, damper, under the trees; he pushed through the undergrowth, the flowers wilting already in his clammy hands, the smell of moist earth and bitter ivy strong.

For a girl, maybe?

Calvin Medway, doctor of philosophy, medievalist, expert on ecclesiastical architecture and economics in the late medieval Europe, author of *The Word as Stone* and *Piety, Plaster and Pence: Finance and Faith in Fourteenth-Century Naples*, had a problem

VIRGINS and
MARTYRS

with his chain. It had started coming off the front cog when he went into a high gear. He dismounted and fiddled with the chain, extremely conscious of the oil on his hands.

The wheels cost £250. Each. The frame was hand-built, and magically light (£725). The saddle was a masterpiece and well it might be at £130. And still you had to wrestle the tire off and fight with the inner tube, exactly as if it were some heap of scrap bought for £30 from an ad in the evening paper.

He engaged the front cog. He'd had much the same problem a few years ago. He recalled the weather being much the same also. And he'd just come away from a meeting with a student, a difficult meeting. He turned the wheel slowly, as the memory returned. Ah yes. Had it been his final meeting with the student, before he lost touch with him? There had certainly been something of a row. A disagreement. Yes. About?

A research outline. Medway had of course been allocated to supervise him, but he had not taken very well to being supervised. This was not entirely surprising: the best students, in Medway's experience, were the least manageable, the most pig-headed. This young man was certainly pig-headed. Was he also unmanageable? In the light of this meeting, it would appear that he was.

"In some ways," the student was saying, "St. Catherine takes over in the medieval calendar of saints from the Virgin Mary. She becomes the new model for feminine piety. She is only a whisker short of divine…"

St. Catherine of Alexandria, Virgin and Martyr, who was tortured by being tied to a spiked wheel; the wheel was miraculously destroyed, and the Emperor Maxentius beheaded her instead. Two hundred Roman soldiers who were watching were converted on the spot: they too were beheaded. Catherine's opened veins were said to produce not blood, but milk.

"Of course," Medway had said, uneasy at the fire in the young man's eyes, the avidity of his posture, the—well the word really was *zealotry* of his whole demeanor, "of course you know that there is no firm evidence of her existence at all…."

"Doesn't matter, doesn't matter," the young man broke in, hot, almost oozing with the urgency of his thought, "it's what she stands for, what she becomes! She broke the wheel. Don't you see? The Wheel of Fate."

Of course Medway understood. The Wheel of Fate was an essential piece of medieval thought: time was a circle, an endless repeating chain of events, unchanging, fixed to the pivot which was the will of God. And everyone, every member of the medieval world, had a place on that wheel, which was also fixed and immutable, be it king or peasant or bishop. To break the wheel was to challenge God.

VIR♂INS *and*
MARTyRS

"Don't you see? It wasn't that she was saved from the ordeal by divine intervention. She defied the wheel. She defied God, threw down the gauntlet, said 'Show me! *Show* me!' Don't you see? There are cults of St. Catherine all over the late medieval landscape, and most of them are pure heresy! Defiant! You see?"

The young man sat back, eyes gleaming. Medway tried to deflect him: such certainty was not a healthy academic starting point. He recalled some mention of the young man having had a vocation, which had not been believed.

"But it's the Church, after all, who create and promote the saints' cults, surely. Isn't Catherine simply another virgin martyr?"

"No!" the youth all but exploded, was on his feet, shaking all over. "You don't understand do you?"

Medway winced in recollection of the violence of the young man's response. There had been something about his appearance that had added to Medway's unease, was it his haircut? Yes. Skinhead crop, and that kind of pugnacious bearing that skins tended to adopt.

In the hothouse atmosphere of a university tutorial room strong feelings were often stirred up, sometimes by the most insignificant-seeming causes. Someone misquoted Tertullian, disparaged someone else's favorite expert. Medway was fond of recounting a story about a young man who had had to be restrained from head-butting another following a disagreement about the meaning of the word "logic." An *almost* true story.

But standing in front of the zealous student who was yelling (all but), "No, you don't understand do you?" Medway had felt a distinct unease. This young man, brilliant as he was, was alarming. It all seemed to mean too much to him. Medway had got the impression that he was creeping round the minefields of a no-man's-land between a passion that was consuming, and one that was *devouring*. Another medieval image came to mind: the serpent that ate its own tail, locked forever into a self-fueling cycle of violence and destruction. The circle was, truly, vicious.

The young man had gone on to publish two papers: "False Gods and Idols: Saint Cults in South America," and the paper that Medway had just recommended to Daniel, the paper that, turning the bicycle wheel in his hand, Medway was sincerely regretting having recommended. Daniel—thin, anxious, desperate—was quite possibly not fit to encounter the fruit of a mind that Medway now believed to be seriously unhinged.

More than just believed, in fact, if he was honest. And more than just "unhinged." Because there had been a third paper, never published, of which Medway had been sent a copy. God forbid that

Daniel should ever read that one. God forbid that anyone should.

*"Some hairs of St. Barbara, virgin."*

Through the trees, leaves crunching underfoot, the air clean and cold now, sunless, the canopy denying all but a ghostly, dim radiance to the forest floor. Small, unseen creatures scuttled noisily into bushes and under the limbs of dead trees. The ferns and ivies bloomed with cuckoo-spit, the ivy leaves shading down to blue and even purple in the faint light. Daniel carried the flowers in his left hand, a limp collection of flaccid stems and drooping flower heads.

He came to classmark NR, racks of collected volumes of *The Journal of Inorganic Chemistry*.

The smell of decay was strong, the floor increasingly littered with broken, brittle branches, and even whole trees propped drunkenly upright, crumbling, rotten now, food for ants and grubs. Something large flapped cumbersomely, massively overhead, crashing through leaves and branches, sending a litter of leaves and small twigs which dropped down around him like confetti at a wedding of giants.

from NZ to P, no classmark O, it could be confused with zero, and P to PK is all one shelf, at PL already

*"some of the hairs of St. Alburga, virgin, abbess of Barking church."*

*simon maginn*

Daniel walked more slowly, more slowly still. He didn't understand why he was here. He had flowers to give to someone. But he wasn't courting. Visiting then, perhaps, in hospital? But this was no hospital. A wedding? But who was there to be married? Sarah Hilyard, she'd been dispatched beyond the realm of husbands and lovers in 1321, all that time ago. Who was there left for Daniel to marry?

*(Daniel.)*

He was close, that was certain. But not to a wedding. They were leaves on his shoulders, not confetti. He was about to turn the corner

PQ

when he realized: the flowers he was holding were flowers for the dead. She was in the next aisle, just round the next corner, and she wanted him

*(find me)*

to give her flowers, she wanted to touch him

oh no. oh no

to show him

I don't want to see, I don't want to look

*(no but look)*

He stood at the end of the aisle; all he had to do was turn his head. And look.

"*pieces of the clothes of St. Aldegunda, virgin.*

"*a bone of St. Sampson, bishop, with one tooth of the same.*"

*(look!)*

☩

VIR𝑔INS *and*
MARTyRS

"Damn you!"

Medway veered against the curb as a lorry pulled past, rocking him in its turbulent wake. The chain was off again. The pedals wheeled round, slack; he mounted the pavement and got off. The *damn* thing was beyond his expertise: it would have to go and be done by the hideously overpriced repairmen who were familiar with Derailleur gears and Witler bikes. *And* he had oil over his damn *trousers* now. Damn it to hell! He almost wished he'd gone to bloody Milan!

Clouds were rushing in from the west, and he glanced up appreciatively. Even on a bike with a dodgy chain he loved a good splash of rain. It certainly looked as if there was a pretty big storm approaching, and the light was going fast.

He ducked into a doorway before it started to come down, dragging the recalcitrant bike with him.

Poor Daniel. Medway was not so hardened by his long experience of students of all kinds that he didn't feel more than a twinge of sympathy. Something quite similar had happened to him during the (seemingly endless) writing of his own Ph.D. thesis, more years ago than he cared to remember. He had been drawing on a source concerning the cost of the construction of a French monastery in 1326: the source turned out to have been misattributed and was in fact at least a hundred years more recent than it appeared. It had blown out a whole chapter, but more importantly it had torn a central thread of an argument. He'd spent six months patching it up, navigating a tricky course round the hole, fighting with himself every day not just to dump the whole thing and become a surfing instructor in Hawaii.

But Daniel, ah there was a young man in trouble if ever he'd seen one!

For a start-off, not to be unkind, but what on God's green earth did he *look* like? Students were supposed to look like hell, it was, as it were, part of the job, but this was surely above and beyond!

One hand in a *most* unsanitary-looking bandage, the other held stiffly at his side, seemingly paralyzed. Most unorthodox. The kind of thing one perhaps expected to see in amateur productions of First World War melodramas, the heroically injured Lord Snot returning from hell-in-the-trenches to Snot Acres and a world that will never be the same again and so on.

The dissertation, likewise profoundly, appallingly flawed, one might even go the whole hog and say *maimed*. Sprawling, confused, in places totally incoherent. Nor did its author appear to be in any condition to pull it all together, assuming such a thing to be possible. No, really the kindest thing would be a mercy bullet through the temple. Metaphorically, of course. Daniel old man, I have to tell you candidly, as your *personal* tutor, that

VIR**G**INS *and*
MAR**T**y**R**S

you've got as much chance of getting this dog passed as I have of being made Bishop. Sorry my dear, but you must *face the truth and be free*, as the benighted Californians say. *Forget* it.

So why, *why*, had he instead recommended that Daniel read that curious and somewhat worrying paper by that *very* worrying former student?

(And why had he, Medway, kept, in his private study, in a locked drawer, another, third, unpublished, paper by the same young man; a paper so alarming, so disturbed that should it ever see the light of day no reputable journal would even touch it? Why had he?)

The rain came down, gusting on the wind that had brought it, and Medway considered the rest of his journey home.

*(look!)*

She was whole, but so thin, it was painful to behold. Skin like white canvas, stretched too tightly over curved sticks. Her cloudy eyes bulged, oversized in the gaunt hollows of her ghastly face. Her mouth was stretched a little, the flesh too taut to close completely, the lips puckered. She was upright, propped up like an ironing board. He had no expertise in such things but she must be, what, beyond a fortnight dead? At least. Skin discolored, blistered, areas where patches of loose flesh had produced regions of skin slip, raw, red. Fatty tissue infiltrated with gas, bloated, if he touched it (her?) there would be crepitation. Strong smell, mingling with the bitter-ivy musty odor of the books. Her right arm was spread out in a parody of welcome, or crucifixion, or supplication. And her *left* arm—

He walked toward, then past her; as he passed he thought she whispered something: it could have been his own thoughts or the brushing of his clothes against the shelves. But he thought she said, "Flowers. I want flowers."

### chapter sixteen

"Miss Bishop?"

Dr. Litherland's tone was hard, as close to anger as he ever allowed it. He motioned to her to get dressed again, and turned away to his desk to make a note on her new record card.

"You can't possibly need me to say this," he said over his shoulder as Wendy smoothed down her loose black dress and shrugged herself back into the fun-fur coat.

"I don't see how you could possibly be mistaken about it. But I'll say it to you anyway, just for the record."

Wendy's hair fell, perfectly still, around her head. No part of her moved.

"You're not pregnant, Miss Bishop, because

VIRGINS *and*
MARTYRS

you're still a virgin."

She remained motionless, freezing the air around her as well, thickening it.

"Aren't you?" His voice retained a hard edge. She was really trying his patience.

"The reason you are failing to menstruate is not that you are with child, but that you are not eating. You will not start menstruating again until you start eating again. It really couldn't be simpler." Silly little girl, he thought, this couldn't possibly be the first time anyone had ever told her this. He didn't yet have her records from her previous doctor, but there was no way she could have been this thin and not seen a doctor, and her periods would have dried up well before she became a medical emergency. A girl of her age, he thought, could easily never have menstruated at all: if she'd started starving herself before her menarche then the whole maturation process might never have got properly under way. Or she might have had a few periods and starved herself to stop them recurring.

Litherland was no expert, but he had had one or two anorexics in his care over the years, and he knew the usual course of the malaise. Her body weight was around 75 per cent of what it ought to be, and all the Feighner Criteria were in place: absence of periods, bradycardia (abnormally slow heartbeat), lanugo, the fine downy hair over her cheeks and down her back as the body tried to keep itself warm. Her breath smelled strongly of peardrops: ketoacidosis, as she burned up her last remaining reserves of fat without replacing them. Beginnings of acrocyanosis, the bluish-mauve coloring at the extremities, as her body shut off the blood to try to conserve heat. Dry skin, brittle nails. Her skin cold to the touch, her eyes wider open than is usual. Oedema in the ankles, swellings, and some degree of postural hypertension. She had seemed dizzy when she sat up on the table from his examination.

Her expression, though her face was pinched and angular in the extreme, was oddly euphoric, rapturous, as she was drenched in extra adrenaline, the so-called "fasting high," which anorexics could become almost addicted to as the condition progressed. Her belief that she had somehow become pregnant while remaining a virgin was bizarre, but then she was very much at the mercy of her mood swings as the slightest shift in blood sugar could send her soaring or crashing. He tried to regard her with more sympathy.

"Miss Bishop, if you wish to conceive a child you will have to arrange two things: you will have to stop refusing food, and you will have to find a nice young man. If you continue to starve yourself you run a grave risk of causing yourself permanent injury: you could easily become infertile, and then you will never be able to have a child will you?"

VIRGINS *and* MARTYRS

He waited for a response, got nothing for his trouble, except a wisp of the peardrop breath. She started to gather her things, her bag, her gloves.

"I would really like to arrange for you to go and see another doctor, a specialist," he said, but she was leaving, his voice was fading. She knew he wanted to send her to one of those rooms full of cheap padded chairs, where the women wept and said unspeakable things to each other. Like last time.

Anyway, he didn't know what he was talking about. She hugged herself, and hugged her special knowledge also. There were other ways to get pregnant. There must be, because pregnant she was and of that there could be no doubt. She knew what she knew. The door clicked shut behind her.

Dr. Litherland watched her go.

If she got to below 70 per cent of expected body weight and stopped eating completely, as she appeared perfectly capable of doing, she would die within ten days. If she didn't drink, within sixteen to forty-eight hours. She needed attention straightaway. He picked up the phone.

### chapter seventeen

The queues inched forward, people with trolleys and baskets containing bumper packs of nappies and toilet rolls, huge cartons of milk and bread. Vast quantities of bread. August Bank Holiday coming up. The end of civilization as we know it. Nuclear winter. Buy toilet roll.

Daniel slunk in and collected a trolley with a desperate, crafty air, looking round uneasily but not meeting anyone's eye.

It was now ten days since he'd last eaten, and he was feeling not weak, but *high up*, buffeted by high, thin gusty winds: he was at altitude. The pain came now in great hot surges, down in his bowels and up in his chest, glowing knives wrenching at him. He would close his eyes and *clench* himself until they passed. He would get blinding headaches in direct sunlight. He sweated at night, dripping, exhausting sweats, so that his clothes were damp when he awoke. He had occasional bursts of thinking about food, but in a rather abstract, oblique way. He turned the idea of it round in his mind, he pictured it, remembered what it smelled like. It was becoming a hazy memory.

His right hand, burned across the fingertips and over the palm, was capable of only rather coarse operations. Holding anything for long was impossible; he could wrench a door open, he could manipulate keys (just), he could turn the pages of books. He could not, however, open a packet or use a tin opener or peel a banana. Bread could be torn at with his teeth, but he didn't have any bread, couldn't buy any because the thought of handling

VIRGINS and
MARTYRS

money was repugnant to him, impossible. Besides this, though, he'd been surprised to find that his starvation had its own momentum and logic: the less he ate, the less he felt the desire to, the less he was able to imagine it. He found, disturbingly, that he could forget about food, totally, for long periods. But he knew that he was using more calories than he was taking in, that if he didn't manage to eat again soon, then a time would come, was not far away, when he would become too weak to fend for himself, when he would not be able to get up. He would die.

As it was, the simple act of pulling himself out of bed was becoming more and more an elaborate confidence trick he had to play on himself, offering illusory rewards, fantastic compensations.

Today he'd had to promise himself that he would, somehow, get some food into the house. How didn't matter, but he would do it. He had no money; even if he had had any he wouldn't, he knew, have been able to use it. The thought of it, the shiny, heavy discs squirming in his palm, his right palm, his *left* palm, no. It had a smell, like blood or the cold, sour soil of graveyards, like the smell of condensation on the taps in that bathroom. No. It was out of the question. He would rather starve.

But of course there were other ways of obtaining food, were there not, he thought cunningly, lying in bed, working up the case. You could, for instance, steal it. It was easy! You just walked into the shop, got out of sight, put something into your pocket, walked out again. Nothing simpler. People were doing it all the time! Small compact items obviously: wrapped blocks of cheese or salami, things like that. Just pick it up, take it away.

It had seemed so easy lying in his bed, the sweat drying on him in the warm morning air. But here, surrounded by all these people (he'd forgotten, of course, that it was the Saturday before a Bank Holiday), jostled on all sides by intent, law-abiding, clean shoppers shoving brightly packaged things into their trolleys, their purses and pockets and wallets stuffed full of *money*, each heading on a circuitous, zigzag route, like the dances of honey bees, to the checkouts where the numb, Valium-crazed cashiers presided over their machines which were *full*, full of—

He wished he'd never come. Despite his nausea and desperation, despite his terrible fear that it was already too late, and that he was just going to drop dead at any minute, be carted away, a bag of bones to be dispatched in whatever way the friendless, the orphans were dispatched: despite this, his overriding feeling was shame.

All his life he'd lived in cities. All his life he'd struggled to look like everyone else, to go unnoticed, be unremarkable. He'd bathed regularly with scented soap, bought shampoo and deodorant, laundered his clothes, brushed his teeth with new and exciting toothpastes. And for what! So he could end up a shabby furtive figure slinking round a supermarket reeking of fear, with that saddest, most banal of crimes—shoplifting!—on his mind. Through the shame cut a blast of anger. Dammit, he had a right to eat!

He shoved his trolley forward with one hand, negotiating the packed aisles, finding that he needed to correct his trajectory every few paces by thrusts with his trunk and thighs. It is skills such as these, he announced to himself giddily, that put men on the moon! Oh yes! The high thin winds sang in his ears, he reeled slightly, feeling a dizzy triumph. He plucked at items at random, chucking them into the spacious, even cavernous trolley. He only had the option of things on his right, but it hardly mattered. The trolley was merely a cover, he would dump it at the checkouts, push through the queues, run out into the harsh, bright sunlight, his coat pockets stuffed with salami and soap and chocolate. He'd eat it at once (well not the soap maybe), just cram it into his mouth, before anyone had a chance to come after him and take him off to the ignominious room upstairs where shoplifters wept and pleaded for forgiveness, for anonymity. He felt shaky with anticipation. Sharp knives of wind bit at his limbs, even through coat and jumper and shirt. And the real terror was not of starvation or insan-

*simon maginn*

ity: the real fear was—*people will see. It will be embarrassing.*

He paraded up and down the aisles; there seemed to be fewer people the further he got from the door. Is that a rule, he wondered, like the inverse-square law? He was in Pet Foods and Household. He grabbed tins of beefy chunks and improved recipes, he had six dogs and a cat, parrots, gerbils, who cared? Today he could have anything he wanted, like a competition-winner. His lucky day!

He rounded the corner, and finally found the chilled cabinets, the cheeses, eight million different kinds, and cured meats, little pies and yogurts.... His stomach yelled at him, a brief, decisive curse in gastric language: you'll be sorry! He selected more carefully now and put the items in the raised wire compartment at the front of the trolley. Those he would transfer into his coat pockets as soon as he could get a moment unobserved.

He glanced behind, anxiously, though everyone was utterly intent on their own purchasing, making intricate compromises between desire and denial: this but not that, if these then not those also. He turned another corner and found himself in an aisle where there were only a half-dozen or so people; the density had suddenly dropped dramatically. He wheeled himself along, and an incision of alarm sliced at him. He grabbed packages and slung them into the trolley, moving fast, keeping his eyes ahead. Another corner (oh no), he rounded it and was in a new aisle and this time there was just one person there, toward the end.

*I know who you are!*

He couldn't get back now, he had to go forward, push past this person whom he knew, get out of sight. The stacks of packages reared up all around. He picked one up and threw it into the trolley: it was full of some kind of gray, powdery material, he couldn't identify exactly what. The person at the other end of the aisle showed no signs of moving

*I've seen all this before!*

so he had to ease past, just squeeze himself past her, she didn't appear to be buying anything, and did she try to whisper to him as he passed her?

*(flowers. I want)*

He slid by, not touching her, holding his breath to avoid her scent, which was whispery, damp paper, falling plaster; he rounded the corner. At last. The aisle stretched away in front of him, completely bereft of people or trolleys or any sign of activity (well, human activity), and he slumped with relief.

Halfway along, his heart rate accelerating to a frantic thumping, he stopped and filled his pockets from the wire compartment at the front. He found that he'd forgotten the soap; he would collect it on his way back, perhaps. The food was the important thing. He made for the end of the aisle, and just for good measure he picked up something

*simon maginn*

on his right, something that gave rather unpleasantly under his fingers. He tossed it in, and found his attention drawn by a little secret scuttling motion on the shelf where it had lain. Some kind of small creature, rustling about among the bags and boxes of what exactly?

He squinted into the trolley: it was difficult to see the labels clearly, it seemed to be very dark at this end of the shop. He picked up the most recent item and saw that it had no label, it was a clear plastic bag of that odd, powdery substance, only now it also had a somewhat *squishy* character to it, as if it were perhaps shredded paper decomposing alongside jelly or human tissue (just for example). He threw it back into the trolley in disgust, and as he did so he saw that other of the packages were also in a similar state of putrefaction, *long* past their sell-by dates, there were small, scuttling movements going on inside several of them, inside the trolley itself....

He heaved it away from him and ran, and as he did so he thought: what exactly is it that I've got in my pockets? Cheese? Salami? Maybe. He dipped a hand into his pocket and pulled out the wrapped object: his fingers dug into it in altogether too pliant a manner for his liking, there was a wee bit too much *crepitation* about it, and he flung it away from him, the other items as well, and bugger the soap! He ran down the main aisle, banging through the

VIRGINS *and*
MARTYRS

relentlessly consuming people and the hideous stacks of detritus all around him and piled up in the trolleys and baskets. He ran for the exit, found instead an entrance where somebody was just coming in, activating the electronic doors, and fled, out into the sunlight.

Halfway home he tore off his coat with one clumsy, trembling hand and threw it into a doorway, not looking to see if anyone was residing there. He was aware of the curious attentions of the people around him, he was conscious of the fact that the itchy, crawling heat of his body was two parts shame to one part exertion. He had, he knew, gone beyond ordinary limits now. He was outcast, a pariah. He was haunted.

### chapter eighteen

Wendy sat at the kitchen table and regarded the plate in front of her. It contained a small wholemeal roll. She picked up the bread knife and cut it carefully in half. One half she took off the plate and put on the table. (That was the wrong half, the bad half.) The half remaining on her plate she cut, again, into halves, and again one of these she discarded, and thus was left with a quarter of a roll on her plate. She picked it up and examined it. She held it close to her nose and sniffed at it—it smelled marvelous, yeasty and doughy and gorgeous. Anorexia, she knew, meant literally "no appetite," but that was wrong. She had plenty of appetite, she was hungry just about all the time: but she had control in equal measure, greater measure in fact. If she controlled what she ate then maybe she could control how she felt, could batten down the panic and the loneliness. And if she could control her shape, then her whole life might eventually start to come right; if she could get her weight down just a fraction more, maybe she'd start to be happy.

She should be happy, she knew: she was pregnant, and so she should be happy. A baby! She'd give it every chance she'd never had, it would be beautiful and cheerful and clever (and thin).

She held the tiny piece of bread in her hand, and with the other thumb and forefinger pulled out the softy doughy center inside the corner of elastic brown crust. She kneaded it into a ball, a smooth creamy marble. She considered slicing it again into halves, but thought better of it, and placed the entire ball of dough into her mouth. She was, after all, eating for two now.

Her mind was a still, flat pond as she chewed, slowly, systematically, all the chaos temporarily abated. Her face was a mask, betraying nothing, and under the mask there was, indeed, at this moment, nothing to betray or be betrayed by. So selective was her attention that the overwhelming majority of things around her simply failed to register. Only certain items ever found their way in, somehow, through the labyrinthine, empty, echoing corridors to the calm pool at the center. Ripples danced over the surface for hours at a time, rebounding off the sides, crisscrossing, finally dying away. One of those fortunate few rose up now from beneath, and splashed gently as it broke surface, sending out delicate wavelets in all directions—"look like you've lost a few pounds there Wendy looks good on you" —and she regarded it, with solemn joy, as the bread disintegrated in her mouth.

She'd spent much of her life feeling cold. Carlisle had been a chilly, white, damp place, long cold springs followed by endless cool summers and then the protracted, stubbornly contested descent into winter, where the air froze and glimmered in the flat light. Her sheets felt damp, always, clammy white cotton that seemed to reject, to suck out, the meager warmth of her body. As she grew thinner, so she became colder—unknown to her, her body was adapting to this by growing a thin, transparent fuzz of fine hair over her cheeks and reducing circulation to the skin. But the cold was everywhere, inside as well as out, like a skin over the world, on everything she touched.

It was less cold in Brighton, though the wind off the sea could be vile, and some of the narrower streets seemed to act as funnels for the wet, frigid streams of air, amplifying it.

She had always been mercilessly aware of her appearance, aware of it in a bewilderingly diverse set of ways simultaneously. She wished, desperately, to be unseen, invisible; and she knew that her face, those stark cheekbones, the bulging eyes, the stretched lips, attracted people's notice. And she knew also that she should be thinner, gaunter, bonier. Her body should be reduced to the absolute minimum necessary so that she could take up less space and be less noticed. She was horrified by the rage, the yearning, the tumult she felt, and she yearned, desperately, ragefully to quieten it, to make it still and small and cool. She starved herself so that she could say you see? I need nothing, not even food: and her grim, death's-head face cried out I'm dying, can't you see that, can't somebody *help* me!

Controlling these conflicting forces was her life. Balancing, negotiating, performing interminable, pernickety transactions, living almost exclusively on the inside where the ravening, appetite-driven monsters prowled behind the fine metal bars: placated by her fiddly little rituals and sacrifices, more or less, but only for the time being, conditionally.

But now she had a new weapon, a new chair to brandish at these tigers. She had an admirer!

Not Keith, with his dirty fingernails and lamentable lapses of self-control; not the old woman, the Dowager, lapping it up in her all-day drinking dens, in nylon blouse and costume jewelry.

No, a real admirer who saw her as she really was, noble, pure; lean like a gazelle, strong, controlled. Someone who could see that she was going to fit in nicely, soon, one day, eventually. He saw the potential in her gross, needy body. He had planted the little seed inside her; his words had lodged in her, were growing and maturing. The messy, banging world had collapsed for her into a vanishingly tiny number of categories, and clear, limpid decisions. Soon she would be perfect.

Daniel was back in his room, on his bed, staring at nothing. The room was uncomfortably warm and his skin felt as if it were changing constantly, melting or emulsifying, like paint that's just been stirred, or soil during an earthquake.

And suddenly she was on him showing him something, oh Christ, a quick flash but not quite quick enough, repulsive, sloppy, gory mess.

Then bobbing about, underneath a great towering structure, the beam of a torch flashing overhead, into the grid of iron struts, encrusted with something, were they mussels? ropes hanging down, immense iron supports.

A vast, booming, open structure, and a sign. Bobbing about. Spray on his face. Then he felt an awful, wrenching dislocation and he thought: my arm!

*(In the house over the water, the great house. That's where he—)*

Daniel gritted his teeth at the pain in his shoulder.

"Why can't you tell me?"

*(Too late. Almost. It's too late. Almost.)*

Gingerly he touched the throbbing, tender shoulder.

She's showing him something, bright yellow, it's moving around, erratically. There's a small notice, sewn into the material, the spray is in his eyes, so he can't see properly. Salt water has got behind one of his contact lenses, it's slipped, his eye has gone into spasm.

Inflata Deluxe Model III. Recreational Use Only.

I don't understand. What's this got to do with— Use Only. Use only according to instruction manual. Read manual thoroughly before use. Maximum safe load 170 lbs. Note: it is dangerous to exceed weight restriction. Manufacturers can accept no responsibility for improper use. Made in Republic of Ireland for JKB Limited, registered office Castle Street, Dublin, Republic...

Spray in his contact lens and the thing is bobbing around, a dinghy of some kind, and there's someone with him.

*(Do you see?)*

"No, wait—"

*(You'll have to go with him. He'll like you, eventually. You must be like me. Like me. You must)*

VIRGINS *and* MARTYRS

"Why must I go with him? I don't understand."
*(Please. Daniel. Find me. I want)*
"Yes yes I know. You want flowers."
*(Flowers. Please I want. It is dangerous to exceed weight restriction! Manufacturers can accept no)*

Spray in his face, a giddy, lurching seasickness, there's a fair bit of swell out there, and with him in the boat….

He became aware that she'd gone.

He opened his eyes, carefully, not wanting to be taken by surprise by anything, but there was nothing, just a warm room and the steady afternoon light.

His left eye was burning, and he lifted his finger to it, caught the slipped contact lens on the pad of his finger and dropped it into the plastic container by the side of the bed. Not much point in having just one in, and his eyes felt as if they could do with a rest, there was a gritty, scoured feeling in them. He lifted the other tiny lens out, and deposited it safely in its container.

The room swam away from him, and he had the not unpleasant feeling of disconnection, of floating, helplessness. A sense of surrender to the true nature of things, which was amorphous, gently blurred, as if seen through milk.

Thoughts turned in his head, but he could discern no real pattern to them. She had had the room before him, he had to starve so he could go in a boat to the house over the water and give her flowers. Obvious really.

But if he did starve, if she wouldn't let him eat, then how could he go and give her flowers? He would *die*, for God's sake. Was that what she wanted, for him to die?

And this, of course, was part of the problem: she was seemingly unable to explain herself at all clearly. She could only give him these pictures, like comic video clips of babies falling off swings and puppies attacking telephones. Only these weren't funny, not at all. She was entirely serious. He thought of the real videos in the next room, those walking skeletons in the death camps and the limitless deserts.

Something

(repulsive, gory)

*something* had befallen her and she had died. She was now trying to tell him something, trying to get him to do something for her; but she was unable to say it, she could only show it, elaborately, obliquely, cryptically. (He didn't want to think too hard about why it might be becoming too late: but was it possible that her ability to communicate with him at all was weakening as she—the word, he declared to himself sternly, was "decomposed.") Was that it? Or was she perhaps just like that anyway? One of those people for whom language is a trick that is never mastered sufficiently to be performed in public, a tool that is never used because the user has no confidence that it won't blow up in his face. (Was she a saint, who had taken a vow of silence? The air vibrated round him as the thought came, but he pushed it away.)

He slept and dreamed of a great ship that came crashing up on to the beach, listing over crazily, its gargantuan steel hull looming over the stones and the lapping waves. He dreamed of an insect with a thousand legs, crouched over the sea, half in and half out, motionless, an insect hundreds of yards long, encrusted with growths and excrescences of all kinds.

He awoke at some time, night time, he had no idea now what day, it could be any day. There was a disturbance in the air which it took him a moment to recognize as the sound of a phone ringing. The phone was in the next room, the same room that contained the videos. Someone, presumably, had made them at some time, had decided to record television pictures of people who were starving, presumably with the intention of watching them. Repeatedly. It occurred to Daniel that the person who had made those recordings was, presumably, a resident or ex-resident of the house.

He raised himself, stiffly, awkwardly; his shoulder was throbbing and he was profoundly dizzy, his body seemed to want to lurch leftward and he was overcompensating.

He pulled open the door and staggered down the short passage.

The phone purred, contentedly, on the arm of the chair in the dark room. He picked up the receiver.

"Hello?" came the voice.

He listened closely, as if expecting some important information like train times or the cricket scores.

"Hello?" The voice was hoarse, cracked, unsteady, he'd heard it before.

"Hello? Is Wendy there?"

He waited for more, attending carefully to the crackles and tiny noises at the other end of the wire. He cleared his throat.

"Who's there?" the voice came again, and Daniel tried to say his name, but produced no more than a curious gulping sound. He tried again.

"Daniel. It's Daniel. Who's this?"

"Is Wendy there?"

He cleared his throat again, excited by this unexpected encounter with the world outside, the real world beyond his room and the library. Maybe whoever it was on the phone could help him.

"Please," he said, and couldn't think what came next.

"Please," he tried again, "she won't let me *eat*."

"Have you seen her?" came the voice.

VIRGINS *and*
MARTYRS

"Bring food. Please."

"Oh crikey." The voice paused, coughed. "What kind of food?"

He considered it briefly, then:

"I don't think it matters, really."

"Well all right. All right."

"Can you come now?"

"Yes. I'll come right away."

"Cheese. Bring cheese.'

"OK. Wendy is there isn't she?"

"Oh, yes. And salami."

"Salami. Oh crikey."

He hung up, crawled back to his bed. He found it terribly difficult to believe that the call had really taken place, that there had actually been a croak-voiced woman on the phone who was at this moment on her way, bringing cheese and salami. It seemed, on the face of it, unlikely. He wished he'd asked her for bread.

He woke again, later, still night, whether the same or some other was unclear to him.

The doorbell was ringing.


### chapter nineteen

Wendy was very weak. The skinhead had to help her out of her black dress, help her to peel off the black tights, the underwear. He held her as she stepped into the bath, steadied her as she settled in.

It could only be days now, hours even. Her legs and arms were reduced to curved sticks. Her hips jutted out, then her hollow belly, then the ribs, stark; they looked as if they could break through the tissue of her skin at any moment. Her chest also was hollow, her breasts simply loose flaps of skin. Her neck stuck up, a pale stalk, from the bones of her shoulders and back.

Her face.

The eyes gleamed out, huge, bright, unfocused. Her lips were slightly parted: already she had something of the death's-head about her face, all bones and teeth and angles.

She washed with stilted little movements; sometimes she seemed to forget what she was doing, and the cloth fell limp in the water. He shampooed the stubble of her newly shaved head, then rinsed it off with a jug, tilting her head back, trying not to get the foam into her eyes.

He took her hand to help her out: the bony claw fastened on him, and for a second he was frightened. It was like death itself gripping you, a hard, inorganic-seeming grip, as of stone or steel.

He wrapped her in a big white towel and guided her upstairs; she wobbled and staggered, her head lolling. She didn't know where she was, she looked stunned.

He sat her down on the bed. I've got something

VIRGINS *and*
MARTYRS

to show you, he said. He left her and she heard him moving about in the attic; he was back minutes later, she hadn't moved. Here, he said. He was carrying a mirror in a painted wooden frame.

He propped the mirror up against the wardrobe, which was full of identical black dresses and black shoes.

He adjusted it to get the angle right, so she could see her whole body, full length.

He stood her in front of it. Look, he said, you're beautiful. He stood behind her and smiled.

She couldn't see properly, but she peered forward, frowning at the reflection.

Almost perfect, he said. You're almost perfect. Soon we will have our mystic marriage. He opened his hand to show her the wedding ring.

Later that day she woke up, and felt terribly alarmed. She made herself move, made herself get up and find the door. He had put her in a white nightgown, very plain. Like a shroud.

She opened the door: it wasn't easy because the wood had swollen and jammed in the frame. Finally she did it.

Cra-*ack*.

She walked down the passageway, holding herself up against the wall. She descended the stairs, two, three, four, turned the corner.

He was coming up to get her.

*simon maginn*

Now, he said, now. You don't want to go wearing yourself out. You must rest. She made a tiny sound, of distress, of hopelessness, of pain.

Now, he said, and turned her round, helped her back to her room, put her back to bed.

Soon, he said. Soon.

### chapter twenty

The Dowager panted up the stairs, resting on the landings; it was a long ascent for an old woman, somewhere between Devil's Peak and Snowdon. The Dowager was sixty-three years old, looked eighty-three, chain-smoked, and visited monthly her elderly mother (ninety-six, looked a hundred and thirty) who was saving herself for her monthly meetings with solicitor and accountant. The Dowager, as a consequence of these meetings, was the recipient of a substantial, if grudging, trust-fund income, which kept her in dog food and 200-packs of whatever cigarettes were cheapest.

Her summers were spent cosseting her dogs; when the nights started drawing in she would become restless and depressed, forget to take her Lithium then take four doses in a day, neglect to cook the Fray Bentos pie before she ate it, and generally become a worry to her social worker who would get her admitted to a residential home for the winter. The dogs would be kenneled at enormous expense, and she would escape regularly to visit them: they would give her mournful but unreproving looks and she'd dab her eyes and count the days until spring.

She huffed up the second floor and called out: "Hello? Are you there?"

The house appeared to be completely unoccupied, and if a hand hadn't appeared and thrown the keys out to her she would have had no reason to believe there was anyone home. She'd peeked into the kitchen: apart from an overturned pan of something or other on the floor it looked long neglected, dusty. Where was Wendy?

She mounted the last flight of stairs.

"Hello?" she called again, and Daniel called back, "Up here," his voice ludicrously feeble.

She opened the door.

She was not at first able to locate Daniel, until he wriggled into an upright position on the bed. She took a step further into the room, squinting at him, then turned round and would have left, quickly, had he not said:

"Wait! Please..."

She turned back and faced him.

"Where's Wendy gone? Who are you?"

"I don't know where she is."

"But she lives here. In this room. What are you doing here?"

"I just moved in, a few weeks ago. She must have moved out I suppose."

"So why didn't she tell me?"

Daniel was suddenly angry at this accusatory line of questioning from this peculiar old woman in ludicrous plastic jewelry and food-stained skirt, who looked, essentially, pissed.

"How am I supposed to know? Who are you anyway? Did you bring any food?"

"Oh. Yes, I did," she said and looked around her in an unfocused and vague manner.

"Oh crikey. I must have left it in the taxi."

"It doesn't matter," Daniel said, weary of the whole business now. "She wouldn't let me eat it anyway."

"Who wouldn't?" said the Dowager, still gawping around foolishly as if she expected Wendy to come out from the wardrobe or under the bed at any minute. The room was hot and the window was resolutely shut.

She turned her attention to the person on the bed, what had he said his name was? Whoever he was, he looked awful: emaciated, pale, exhausted; he was breathing rather fast and shallowly. She took a step closer to him, cautiously, and he could smell the alcohol on her breath as she peered down at him.

"Are you all right?"

He closed his eyes in exasperation. How could anyone be so dense?

VIRGINS and
MARTYRS

"Well what do you think, for God's sake. Do I look all right?"

"Actually, no." She giggled nervously. "Not really, come to think of it."

"Please. Get me out of here. I've got to get out, I've got work to do, and I can't do anything here, she won't let me. Please. If I could just get out I think I'd be OK, she wouldn't be able to find me."

The Dowager frowned, seriously.

"Crikey!" She backed away again from him. "I'll ring a taxi shall I?"

Daniel was amazed at the good sense of the suggestion. Why hadn't he thought of it himself?

"Very good idea," he panted, and closed his eyes as faintness and nausea swam up inside him. "Excellent idea." He felt vertiginous, giddy.

"Where's the phone?"

"Next door." He gestured feebly at the wall dividing his room from the next. "In there."

She trundled away to find the phone, and he tried to lever himself up into a sitting position. He suddenly felt much worse, exhausted, too weary to move or even just to lie still anymore.

"Tell 'em to hurry up!" he called out, as consciousness fell away all round him. "Tell 'em it's urgent!"

It took her about three minutes to get down the stairs to open the door for the taxi driver.

"Would you mind helping me down with something?" she asked and he, seeing a frail old lady who was clearly out of breath, agreed.

"Right at the top of the house, I'm afraid," she said over her shoulder as they plodded up the stairs. She had to stop, abruptly, and the taxi driver held her arm.

"Take it easy, love. No hurry," he said kindly. He had the clock running.

"I get a bit wheezy," she said, "particularly in the heat, you see."

"You should be taking it easy, at your time of life."

"I'm only sixty-three. You wouldn't believe it would you?"

"Don't look a day over twenty-five," he said, earning his fare. "Is it much further?"

"A bit. Shall we stop for a minute?"

He held her arm and helped her into a sitting position on the stairs.

"Fag?" she breathed.

"Twist my arm then." She gave him a cigarette of a brand he'd never encountered before, and they smoked in companionable silence, apart from the sound of her lungs like the bellows of an antique harmonium.

"Bloody doctor keeps saying I should give up!" she said, spluttering, putting her hand to her chest for a good old cough.

VIRGINS *and*
MARTYRS

"Well that's doctors for you," said the taxi driver sagely. "Always think they know best about everything. I heard there was a study done, Finland I think it was, and the people what smoked lived, on average, *ten years longer* than the ones what didn't."

"Crikey!" she said and looked at him admiringly. "I never heard that one."

"Yeah, well they don't tell you things like that do they? Vested interests, see." He narrowed his eyes significantly.

He took her cigarette end from her and ground both of them out thoroughly on the staircarpet. "Don't want to start any fires now do we?" he said in a playfully scolding voice, and she giggled, then coughed more.

"Right. Better get on then, I suppose," she wheezed.

"Give us a piggyback will you?" he said, and she tried to laugh and had to sit down again.

"There he is," she said, finally throwing open the bedroom door and pointing to the bed.

The driver approached, with the air of one who has seen enough of the world to adopt a healthily cautious manner. Not that he was *scared* or anything.

"Is he all right?" he said, and the Dowager wheezed behind him, "I think he's just asleep."

*simon maginn*

The taxi driver put out his hand and gave Daniel a gentle push. No response.

"Listen love, I don't want no one dying in my cab," he said. "You'll be better off with an ambulance."

"No, he's all right," she insisted. "I was talking to him just a minute ago. He said he wanted to go out, so I said I'd get a taxi. He was all right then. More or less," she added truthfully.

"Yeah well he's not looking so hot now is he," said the taxi driver, unable to keep the fear out of his voice, and the Dowager leaned over the collapsed figure and shouted at him.

"Wake up! Taxi's waiting."

Daniel stirred sluggishly. His tongue came out of his mouth, mollusc-like, and moistened his lips.

"Mate?" the driver bellowed at him, in a no-nonsense, let's-get-this-show-on-the-road way. "Oi. mate. Let's go!"

Daniel opened his eyes: the room was the familiar milky blur, darkened by great figures looming above him. He struggled into a more upright position.

"Contact lenses," he said, and the driver turned to the Dowager. "What did he say?"

"'Friends,' I think, wasn't it? It's all right," she called out to him in her broken, unmusical voice. "We're your friends. You're all right now." Then she had a brainwave. "I know," she said, "I'll give him

VIRGINS and
MARTYRS

one of his pills, that'll get him going." She produced a plastic tub of Haloperidol from a pocket and shoved two of them into Daniel's mouth. He swallowed, with some difficulty, and she turned back to the taxi driver.

"He'll be all right, now he's had his pills," she said, adopting what she believed to be a sober, responsible demeanor. The taxi driver agreed to take her seriously.

"OK mate, let's have you," he called out, grimly cheerful now, and took hold of Daniel's arm.

"No!" Daniel called out and managed to fight him off. "No, I'm fine really. Just give me a minute."

He stood and the milky room swayed and contracted. He was much dizzier than he realized. He half fell backward onto the bed again, and bashed his arm against the wall.

"Fuck."

He stood up once more, aware of the attentions of his two helpers.

"Really," he said as accurately as he could, "I'm perfectly able to mange, thank you," and the taxi driver whispered to the Dowager, "What did he say?"

By the time they'd reached the last flight of stairs it was essentially a battle to keep Daniel on his feet and moving. The taxi driver was propping him up on one side, the Dowager on the other and slightly behind. He was trying to brace himself against the wall. His balance was undependable and the problem was exacerbated by the apparent paralysis of his left arm, which he was trying to keep out of the way. He seemed to be slipping in and out of consciousness. And, curiously, he appeared to be getting heavier all the time, floppier, less maneuverable.

*(Daniel)*

They reached the hallway leading to the front door; his legs gave way and the driver and the wheezy old woman had him now, supported him completely, one on either side. They were all but dragging him toward the front door.

*(Daniel)*

"Nearly there," chanted the driver, intoning the words without thought, "nearly there son. Nearly there. Few more steps. That's the way."

They reached the door: the Dowager twisted the lock but it was stiff.

*(Daniel. I want)*

"Flowers," he murmured, "you want flowers," and the door abruptly opened. All three staggered somewhat, and then they were out on the pavement in the still, warm night. Daniel crawled into the back of the taxi and lay on the seat, his left arm sticking out awkwardly. The driver looked anxiously at the Dowager as she got in beside him.

"Do you think we should cover him with something?" he said, and went to the boot to dig out a blanket, a brightly-colored tartan affair.

VIRGINS *and* MARTYRS

He took his seat behind the wheel, and glanced at the clock.

"OK love. Where to?"

They drove, sedately, along the main arterial which led through the depths of darkest Hove and on to Worthing, then on again along the endless, sprawling conurbations of the South Coast.

It was a wide, spacious, well-lit road, with big detached and semidetached houses on either side, many of them enjoying a new lease of life as nursing homes and dental practices and private schools.

"Hove was laid out on the same ground plan as New York," the taxi driver said to break the silence. "Did you know that? First Avenue, Second Avenue." He paused at a red light.

"Third Avenue," he added, just for the sake of completeness.

Daniel lay flat on the back seat, his eyes open, watching the lights flash by. He lay quietly, only moving his eyes, as they followed the course of the streetlights. It had been raining: the car was making a faint squishing sound.

He felt he should speak, "Stop," for instance, or "where are you taking me to?" but he seemed to have forgotten how to do it, what muscles to use. Instead his eyebrows lifted slightly. It didn't matter too much though, because he was certain that

Wendy wouldn't allow him to leave the house now, she would get him back somehow. He realized, and his eyebrows again lifted, that he had absolutely no idea who this old woman was. Some funny friend of Wendy's seemingly. He had perhaps been foolish to entrust himself to her. The thought played in his head, but only very quietly.

The car again slowed to a halt: the Dowager said "Straight over at the lights," and the driver said, "Can't go straight over, love: diversion, see." The car turned right and accelerated away.

"Is he all right in the back there?" the driver said, and the Dowager craned round to look. Daniel was lying perfectly still, his eyes open but hardly moving now, and his left arm protruding woodenly. He was pale, milky-white except round the eyes where he had a faint bluish stain, and his lips were the most delicate of coral pinks, crusted, very dry. He seemed impossibly insubstantial, and she couldn't be entirely sure that he was breathing. Wrapped in the tartan blanket, he looked like a wraith.

"He's fine," she lied. "I think he's just having a little nap."

"For Christ's sake, another one!" the driver said, and obeyed a second diversion sign, forcing them into a left-hand turning.

It was darker here, and the houses were tremendous, gloomy forms, lurking mutely behind the wet

VIRGINS and
MARTYRS

trees. The driver steered cautiously between the cars parked on either side, weaving through.

Daniel floated freely, only faintly conscious of the car's motion and of the sporadic, increasingly anxious conversation between the two blurred forms in the front seats.

"Try this next left, here," said the Dowager, but in truth she was not at all sure which direction they were traveling in: the driver shrugged and signaled, and—

(uh-oh, here we go again, Daniel spoke to himself in eyebrow language)

"Shit!"

The car braked abruptly and the driver looked angrily at the Dowager who was staring around gormlessly, vaguely, trying to penetrate the dim, black, glossy wetness outside.

"Dead end," said Daniel, and "Dead end," said the driver. He put the car into reverse and glared furiously into his mirror, and behind him. He couldn't see a damn thing. They got back out onto the road they'd turned off and continued into the blackness.

"There's no point, don't bother, she won't let you," said Daniel's eyebrows, and sure enough the road widened out, turned into a crescent that ran round the edge of a small, black-green park with indistinct lavender railings and dripping, dimly seen trees overhead. The car's headlights gleamed on the trees and bushes. The crescent circled the park, and they came back to the road they'd just left.

"Head back for the main road," the driver muttered, and the Dowager peered suspiciously round at Daniel, who was motionless, as before.

"We should really get him home," she said, not liking the look of him at all. His eyes had become filmy, as if he was flying through clouds which were dusting his eyeballs. As if he'd died and gone to heaven, floating among the clouds. She fretted at the memory of who it was he reminded her of and found herself back at St. Maris Stella Convent, gazing up at a panel in the dim little chapel where the girls had to go to fidget and pass each other notes every Sunday morning. It was the clouds in the eyes that had prompted her. Someone lying down with a pink-faced angel hanging over him: the angel had a bright gold halo and enormous feathery wings. The person lying down was on a particularly uncomfortable-looking platform in a kind of open shed, and his arm was trailing on the ground. His eyes stared up at the angel, who was gazing down at him with a very soppy kind of expression, probably intended to represent "Adoration" or perhaps "Compassion." It had all meant something but she couldn't remember what.

I shouldn't really have given him those Haloperidol, she thought, and giggled. They were back on the main road again now, traveling in the direction they'd come from, the opposite direction from the one they wanted. East. She jerked her head back, abruptly, and called "Stop!" The driver slammed his brakes on, and everyone was flung forward; Daniel rolled off the seat and onto the floor, and his arm caught underneath him.

The driver again turned to the old woman beside him.

"What?"

"I thought I saw someone," she said, still twisted round to look out of the window, behind her. The street was entirely empty. "Someone I know," she added. "I could have sworn…." She shrugged apologetically at the driver, who, wearily, drove on.

Daniel, now wedged below the front seat, watched the driver's feet as they shuffled on the pedals. He could no longer feel anything. His left arm had been the first part to leave him, now there was nothing at all, except perhaps a faint, pale grittiness in the eyes, unaccustomed as they were to prolonged use without contact lenses. He had become completely tangled up in the tartan blanket, and he thought, slowly: this is how it must feel to be dead. Shrouded, immobile.

"*Shit!*"

The driver's voice again: Daniel was unable to take a very active interest. He knew broadly what was going to happen already. Well, he knew how the ride would end anyway—he would be back at the house. It occurred to him that he didn't have his keys—he'd have to break in. Maybe the taxi driver would help him. Or maybe this peculiar woman was some kind of a burglar. The thought struck him as funny, but he was unable to laugh or smile: his face just wouldn't work, not even the old reliable eyebrows. He had become a piece of cardboard with his name on it.

The driver had pulled to a halt, in the middle of the road, and was now getting out.

"What's the matter?" the Dowager asked in her cranky voice, and the driver called back to her, "Can't you see it? There's some bloody—*thing* in the road," he said, and then Daniel could hear him grunting disgustedly.

"What was it?" the Dowager asked as he got back in the car, but there was no reply. He slammed the door grimly and started up again.

"Jesus H. Christ," he said thickly after a few minutes.

Apart from the squish of the tires over the wet road, and the occasional squawk of something unintelligible over the radio, there was complete silence in the car. The feet in front of Daniel's eyes rested comfortably on the pedals as the car picked up speed.

"I'll take us up onto Church Road," the driver commented briefly, "get away from these diversions."

VIRGINS *and*
MARTYRS

Daniel closed his eyes, tight, as the driver swung the wheel round. He didn't want to see the

*crash!*

as the driver's foot leaped onto the brake, and the car threw itself halfway up a lamppost as he tried to avoid the person who had just come out of nowhere, right out into the middle of the road, a woman in a fur coat; his last thought, before thought left him, was: she didn't have her coat on properly, she must have been in a hurry, she only had one arm on. Then his eyes closed as his head began to sail gracefully toward the windscreen. The headlights flung their identical parallel beams irrelevantly up into the sky.

Daniel was jammed back against the rear seat supports: this seemed to disentangle him from the blanket, and the impact released a great hilarious burst of adrenaline into him: he reached up with his good arm and unfastened the door, which swung open due to the absurd, unplanned-for angle of the car.

He crawled out, fell to the road and heaved himself upright against the car. The tartan blanket languished, shed, inside, like a sloughed skin.

Daniel started walking, propelling his legs forward against their will, putting one foot in front of the other. He didn't look back. Soon the sirens of the emergency services would start their mechanical wailing, slicing through the still night.

*simon maginn*

He had no keys, so he rang the bell. What else was there to do?

The rain had started again, and he stood in the dropping air. Shock was catching up with him, and the adrenaline was reacting badly with the Haloperidol. He could feel tears trickling down his face. The house was in darkness. Why should he think it would be otherwise? What was the point of standing here in the rain, in the middle of the night?

Then he saw it, the wobbling, refracted shape emerging from the gloom, approaching through the distortions of the fluted glass.

"Daniel? Dear God, what's happened to you?"

It was the skinhead. He hustled Daniel in, and shepherded him up the stairs to his room, where Daniel collapsed onto the bed. Before he passed out he thought he smelled the most delicate whiff of perfume, or was it just dead flowers, freesias or hyacinths, one of those sweet, heady smells. Then blackness came for him and he succumbed to it, happily, happily.

PART

*three*

THE HOUSE OVER THE WATER

### chapter twenty-one

The light in the room was mild, benign. He lay still on the bed, full of the food the skinhead had prepared for him, replete, like a baby after his bottle. On the verge of napping.

After he'd collapsed on the doorstep he'd continued to have a kind of fragmented, muted sense of what was happening, refracted, as if he were seeing it take place through the fluted glass of the front door. The Dowager's chemical cosh hadn't quite obliterated his senses, but it had certainly interfered with them fairly substantially.

The skinhead had been appalled and alarmed at his condition. He had also been somewhat horrified at the condition of Daniel's room and had taken it upon himself to tidy it up. With Daniel safely deposited onto the bed, he had cleared up the bags of clothes and the other detritus that had accumulated round it. He'd opened the window and gone round everything with potpourri polish and a duster. It still looked pretty shoddy, but it was unquestionably an improvement. He was no stickler, he thought, but he had at least a rudimentary sense of what was orderly and hygienic.

The bed itself, he decided grimly, was neither of these things. The one remaining sheet had come adrift at the top and along one side, revealing the ugly floral print of the mattress. No underblanket, he noted primly. That meant that Daniel's sweat would have impregnated the mattress. He considered turning it over, then remembered, and decided not to. The duvet was emerging from its cover like a pallid maggot escaping from a piece of carrion, gray, begrimed, malodorous. The duvet cover itself, an unattractive affair in geometric slabs of blue and white, was discolored in places, stained, and grubby overall.

He managed to get Daniel sitting up on the bed, his head lolling groggily, like a drunk.

The skinhead gently pulled the duvet away, and then untucked the sheet until it was free from everywhere except where Daniel was sitting on it. He lifted him carefully by the shoulder and whipped the sheet away. Daniel slumped down again, and the skinhead thought, too late, *the pillow*, as Daniel's head fell onto it and he lapsed back into immobility, smacking his lips. Oh well, he'd come back for it another time.

He gathered up the limp, sweetish-smelling bundle and carted it off, dumping it by the front door.

Daniel himself was more of a problem. Even in optimum circumstances the human body, he well knew, is an incorrigibly unsanitary item, and Daniel was quite some distance from anything approaching an optimum.

He sighed and, overcoming his resistance, approached the bed where Daniel stirred and grumbled.

VIRGINS and MARTYRS

"Come on then. Let's get you going."

With much patience and a certain amount of ingenuity he contrived to persuade, cajole and partly carry Daniel into the bathroom. Daniel's eyes flickered open as the two stood, swaying together at the door, and he made a sound of some sort, whether of complaint or inquiry or merely comment being unclear. The skinhead sat him down, propping him up against the side of the bath and squatting down in front of him.

"Daniel?" Daniel murmured something from a dream about a cavernous deserted building and an adding machine.

"Daniel? I'm going to get these clothes off you now. OK? Help me if you can. OK?"

Slurred sounds, like a drunk explaining how a car engine works. Cadenced but without meaningful content. The skinhead smiled.

He reached forward and took hold of Daniel's left arm, then dropped it again instantly, as the arm shook, a shock like a live wire jolting his hand. The skinhead looked curiously at him. "Well well well," he said, and grunted, rocking on his heels.

He went down to the kitchen and rummaged around under the sink where some yellow rubber gloves lurked, rarely used. He pulled one onto his right hand, then, with some difficulty got the other on over it. He returned to the bathroom.

Again he grasped Daniel's arm, without any problem now, and with his left hand pulled at the sleeve of the jumper.

"Bend your arm now, come on now, help me," he muttered, and gave Daniel's arm a little push at the elbow. The arm bent and the sleeve came away; the arm was now loose inside the body of the jumper.

He repeated the procedure on the other side, then braced Daniel's neck down and grabbed the jumper from behind. It jerked up and, with some reluctance, came up over Daniel's head, sliding over his hair. Finally it came away, and the skinhead chucked it into the corner. Daniel seemed to be receding further into unconsciousness. The skinhead stood up to relieve his calves and rested for a moment. The remaining clothes, he knew, would be easier.

Ten minutes later he had the shirt, shoes, socks, trousers and underwear piled up in the corner. He returned to the kitchen and got a bin bag, shoved all the clothes into it, and took it down to the front door with the bedding. Important to be orderly.

Back in the bathroom he ran the hot tap: it took a few seconds to get up to temperature and he dangled his fingers under the jet of water, staring vacantly at the wall.

When the water was hot he put the plug in and turned on the cold as well. He filled the bath three-

VIRGINS *and* MARTYRS

quarters full and poured in a little Alpine Meadows Radox. He tested the water.

"OK feller, bathtime."

Daniel by now weighed pitifully little, but even so he was 95 percent dead weight and without co-operation even the slightest human form was hard to move around. The skinhead took Daniel by the right hand and got him, approximately, standing, then hooked him below the knees; he knelt to take the weight and lifted, a good, if slightly unbalanced, clean lift. He lowered Daniel into the water, positioning him so that he was half-sitting, his head leaning back against the cold rim.

There was a purple face cloth behind the taps and the skinhead sloshed it around in the water, then started applying it to Daniel.

"Daniel?"

There was no response; his awfully thin chest rose and fell almost imperceptibly. The skinhead lifted an eyelid; nothing there.

"I'm going to stick your head under, guy. Just for a second. Just to get your hair wet. OK?"

He took hold of the top of Daniel's head and rested his other hand on Daniel's neck. Then he gently lowered the head down until it was completely immersed. He moved it from side to side for a few seconds, then lifted it clear again. Daniel spluttered and his eyelids fluttered open.

"Uh?"

Daniel lifted an arm in a slight, laconic gesture of some kind, let it fall again. The eyes briefly registered the pale blue tiles and the squat chrome taps, then closed down.

The skinhead let Daniel's head fall back against the rim of the bath, and combed the wet strands of hair off his forehead. He cleared the water out of his ears with a gloved finger and dabbed the corner of a towel against his eyelids.

"Christ where did you get that haircut?" he said, and laughed. "Did you get the fellow that did this to you?"

He ran a speculative finger over the uneven stubble of Daniel's jaw and went to find a fresh razor and his shaving brush. He worked quickly but steadily and only nicked the skin once, over the lip. It bled hardly at all.

"OK chap. Now I'm going to let the water out before I try to get you out of there. Because if I should happen to let you slip, well a person can drown in a few seconds as I'm sure you're aware. OK?"

He pulled out the plug, and Daniel, right down at the center of a dark, deep dream, thought he could feel his blood being drained from his veins as the liquid slipped over him and tugged with the gentlest of caresses at his skin and through his fingers and toes.

The skinhead, returning from the sink where he had been scrubbing his hands and fingernails,

VIRGINS and
MARTYRS

dried Daniel's head and shoulders and arm and lifted him out, placing him on a large white towel laid on the floor, where he finished drying him off. He put a hand towel over his waist and crotch, and then, bending from the knees as before, lifted him up. Daniel's head hung back, and his arms fell outward. The skinhead had to twist him to get him through the bathroom door, and then had to sidle sideways up the stairways. He kicked and kneed open the door to Daniel's room and laid him on the bed.

"OK. Just one more thing, and I'll let you sleep in peace. Just wait here. Don't go away now." He went down to the kitchen and rummaged around in a drawer, then came back upstairs carrying a small yellow box.

He picked Daniel up again and sat him in the chair by the window. He put the towel round his neck, then ducked down to find a plug.

"OK sir. What's it to be?"

The device whirred into life: hair clippers.

He dropped oil onto the vibrating blades from a tiny tube. He snapped on the number two attachment.

"Number two all over. What do you say?"

He held Daniel's head still and applied the shaver to the back, carving a neat path through the wet hair. A drop of oil trickled down his fingers and onto Daniel's forehead.

*simon maginn*

The shorn bits of hair fell onto the towel and the floor. Much of it seemed to find its way onto the skinhead himself, gluing itself to fingers and sleeves.

Daniel's dream rattled as the shaver tingled the prominent bone behind his ear, rattled and shivered and fragmented. The shaver whirred, carving trench after trench through his thick wet hair, fracturing and troubling his dreams. The curves and troughs of his physiognomy emerged, as did a small curved scar near his crown.

When the skinhead was satisfied he brushed the sharp little fragments away as best he could and removed the towel. He stood back to observe his work.

"Yes. Definitely."

He lifted Daniel off the chair and deposited him carefully back onto the bed: he disappeared and returned with a brown sleeping bag.

"Just until I've got your laundry sorted out," he said. "Hope it'll be OK." He gently, solicitously covered Daniel's unquietly sleeping, cleaned, shaved body with the bag and, flicking off the light, softly shut the door and tiptoed away.

Loulie fretted at a corner of a rug by the front door, her big expressive eyes fastened on the letterbox, where the key hung on a length of string. She sighed and rolled onto her side, scratching at her swollen belly. Her nipples were hard little protuberances now, dark, and they itched. She whined softly and sat, awkward, bulging out all over the place. The only really comfortable position was standing, and her legs were tired. She was waiting for the hand with long broken pink nails and heavy jewelry to reach through and pull up the string. She'd been waiting for hours.

As had Cathy Slater, the Dowager's long-term social worker and unofficial (and increasingly unwilling) dog-minder.

The way it usually went was that the Dowager would ring her, Cathy (at home, at work, the woman didn't seem to draw any distinctions), with some kind of emergency. She was ill! Her legs hurt! She was lonely, *darling*! Cathy would allow just a trace of hardness into her voice as she explained that she was busy, she had a case conference or a meeting or a dinner party to go to. Or just basically a *life*. But the Dowager would wheedle, sound hurt; if necessary she'd cry, sounding for all the world like a frail old woman with a mental health problem who lived on her own with only her dogs for company. In short, like a client. It was bloody blackmail and she knew it.

Cathy would put the phone down, furious, guilty, manipulated, and get into her Metro. Once she'd been on her way to a funeral, all ready to leave the house, in tasteful black and discreet accessories, her hair in an experimental French pleat.

She'd been feeling pleasantly serious; it was a relative but not a close one, and she'd been enjoying the sense of herself as a sorrowful but sexy woman, aware that the black looked marvelous on her.

"Darling? I can't get the *light* to come on."

"It's the middle of the day, Molly." (Cathy was allowed the privilege of addressing the Dowager by name rather than title, an honor that was, in practice, accorded to just about everyone except policemen, taxi drivers and certain shopkeepers she'd fallen out with.)

"Is it? I must have dropped off. I don't know where my Lithium are. Is it today I'm supposed to have my blood test?"

"Your blood test is on the first of the month, Molly."

"Is that today darling?"

"No. It isn't. And you keep your Lithium in your small bag, which you keep in the alcove by the gas fire in the back room. Don't you."

"Do I? But what about the light? How can I see anything?"

"Molly. It's broad daylight."

"Yes darling, but what about *later*? It'll be dark *later*, won't it?" she added cleverly. Oh yes, very bloody cleverly, Cathy thought. Call yourself prematurely senile? Not likely.

"Yes Molly. I suppose it will."

"And I can't get the cooker to come on. I've been waiting *hours*. It just *won't*."

VIRGINS and
MARTYRS

"Molly, now I think we've been through this before, haven't we? You have to switch it on, at the wall. We keep it switched *off*, don't we, so it won't start a fire. Your idea, as I recall. There's a switch. It's marked 'cooker'...."

"Oh *darling*..."

"And you push it to 'on'...."

"Can't you come? You're so clever with things. Darling?..."

So she'd gone, impeccable in black, and the Dowager had just had to pop out for something, and had returned after the pubs. Cathy had had to pay the taxi. Molly had accused her of not feeding the dogs right. Loulie had a funny look in her eye, she'd said.

This time it had been:

"Cathy? There's a man in the spare room!"

"Oh Molly there isn't. How could there be?"

"I don't *know*, darling. He must have got in the window or something."

"There isn't room to stand in your spare room. I can't get in. How could anyone else?"

The spare room was an infernal region infested with old budgie cages and suitcases and an enormity of bulky personal effects; stacks of magazines; small, odd, pointless items of furniture, stuffed with crockery and little statues; the whole lot generously scattered with birdseed.

"But I *heard* him."

*simon maginn*

"Did the dogs bark?"

"Yes!" she hissed triumphantly. "Yes they barked like crazy! Loulie was practically hysterical!"

Just for a change, thought Cathy. Loulie was the real mental health casualty in that ménage.

"All right." She sighed. "I'll be over right away."

"And could you bring some crackers? Those nice little ones, you know."

That had been at about nine p.m., and it was eleven now. The man in the spare room had gone by the time she arrived, he had presumably left by the window, the way he'd come in. Cathy had gone through the ritual of opening the door of the spare room and shouting in.

"Oi! Man in the spare room! What's your game?"

But the Dowager had seemed to lose interest by then, and was looking for her lighter and keys. She'd suddenly remembered that she had to pop in next door, she would only be a minute....

"I'll wait an hour, then I'm leaving. I mean it Molly. Loulie can chew through every wire in the place for all I care."

"But I'll just be a *second*. But you will keep an eye on her won't you, I think she's feeling the heat a bit. In her condition, poor little *lollipop*. Don't let her drink too much, she's getting a bit loose. Particularly when she gets excited. I think it's the pressure on her little *kidneys*. *Yes*." Molly beamed at Loulie and her kidneys, and disappeared.

VIRGINS and
MARTYRS

That had been nearly two hours ago. Cathy sat in the cluttered back room surrounded by the litter of ashtrays and newspapers. There were small framed photographs of dachshunds: to the untrained eye they looked pretty much interchangeable. If she's not here by half-past, she thought, and the phone rang.

"Are you a relative of Margaret Sillcott?" Cathy had had to think for a moment.

"You mean Molly? Well not really. What's happened?"

"This is Sergeant Collier, Hove Police. I'm afraid Mrs. Sillcott's been involved in an accident. She's been taken to Accident and Emergency at the Royal County. They need someone to act as next of kin. Do you know if she has anyone?"

She'd be hours at Casualty, Cathy knew. She regarded the dogs who'd gathered round her feet as she spoke, looking up at her suspiciously.

"Oh for Christ's sake!" she said, and Loulie backed away, bared her teeth, growled.

Outhwaite was hanging around the Communications Room when the call about the accident came in. He had no legitimate excuse to be there, and was reduced to making small talk with a bored constable who was about to go off duty. Quarter to ten.

Outhwaite should have been at home, hours ago, sitting in front of the telly while Sean sat upstairs in his bedroom counting the bricks on the wall opposite his window. If the number came out wrong he'd start shouting and wake up Grant.

Sean had been assessed as fit to live at home, was no threat to himself or anyone else, and was able to feed and groom himself. He attended a day center where he stared out of the windows and counted the cars. It was an Obsessive Compulsive Disorder, they'd said, and there is no treatment, no cure. Sean would come to a standstill in front of traffic lights and count the cars waiting for green: if they were not the right number he would wait until fresh cars came along to make up the sum. If the queue of cars was released before it reached the right number he would become enraged and refuse to move, waiting for red again. Seventeen years old, and strong. He would need supervision all his life.

He spoke quickly and excitedly, ducking his head repeatedly, making curious, arbitrary statements seemingly from another world. Outhwaite had on more than one occasion felt that there was a patterning to his speech, beyond its obvious meaning. Outhwaite believed Sean counted his words, tailoring his statements to a preordained number. Outhwaite had absorbed the expert opinions, acquired over a long period, each the result of long waiting, long hoping, for him and Karen. And yet there was a place within him that believed that what the boy really needed was a bloody good thumping and a few words of warning about what he was doing to his mother, his brother. His father. This was why Outhwaite so often found himself hanging around the police station long after his shift had ended, long after he should have been at home, with Karen. Why he would sometimes glance at his car clock and see that he had been parked somewhere for an hour, an hour and a half, just sitting, delaying. He crept into his house late several times a week and had become adept at sliding in between the sheets without waking Karen.

So the call when it came was a welcome break from the conversation with the bored constable, which had become something interminable and futile about the comparative fuel efficiencies of their cars.

Outhwaite listened to the details of the accident as they came through: they immediately struck him as odd. Phones rang distantly, and he could hear a WPC out in Reception arguing with someone, as the young constable with the fuel-efficient car wrote down the story.

A taxi involved in a single-vehicle incident on a stretch of road which, at that time of night, was all but deserted. Wet road, but perfect visibility.

Odd, to say the least.

It was none of his concern, of course, but he was interested. He rang through to the office of the taxi company, and his skin prickled when they told him the address the fare had given. No. 8 Adelaide Street. The house he'd searched, what, ten days ago? The house where there had been a polite, shaven-headed young man, and a hank of human hair on top of a wardrobe (and wasn't there something about that?). The house that had been silent, deserted, like, he'd thought, a shrine. Rooms inhabited only by furniture and dust and muted light. A haunted young man who had come to him and told him—something. Some insight or hallucination or vision, concerning the Lady of the Lake arm. Who had not been present when they'd searched. Where was he now, Outhwaite wondered, this untidy, intense young man? He thought of him, obsessed, terrified, holed-up in that house: and he thought of Sean lying on his bed, patiently counting the world, juggling the number, trying to make it all come out right. He couldn't help Sean, no one could. But that other one—

He would make inquiries.

After he'd left, Constable Warren picked up the phone and dialed.

"He was here again," he said when the phone was answered. "You know, Outhwaite, the one-armed-bandit man." He listened, then laughed loudly. "Yeah, well at least he's 'armless," he said, and winced in mock pain at the joke. "Got a bit of a bee in his bonnet, it would appear. Still, maybe he's got something up his sleeve." Another grimace of pain. He listened again; "Poor old bugger. You know what I think? I think someone should give him a hand."

### chapter twenty-two

The next morning, the skinhead watched, smiling, as Daniel ate. Bland, pappy even, but, he assured him, if he really hadn't been eating for nearly three weeks, then he'd have to build himself up slowly. His stomach would have shrunk, and if he ate too much too quickly he could injure himself.

Daniel spooned in the pap; he was feeling a lot better. The car crash had seemed to mark an end to the confusion, the weirdness, the visions. Whatever it had been about, it was over. The skinhead had turned up, it seemed, just in time, and now here he was, clean, shaved (he ran his hand over the new stubble thankfully) and sitting up in bed, with clean white sheets and pillows, eating this—well, whatever it was.

"Good for ya, fella. Get it all down now."

Which Daniel did: it seemed rude not to, and he was after all *starving*. Not just literally either: he realized as soon as the first mouthful entered his mouth how simply hungry he was, and how good it was to eat anything, even something as tasteless as this stuff, this porridge. If something could be offensively bland, he thought, then this is it.

He was going to get up later and go to the library. He still had time, though he was really going to have to go for it. The skinhead had told him the date and he'd been amazed: still only late August! He'd somehow thought it was much later in the year: he'd had the feeling of time flooding away from him, hemorrhaging away, uncontrollably, but in fact his mental health problem or whatever you wanted to call it, had actually only taken up a matter of days.

And here he was and he was as good as new. Thin? Christ yes, not half! He plucked incredulously at the wasted flesh on thighs and chest, and was astounded at how his sense of himself had similarly shrunk away—almost to nothing. If the skinhead hadn't found him in time, he was certain that it would have shriveled away completely, that he would have died. How close he'd come he couldn't know.

Shaky also. His legs, through starvation and lack of use, also probably through the shock of the crash (he remembered that it had happened, but not how or why, or even what his part in it had been: but it had definitely taken place, and unquestionably to him) were less than 100 percent trustworthy. When he tried to stand he wobbled, swayed like a drunk, giggled, had to be helped. But he was improving hourly, he could feel the life charging back into him. He would be able to climb onto the bus and, at the

VIRGINS and
MARTYRS

other end, ascend the steps to the university library, and get back to work. It wasn't too late!

The skinhead took the bowl away and Daniel looked round for his clothes. His briefcase. His contact lenses. He saw the clean, orderly room arranged neatly around him.

"Where are my things?" he called out, and stumbled to the door, calling down the stairs to the skinhead's retreating back.

"Where are my things?"

The skinhead turned.

"Oh yes. I'll bring it all up. In a minute."

Daniel stood in loosely hanging white trousers and a large clean white shirt. "Just until I've got your things laundered," the skinhead said. Daniel put in his contacts, and the world rushed at him, sharp, businesslike, uncompromising.

The skinhead stood back and regarded him.

"Looking good, feller. Good as new. Better."

Daniel smiled uncertainly, and felt the unfamiliar way his face responded. It didn't really seem to belong to him anymore. But it would come back, he had no doubt.

"Are you sure?" he asked, and the skinhead said, "Would I lie to you?"

He walked to the bus stop; it was a cool cloudy day, and there was a pale, soothing breeze coming off the sea. He glanced into the launderette as he passed. People were in there doing their laundry, a scene of good order and irreproachably sensible hygienic procedures.

He showed his pass, then climbed up to the top deck of the bus, though the stairs tired his legs.

The skinhead had apparently taken his clothes away to be washed, and had collected up the briefcase and the contact lenses more or less by accident when he'd tidied the room. Perfectly understandable. Daniel checked through the papers in the briefcase: they all seemed to be in order. Glancing through his dissertation he was struck by how much sense it made. It was by no means the chaotic jumble it had become in his mind recently. Just a little knocking into shape and it would be ready to go.

(Bathing him, also, was a quite reasonable thing to have done, in the circumstances. Wasn't it?)

He had to rest halfway up the steps to the library, and again at the top. It seemed to be a terribly long way, and the muscles in his legs were hot and singing. The borrowed clothes chafed against him in all sorts of unexpected places.

(And as for the haircut, he was grateful for it. From glances in windows and car wing-mirrors, it was clearly a vast improvement. Possibly the skinhead could have waited until he was awake to ask his permission. But he must have just thought

VIRGINS and
MARTYRS

that he might as well do it there and then. Nothing to complain about there. Surely.)

Inside, the library had the same airless, baked quality that his room suffered from, heat trapped and circulating slowly around the huge web of shelves, books and stupefied students. He found a free desk and dumped his case. He sat down, and for a moment just waited, looking straight ahead. Waiting for something to happen, a voice, a smell, anything.

Nothing.

He got down to work.


Outhwaite found the Dowager in the Veronica Smallwood ward, also known as Female Surgical. She was sitting up in bed in a pink hospital nightgown, her face ashen and lined, her short-cut hair hanging stiffly over her features.

"Mrs. Sillcott?"

She scrutinized him closely.

"Yes."

"I am Detective Inspector Terence Outhwaite."

"Oh yes?" She had an abiding suspicion of the police. In any little disturbance they always seemed to be on the taxi driver's side.

"Do you mind if I ask you a few questions? About the accident?"

"Yes?" She gave no sign of understanding his question, showing him a face full of incomprehen-

*simon maginn*

sion and querulous anxiety. It used to work with Cathy Slater, before she'd wised up.

"I understand that you were on your way to No. 8 Adelaide Street."

"No."

"No?"

"No I wouldn't say that exactly." She smiled, and gestured helplessly. It was all too confusing, the gesture said, for someone so elderly, so female.

"Could you describe to me how the accident happened?"

"Have you got a fag?"

Outhwaite sighed, looked around.

"I don't think they like you to smoke in these places," he said, and she winked.

"I'll save it for Ron."

"I'm sorry?"

"Later. Later Ron."

He smiled uncertainly and she scratched her ear, leaning forward confidentially.

"I'll hide it down my cleavage and sneak into the toilets later." Outhwaite, to his amazement, found that he was blushing at the mention of her cleavage. He looked nervously around, then reached into his jacket pocket and took a Benson and Hedges out of its packet: she winked again and carefully placed it inside her nightdress.

"Your face and my arse," she declared, and Outhwaite recoiled. Was she *mad*, this woman?

VIRGINS *and*
MARTYRS

"A match, stupid."

He passed over a book of matches which was secreted alongside the cigarette.

"Mrs. Sillcott—"

"Viscountess. You can call me Dowager," she said, properly, primly now, remembering her dislike for the police. Outhwaite, nothing abashed, declined the invitation.

"Mrs. Sillcott, I'd like you to tell me why you were going to Adelaide Street yesterday night. Do you know someone there?"

"No. I used to know someone, but she went away. Disappeared," she said.

"What was her name?"

"Didn't tell me where she was going."

"Can you tell me her name?"

"Wendy Bishop. Little slip of a thing she was. I knew her boyfriend, ugly little sod but there you are. He used to buy pills off me, pound a time. Ooops! Shouldn't be telling you that now should I?" She giggled. "Anyway she wasn't there long. Wouldn't let me go to see her there either. Funny girl really."

"How would you describe your relationship with Miss Bishop?" Outhwaite asked. He was more or less on autopilot, just going through the motions. This wasn't leading anywhere. So he almost missed it when she said:

"Nice long hair she had. Very black. Between you and me I think it came out of a bottle. But she was very proud of it. She thought she looked like Cleopatra. I told her Cleopatra had a bit of meat on her, she wasn't all bones. She never took any notice though."

The woman in the next bed coughed on, methodically, mechanically, like a perverse child's toy: middle-aged Barbie with Emphysema. Outhwaite was silent for a second as the image of a dusty hank of human hair on top of a wardrobe came to him. Used to be a bit of a hippy. Took such a lot of looking after. I never missed it.

"Mrs. Sillcott, can you think of any reason why Miss Bishop might want to cut her hair? Cut it completely off, I mean?"

"What're you talking about?" she said, tiring of the interview. She started looking around for a nurse. "What would she want to do that for? What kind of stupid question is that?"

"You say she disappeared. When would that be?"

"How do I know? What're you asking me all these things for? Like a common criminal!" She sniffed, unconvincingly, and closed her eyes, allowing her hands to flap slightly on the blankets. "Why don't you ask *him*, that taxi driver? You're always on their side you people." Her head sank back on the pillow. "Poor little lollipop," she murmured.

Outhwaite hadn't finished yet.

"Why did the car crash, Mrs. Sillcott? The hospital tested Mr. Steadman for alcohol, but he was

VIR**G**INS *and*
MARTYRS

clear. There was no reason to crash that we have been able to ascertain."

"It was all those diversions, and then she just came running out in front of the car, waving."

"Who did? Who came running out?"

The Dowager paused, genuinely uncertain now. Could her recollection really be accurate?

"I think it was her. Wendy."

"She ran out in front of the taxi you were traveling in? Are you sure?

She shrugged disdainfully.

"It certainly looked like her. Same coat and everything, same hair. *I* don't know." She shook her head. "Where's my lollipop?" she said, only half playacting now, "where's my little petal-pie? It could be any day now."

Outhwaite leaned in to her.

"What could be?"

"My lollipop. She is in an interesting condition. She is with child."

"Wendy? Wendy is pregnant?"

"Is she?"

"I don't follow—"

"I don't know what you're talking about. My lollipop," she said with dignified finality, "is a dog. By which, of course, I mean a bitch." She waved an arm grandly. "Nurse! This man is insane! Nurse!"

Outhwaite retreated, the sound of coughing following him down the ward.

Daniel was scribbling furiously, pausing occasionally to run his hand over his unfamiliarly bristly head. He was on to something.

Dr. Medway had been, as usual, absolutely right. It wasn't Buckley F. Tsasze and the medieval economy he needed to incorporate into the argument, it was that other essay, about the saints. It was all becoming clear: the witches and the saints were almost interchangeable, at least as far as their biographies were concerned. Opposite sides of the same coin. It was almost as if the same person could become either thing: the difference was purely in the interpretation.

Take his own Sarah Hilyard, for instance, his beloved. She saw visions from an early age, was reported to fast and mortify herself regularly, and refused to rush into the marriage that her father had arranged for her. This could be the story of any number of medieval virgin martyrs. St. Benedicta, for instance, or even Catherine of Siena. The difference seemed to be largely in the fact that Sarah continued to live with her family, and gave a more colorful account of her experiences. But Sarah was tortured, starved, imprisoned, tried and finally burned, with her ashes being scattered on a dung heap, whereas Catherine of Siena lived an exemplary if somewhat uninteresting life cloistered in a Dominican convent and was celebrated after her death, her bones becoming a venerated relic, cur-

VIRGINS and
MARTYRS

ing the desperate peasantry of fifteenth-century Europe of their rheumatics and their dropsies. An ancestor with friends in high places, the highest.

But the outcome could have been so different so easily! If only Sarah had been a little more circumspect, a tad more sensible; if she had been demure and pious and basically dull, then hers could have been the bones fingered by the anxious hands and kissed by the cracked lips of the farmers and merchants; and if Catherine had had any life, any fun, in her at all, she could so easily have become a torturer's plaything, her tender, emaciated body cowering bruised and bleeding on dirty straw in a damp cell somewhere.

Sarah had been so young, so foolish, at her trial! She thought the world was hers to enjoy, and instead she found a world intent on nothing but dragging her away to the interrogation cells. The inquisitors and witchfinders were the serial killers of the medieval world, licensed and employed by the Church and fed a steady diet of young, predominantly female, victims.

And yet no less victims were the saints, those poor, driven, deluded creatures, performing their appalling acts of self-mutilation, denial, torture, and often meeting early, avoidable deaths; the whole process overseen, validated, applauded by the same Church.

(thin when they died they were all thin)

*simon maginn*

His pen scratched at his paper, as the library yawned and lolled around him. His words came faster, becoming less distinct, more abbreviated, sketchier, until they came to resemble merely the trails of insects. His head was full of thoughts, twisting, turning, blurring. He had to get it all down.

"Daniel."

He froze, the pen arrested in full flight, the blood banging to a halt behind his eyes. He didn't turn round, couldn't turn round, all time had stopped.

"Daniel? How's it going?"

His head turned on his neck, stiff, like a long-disused piece of automation. He could feel his eyes bulging with the force of the blood behind them.

"Are you OK?"

Daniel stared, only slowly recognizing that this was a real voice, coming from a real person, a person he knew, someone he'd been in a seminar group with.

"Hello," he said, the word clanging madly in his ears, "yes. Yes I'm fine. You gave me a bit of a start."

"Sorry 'bout that. Hard at it I see?"

"Yes." Daniel hunted for this person's name, but only came up with a picture of a wall. Hadrian? Adrian?

"Nothing like leaving it to the last minute eh? I've only just got mine out to the typists." He laughed, and Daniel tried to laugh as well, but was

VIRGINS and
MARTYRS

distracted by the light glancing off this person's glasses, and wasn't sure he was doing it right.

"Someone told me you'd moved house?"

"Yeah." There ought to be more, but somehow there just wasn't. Daniel wanted to get back to work.

"Well anyway. Stay in touch yeah?"

Funny, Daniel thought, how people kept saying that to him.

"Yeah," he said. "'Bye," and tried to block the sound out as it reverberated in his skull, like the buzzing of a pair of hair-clippers. Nothing wrong with that. Was there?

"Nothing wrong with that," he said, and frowned. That wasn't the right thing to say. Still, never mind about that. He had to get it all down. On paper. Knock it into shape. He turned back to his work.

He blinked and put down his pen: he was unable to read the page he had written, it was just scribble, dots and dashes, little scrawls and curlicues. He flicked back to previous pages—it was all just scribble. Rubbish. Meaningless.

He stood up, and for a moment thought he could detect that scent, that powdery, dry-paper smell of Wendy, a fortnight dead or beyond—

No, that was finished, he assured himself, all finished,

(thin so thin)

and he was *himself* again (except that he was wearing someone else's clothes and had someone else's haircut and was living in a house that was not his either), no more hallucinations, no more

(visions?)

*weirdness*, that was over!

He marched away; he needed to find a Butler's *Lives of the Saints*. He needed to check a detail, something about—something—

He strode off, determined, through the close, somnolent air, left arm held stiffly, right arm now free of its bandage but still sore, eyes bulging. The books roared and howled their fury as he passed.

Outhwaite was waiting for a break in the traffic.

The taxi driver, Steadman, had been stunned and confused, but had been definite about one thing: someone had stepped out in front of the car and he'd had to swerve violently to avoid her. He'd asked about his passengers.

"Passengers? You mean passeng*er*, surely, the old woman, Mrs. Sillcott?"

"And the other one. Friend of the old woman's. Looked like he'd maybe had a little bit too much of something."

"Can you describe him to me?" Outhwaite was intrigued—why hadn't the Dowager mentioned this other passenger?

"Skinny lad, twenty-odd, none too clean, something about the way he looked, something in his eyes."

"Haunted?" Outhwaite had prompted, inspired, and Steadman had regarded him oddly, looked away.

"Could be. Yes. Do you know who he is?"

"Where did you pick him up?"

"8 Adelaide Street."

"Wait." Outhwaite held up his hand. He was confused. "Wait now. You picked him up at the address in Adelaide Street, and Mrs. Sillcott as well?"

"That's it."

"But the car—when you had your accident, you were traveling toward Adelaide Street, not away."

"We got, sort of, turned around," Steadman said, and his face clouded, became vague. He squinted and fingered the dressing on his head. "Diversions," he said, and then looked up at the ceiling and clucked his tongue, as if debating with himself the veracity of what he was saying.

"There were no diversions," Outhwaite said. "You must be mistaken."

"There was something in the road." His face began to crumple. "I don't—let me think for a minute now—" he'd said, and had become restless, upset: a nurse had come over to the bed and Outhwaite had left.

Outhwaite knew taxi drivers. Alongside bus drivers and motorbike couriers, they were very often the only reliable witnesses to traffic accidents. An old woman is knocked over by a driver, who doesn't have time to stop and see if she's all right. His house is on fire maybe. At any rate, he accelerates lustily away from the scene. Police and ambulance are called. Witnesses gather, people who saw the car, saw the woman, saw everything. The first question is: what was the registration number of the car? Did anyone see?

Immediately the witnesses go into a huddle: a few minutes later a spokesman emerges and delivers a majority opinion, a compromise, containing elements of all their disparate sightings. A registration number, certainly, but you can bet your shirt on the fact that it is no registration number currently in use, or if it is then the car it belongs to is at this moment several hundred miles away and of entirely the wrong make and color.

Then a taxi driver will step forward, and his registration number will turn out to be the exact one. Venal, stupid, not infrequently violent, terrifyingly aggressive drivers and subject to all sorts of appalling and vicious opinion: but they were excellent witnesses, *beautiful* witnesses, the best.

And yet here was one, didn't seem to know what road he'd been on, was inventing imaginary diversions where none existed, crashed his car on an empty stretch to avoid someone who seemingly just appeared in the middle of the road, then disappeared again. Admittedly, this Steadman had had a bad knock on the head and was, probably, still to some

VIRGINS and
MARTYRS

degree in shock. But even so, it didn't tally. Steadman was entirely the wrong type to hallucinate obstacles in the road.

And he was also altogether the wrong type to agree so meekly that one of his passengers might be "haunted." Outhwaite's suggestion should have been met with amusement, derision: instead Steadman had looked shifty, evaded his eye, agreed. No, it made no sense.

An oncoming car slowed and flashed his lights and Outhwaite edged forward.

But the thing that troubled him more was that there had been three people in the taxi when it crashed, and only two when the emergency services arrived. There was one unaccounted for, and he was, Outhwaite had no doubt, Daniel Blennerhassett.

So where is he now, Outhwaite was thinking again, where in God's name is he now? And why is he hiding?

Daniel stood, transfixed, with the book open in his burned right hand. He'd found the Butler's *Lives*, but had instead reached for an oversized book on the bottom shelf, an illustrated book, and he'd opened it, or it had perhaps simply fallen open to a page, and he stood now, his gaze fixed upon it, his eyes devouring it.

It was a reproduction of a fourteenth-century altarpiece, of the Florentine school. It showed scenes from the life of St. Julia, a fifth-century virgin martyr. Eight dim, murky, crowded little panels, but the colors were still there, the brilliant pigments, vermilion, scarlet, and in places flashes of somberly glowing gold, the boards dusted over with the fading of centuries.

The figures inside the panels were frantically busy, performing their significant actions and holding their poses, crowding in from the corners of the panels, standing in awkward huddles. The saint herself, in contrast, was alone, separated. She simply stood, crowned and haloed, as the figures in her story cavorted around her.

It was a common enough story: steadfast Christian meets wicked heathens and neither side budges an inch. In the case of the unfortunate Julia, she was accompanying her master on a sea voyage. The ship docked at Corsica; the governor of the island, one Felix, demanded that she come ashore and worship the idols, which she of course refused point blank to do. Negotiations, at this stage, broke down, and he beat her, around the face. The red smears of her blood were the focal point on the fourth panel, resplendent against the cluttered surroundings. She stood, leaning slightly forward, in the prow of the ship. Her crown and halo were not disturbed a jot by this beating.

In the next frame she was on the floor, being dragged by her hair. The purpose of this, apparently,

VIRGINS and
MARTYRS

was to pull the hair out, though she still had it in later pictures. There were three men pulling her, and about ten watching from a curious little raised platform with a flat roof. Felix was prominent among them. Inevitably her crown and halo had slipped by now.

And yet here she was in frame six, miraculously attired again in her golden accoutrements, her celestial accessories. And well might she be, for in frame six she was hanging from a poorly designed timber construction, arms akimbo, face raised to heaven. She had been crucified, and her soul, in the form of a dove, was ascending to meet its glorious reward, the special reward that is promised to virgins and martyrs.

The remaining two frames dealt with the removal of her body and its transportation to the island of Gorgona, where she was enshrined.

But the detail that was making Daniel hold the book right up close was in frame seven.

She was being picked up by the monks from Gorgona, three of them, shadowy, cowled figures with prominent tonsures. Two of them were supporting her, as the blood flowed, rich, deep, viscid from the crucifixion wounds on hands and feet. No neat stigmata these, but rough, ugly gashes. Her dress had slipped, hardly surprising in the circumstances, to reveal the ghastly, unspeakable thinness of her shoulder and breast.

*simon maginn*

But the detail that had stopped Daniel in his tracks, had, literally, caught his eye, *trapped* it, was what the third monk was holding in his clasped hands.

Flowers.

### chapter twenty-three

Outhwaite was parked at the end of Adelaide Street: he could see the door to No. 8 in his offside wing mirror. He had been there for the better part of an hour, watching the light fading from the rooftops and around the chimney stacks. The seagulls nesting on the roofs squawked and shrieked, unearthly, desolate utterances. The males were picking out nesting places, marking territory by the strength and duration of their cries, flapping about with tiny pieces of twig and leaf, building the nests. The females stood around, being timidly approached and flapped at by the males, until they felt threatened: then they retreated a few paces. These tortuous attempts at completely unprecedented cooperation (many of the birds would be trying all this for the first time) brought forth prodigious bursts of shrieking, wailing, sobbing and a repertoire of other calls, as they tried to communicate to each other the scope and complexity of their plans and desires. To Outhwaite it seemed to sum up the sadness in the

VIRGINS *and* MARTYRS

world. Forlorn, thwarted, endlessly trying. And, he supposed, it all must work out eventually. There seemed to be no shortage of seagulls.

The calls of the birds reminded him somewhat of Sean's curious, formal, stilted statements. Attempts to speak by a creature badly equipped for communicating, but determined to try.

Daniel had come to him, and he had been reminded of a child. But tucked away inside that impression was another one, that Daniel knew more than he was saying. And the undeniable truth was that Daniel had known something he couldn't have known. Daniel had also had, on top of the wardrobe, a hank of human hair. The skinhead had said it was his own, but Outhwaite had been wholly convinced that he was lying, improvising that story about a change of image and keeping the hair as a souvenir. It just didn't ring true. Outhwaite had felt that he was covering up, trying to protect Daniel.

And now this same Daniel, this unhappy child with his impossible knowledge was involved in an accident, and left the scene before the emergency services arrived. Before the *police* arrived, Outhwaite corrected himself precisely. Why?

What was he up to, this Daniel Blennerhassett? Hide and seek? Why had he come forward in the first place?

It was true, Outhwaite knew, that criminals often brought about their own capture, consciously or not. He didn't quite believe that criminals sought police just as much as police sought criminals, but he often felt that the process was far from one-sided. Criminals left clues, trails, they made idiotic, elementary mistakes, or they just plain walked into police stations and confessed, wept, pleaded for forgiveness. Even the good-class criminals, the professionals, sometimes. Had that been Daniel's intention, to seek forgiveness, an intention that he had finally balked at like a horse refusing a fence? He had walked in to confess, and had quite simply changed his mind halfway through. Was that possible?

And there was, of course, another side to it, a side that Outhwaite would have to have been deaf and blind not to be aware of. He was becoming The One-Armed Bandit, and it was about time someone Gave Him A Hand. He was personally associated with the case, he was in charge of it, and it was getting precisely nowhere. How long would it be before someone suggested that his personal difficulties (meaning Sean, and the known fact that Outhwaite would rather do just about anything than go home) were starting to affect his efficiency and maybe he should take some compassionate leave? To a policeman, wife and children and home were as essential a part of the job as a car and radio. A policeman having a touch of the domestics, *and* a high-profile case which was, effectively, stuck in a ditch, was fair game for comment.

VIRGINS *and*
MARTYRS

This meant that Daniel's movements and whereabouts were of more than casual interest at this time.

Of course there was no suggestion that procedures would not be followed to the letter. It was the law. There was no possibility that Daniel, should he be innocent, would be found guilty, or that when once again he appeared in a police interview room he had anything to fear.

But should he be guilty—well, Outhwaite was fairly certain that when he had Daniel in his sights again he would not be getting away quite as easily as the last time. That was all.

Because whatever he was, victim or accomplice or miscreant, innocent or guilty or anything in between, Outhwaite was finding himself clearer and clearer about what type Daniel was: he was police property. They had business to discuss, when he finally turned up.

And Outhwaite knew he would, sooner or later. The seagulls on the roof would, after an immense amount of chasing and evading and generally carrying on, nest together, and the suspect would find the policeman.

Particularly if the policeman in question happened to be parked at the end of the road, patiently waiting.

††

The book weighed heavily in Daniel's skinny, enfeebled arms, and the strain of holding it up was setting off vibrations in his arm and chest and back muscles; he stood trembling, and the hot air formed a close, suffocating skin over his meager bones.

A metallic voice rang out over the tannoy:

"This library will be closing in fifteen minutes. Would users requiring counter services please make their way to the ground floor as soon as possible to avoid queues developing—"

The announcement continued, starkly bureaucratic, as Daniel held the book open in his arms.

The pictures were an account, in all its important details, of the story that had been given to him in fragmented, allusive form by Wendy. A body, skeletally thin, scourged, battered, hung up on a makeshift framework, nailed by hands and feet, an approximate replica of the original crucifixion, with the exceptions that this had happened six centuries later and the victim here was female.

But this death had taken place almost thirteen centuries ago. Wendy couldn't have died more than six weeks ago, if the items in the room were a reliable guide. She couldn't possibly have met the same raw, messy, bloody fate as St. Julia.

No. No. Those things didn't happen anymore. Nobody was martyred anymore, that particular inglorious chapter of Church history had been closed, for centuries. Hadn't it?

VIRGINS and
MARTYRS

(Not the Church then. An enthusiastic amateur?)

No, it was absurd, outrageous, ludicrous. His hands clung onto the book; his arms had locked into position, and he was not aware that his entire body was now shaking violently, vibrating with sympathetic tension, rattling. Something fell onto the page, *splat*, a drop of sweat, blurring the image over the face of St. Julia and her golden crown, and for a moment he saw Wendy's bland, dead-fish face and cloudy eyes gazing up at him.

*(Daniel. Daniel. Daniel. Da)*

What was she telling him? That

(someone)

had strung her up somewhere, nailed her up, whipped her until her skin was shredded, a tender, runny mess (soft and moist like pizza) and that she had hung there—for how long

(beyond a fortnight? Oh definitely)

No.

Another drop fell to the page: it landed on the cloak of an angel, scarlet, and Daniel gazed at it, a blurred, contoured mound of redness. Uh-huh, he thought, now I'm sweating blood. Only to be expected I suppose. After all, if I'm to believe you, that your death was some kind of monstrous reenactment of the death of St. Julia of Corsica, virgin and martyr, then yes, I can believe that I'm sweating blood.

*simon maginn*

Abruptly he found that he was shaking so violently that the book, an old, dusty volume sewn into a cloth spine, tore.

He thought he understood now. He was to find her appalling, mangled body, to bring her remains together, to bury them as human remains are buried, to lay flowers over her. The old phrase came to his mind, lay her to rest. *Requiescat.*

And all this she was telling him in a cryptic, encoded manner, perhaps because she couldn't speak in any other way, or perhaps because her ability to tell him anything was deteriorating along with her awful remains.

And he had been selected as the agent of her wishes because he had moved into the room that she had inhabited, slept in the bed that she had slept in, lain in the bath—

*(There's more)*

The book slipped slightly in his clammy hands, and he noticed for the first time a slip of paper sticking up from further on in the book. A badly cut page? No, it was a different kind of paper from the rest. Brittle, yellowed.

Newsprint.

*(Look)*

He turned the pages until he came to the place marked by the slip of paper, which slid out and fluttered to the floor. He reached down to pick it up. Part of an advert for an indigestion remedy, part of an article which mentioned the word "league" a number of times.

*(Look!)*

He turned it over.

There was a coupon at the bottom of the slip: and as he read what it offered ("Yes! Please send me—copies of *How to Handle those Little Hitlers* at £9.95 each") he remembered where he'd seen the other half of this slip of paper: in the drawer, in that ugly, nestlike pile in the drawer in his room. In *her* room.

He looked at the picture that the paper had marked, and a great gust of fear came bellowing up from inside his chest: he clamped his teeth shut to keep it inside, but it leaked out round the corners of his mouth, a high, sibilant whistling.

Someone hanging from a wooden frame, upside down, his body emaciated, his head swollen with blood, his hair hacked off, blood streaming from wounds on hands and feet.

The martyrdom of St. Peter, apostle.

Outhwaite drove a Rover 214 Sli; and among its more serious attributes, it was capable of electronic wing-mirror adjustment. There was a four-way toggle switch on the dashboard, with arrows for left and right, up and down. Particularly useful for the near-side mirror obviously—after all, the off-side was only on the other side of the window. Of dubious value in ordinary driving situations, this gadget really came into its own in any kind of surveillance, since it enormously increased the range of visibility. Not only could he get a completely clear line of sight up the entire length of the short street, but he would be able to track any suspect as he moved. It also meant that you could sometimes obtain curiously privileged glimpses into windows of houses and other cars, which while perhaps having no strictly material bearing on the matter in hand, could nonetheless provide innocent diversion through the long watches of a prolonged (unauthorized) surveillance.

Like this character with the racing-green Peugeot a few cars down on the other side of the street. Baseball cap and dark glasses. Outhwaite watched with muted amusement as the figure bobbed about with his tailgate open; he was removing all those things that accumulate in the trunks of certain people's cars, things that over time seem to acquire an almost magical significance, like good-luck charms. Particular rags, empty tins of WD40, an oil can that found its way in five years ago and had never come out again since. Outhwaite was amused at the mood of determination that had clearly overtaken this person: today was the day, and this was the hour that he was going to clear out the lurking detritus that was infesting his boot. Maybe he was intending to sell. Or he was perhaps

VIRGINS and
MARTYRS

planning a trip and needed the space. Or was he possibly just possessed, consumed with the urge to be free and clear of it. Stuff it all into a bin bag and be done with it.

What was he doing now? Outhwaite nudged his rocker switch, but he couldn't quite get the right angle. The baseball cap was posed in midair and seemed to be vibrating. He stood up straight again and wiped his face with his forearm: Outhwaite could briefly see a flash of yellow in his hand. A cloth, or maybe a rubber glove. He was actually washing the inside of his boot, scrubbing away.

Above and beyond, surely, Outhwaite thought. File under f for "fanatical." Something tugged at the side of his mind and he frowned, blinking rapidly, but it wouldn't come, and he was disturbed by a sudden insanity of screeching from a nearby rooftop, a sound so deranged and disordered that it could only emanate from a seagull crazed with lust, stubbornly demanding requital. It momentarily drove all thought away from Outhwaite, and then his eye was caught by a movement, but not from his carelessly positioned wing mirror; this was happening directly behind him and he tilted his rear-view mirror (manually) to snatch a glance of someone entering No. 8. No one he knew: this was a shaven-headed person all in white. He thought he'd pretty much sorted out the personnel at No. 8 and was surprised at this new arrival. He had a key, whoever he was. Must be a friend of Daniel's or that other one. Should he go and question him?

No. He didn't want to be seen, and it was Daniel he was waiting for. Questioning this new person would just be an excuse to get out of the damn car and move his legs. No. Keep your cover. Patience.

### chapter twenty-four

Daniel arrived back at the doorstep of No. 8 as the light was starting to fade. Whatever horror shows Wendy might treat him to, he still had to come home, if only to pick up some of his books and clothes. He could hardly just leave everything behind, that wasn't really an option, because even on the radical economy diet he'd followed lately, even with his inability to touch the little money he had available, he was still a graduate student on a graduate student grant, and that meant poverty.

And in any case, where was he to go? Back to Montpelier Road? They'd already filled his place. Home to his mother and her endless intimate concerns about him? Hardly. He knew no one in Brighton or Hove Actually he could stay with. He had an address for his brother Mike in Coventry, but he knew he could never use it. And how would he get there anyway? Hitching? He hadn't the faintest idea how, and somehow he didn't think that Wendy would let him get very far.

And, dammit, was he going to let himself be hounded out of another house? It had been his own choice to leave Montpelier Road but it had still felt like a failure, as if he'd conceded defeat.

(*And first of all, in the flat where his mother had moved around, singing, where she had finally lain down one impossible day and turned to the wall—he had been carried out of there, struggling in the arms of a woman he didn't know, trying to grab hold of the door handle.*)

Was he going to let that happen again? He prided himself, if on nothing else, on his tenacity. He got through things, he stuck things out. Not, he conceded, the most exciting of virtues, but his own.

And he was *damned*, he felt suddenly, standing on the doorstep, if he was just going to be meekly driven out of this house as well. Whatever was in there, he would face it down.

Daniel Daniel Daniel, he heard Dr. Medway saying, in his effortless, urbane voice, all these melodramatics on doorsteps, do you really think you're cut out for this?

He was holding the key in his hand. His key, his door, his *house*.

He turned it, the door swung open and he could immediately smell it, a faint but fantastically evocative smell, and he was momentarily rooted to the spot as he tried to place it. It was a smell from his late childhood, that eerie, troubled time before the drama of adolescence set in and twisted everything round.

He'd been living in Solihull with his adopted parents, and Mike, his only sibling (a word they used often and which carried for him a curious, hissing, menacing quality, as if the person referred to was liable at any moment to try to bite his ankle) was fifteen and deeply involved in Getting Into Trouble, a pastime that his mum and dad seemed to find more absorbing than Mike himself. He would stand in the hall with the ugly watercolors of Paris and the ornamental phone table, as his adopted parents in outraged unison confronted him with coming in at this time/in this condition/as cool as you like or whatever the offense was, and Mike would be saying "What? What?" in the true voice of adolescence, shrill and falsely indignant.

Daniel, thirteen and still a child, watched from the doorway and hated them all, hated Mike for his idiotic, paltry misdemeanors, hated his parents for their apparently limitless capacity for righteousness, hated the well-kept-up, ostentatiously luxurious house, where he was perpetually worried about damaging things. He was as yet innocent of his true relationship to them. Mike, the hissing sibling, who was two years older and considerably wiser, had for the last twelve months been wearing a wide and varied selection of smug smiles, knowing and pitying by turns. Daniel, as far as he had assumed that this meant anything, had thought it was merely part of Mike's unattractive metamorphosis into a Young Adult (another of his mum's phony labels).

It had been a hot summer, heavy, overcast. They were to have a day out in Droitwich, a spa town about an hour's drive from Solihull. There were indoor brine baths there: his mum had an assortment of ill-informed beliefs about their therapeutic value.

Inside the unprepossessing brick building there was a world of salt and painted iron, dripping, pitted, crystal-encrusted railings and showers where the woodwork was blistered and flaked. The air was acrid with the corrosion of metal and wood, a pungent, irritating miasma, tickling the nostrils and the back of the throat, warm and misty and sharp.

Mike and he were hanging round the shallow end, Mike self-consciously cool in new black Speedos and a recently acquired muscular structure. His mum and dad were off somewhere, wallowing about unattractively in therapeutic mineral solutions. Daniel had suddenly found himself being dragged by one leg into the pool: Mike had decided that some aggression-thinly-disguised-as-horseplay was in order. Daniel had grabbed hold of the rail that ran along the pool just above water level, and held on. He had managed to lock his elbow round the rail, but Mike was grinning and yanking at him, pretending to misunderstand his protests.

*simon maginn*

"Off me, get off me!": his arm was well and truly stuck now, bent awkwardly between the wooden rail and the tile of the pool wall. He lashed out with both feet and, as his teeth cracked against the rail, he suddenly had a mouthful of strange, silky salt water and splinters of paint. He kicked out again, harder, and caught sight of Mike's idiot face, his teeth flashing, his eyes red with salt water, his black hair dark against his forehead and ears. For a few moments he was certain that Mike had genuinely taken leave of his senses in the ferocity of his mood, had become possessed by a grinning, muscled, furious devil. Daniel had screamed, thrashing, and was abruptly released as a fat hairy father-of-three wrenched Mike away and shook him by the shoulders, yelling into his face about sense and shoe sizes. Mike glared back at him, insolent, sleek and, temporarily at least, malevolently handsome.

Daniel had got his balance back, extricated his grazed elbow from its trap, and slunk away to be sick in the toilets.

And here was that smell again, dripping wet wood and corroding iron. He crept up the stairs, his heart banging viciously against his skinny ribs, ready for anything, on total alert. There was nothing though, and he slammed his bedroom door behind him, inarticulately grateful at being unmolested. He dropped the dissertation onto the table—the plant, he noticed, had stuck up a hard, dark green shoot—and, shaky from his exertions, lay down on the bed. Just for a moment. A handful of rain flung itself against the window, big fat drops. He went to the window and opened it: the air was cool and creamy, deliciously moist. His burned right hand throbbed gently. He put out the light and lay down again. Watched the ceiling.

Listened.


He was dreaming that someone was walking on his head, or rather that there was a bird in the room, banging against the ceiling. It dropped to the floor, somewhere nearby.

He sat up with a jolt. The echoes of a sound were reaching him, a largish sound that had very recently taken place just outside the door. And could he hear footsteps fading away out of earshot?

Surely not. A cool draft rattled the window in the frame. That was probably what had woken him up, just the wind. (Not someone moving around over his head, in the attic, dropping down from the hatch outside his bedroom door, creeping away downstairs?)

No. Surely not. He lay down again. His body felt singularly rigid, his breathing shallow and irregular. At one point he became convinced that he had stopped breathing altogether, and forced panicky air into his throat. His eyes closed, then flew open again, locked feverishly on the ceiling. It took him a moment or two to understand what was the matter with him: then he realized. He was scared stiff.

And oh Christ he could hear someone moving through the house, all but silently up the dark stairs and along the warm, dusty passages.

*(you lie very still, he doesn't hurt you if you lie very)*

Adrenaline surged into him, washing about, creating panic but not motion. He could smell himself, his panic, as he lay, feverish, motionless. A muscle in his jaw went into spasm as his teeth locked shut, as if with tetanus. This was no fasting high, this was just fear cooking his chilled body, his wasted muscle flesh, creeping over his cheeks and neck. The endokinins lit up his brain, simultaneously brilliant and somber, burning branches in a nocturnal forest, euphoric and tranquilizing, calling out from corners, beckoning him into shadows.

No lights on the stairs or landings, no streetlights to shine into windows, no moon. Unless whoever it was was carrying a torch or a candle he would have to move slowly, feeling his way forward, stroking the walls, testing for the last step. Slowly. Of course he knew the way, knew the obstacles, had perhaps made a mental note of the number of stairs in each flight. Was perhaps practiced at navigating the house, silently, in darkness.

*(be still, he'll bring you to me)*

Oh Christ he didn't think he wanted that to

VIRGINS *and*
MARTYRS

happen, really, all things considered, no offense mind.

He was on the landing below; Daniel's over-sensitized faculties were sensing him, smelling him, that rich, nostalgic smell, was it something to do with the wrappers of toffee-apples or

*(yes yes)*

Daniel jerked in shock as he heard a sound from directly below, a sound that he knew instantly, the unmistakable *bik-bok* of the bathroom light cord.

But the door didn't shut, nor did the little bolt slide into place. So: light on, door open.

Now he was coming up the stairs to the top floor. Perhaps he was going to do something in the room next to Daniel's, the room with the phone and the television. And the videos. The videos of starving people, emaciated people, dead people.

No, he was past the door now, OK maybe he wanted to get something out of the attic. But he'd just come *out* of the attic hadn't he?

the rubbery scent of deck chairs left out in the rain or

(but what would he want in the attic, what was there in the attic?)

*(don't you remember? don't you remember that it is **dangerous** to exceed the recommended load and that the manufacturers can accept **no responsibility**)*

He was right outside the door: Daniel was aware that his own muscles were aching with the strain of

*simon maginn*

his rigidity, that his eyes were locked on the ceiling, that he couldn't move. The part of his brain that issued commands to limbs had gone away, and the most he could aspire to in that direction was to remain rigid, chilled, like

(had he climbed into bed beside her, had he touched her arm, her cheek, had he tried to rouse her and found her flesh cool, solid, densely packed?)

Cra-*ack*.

A little light fell in, a darkness more washed, more transparent, as the door opened. The skinhead came in, and Daniel could immediately smell it on him, rank, strong, clear.

Salt water. The sea. Wet iron. Rotten wood.

The skinhead approached the bed and Daniel felt himself, his *self*, disappearing, slinking away, leaving only the gross, clammy, rigid form in the bed, and the eyes locked onto the ceiling. The skinhead's hand reached down toward his face (not my eyes!) and then the gentlest, tiniest motion: even in the dark he could sense the world swimming away from him as the contact lens was removed, with infinite care, then the other one. (Not my eyes!) A sound of some sort escaped his lips, as the skinhead reached down again and pulled away the duvet, slid warm hands under his shoulders and thighs, and lifted.

The skinhead twisted and lifted him through the door and down the stairs; Daniel realized at some point that the skinhead was wearing only boxer shorts, the heat from his body was reaching Daniel all over, wherever their flesh met. They turned the corner of the stairs, the skinhead again adjusting his burden to get it round the corner.

There was more light now, spilling out from the bathroom.

*(still be still)*

In truth he couldn't do otherwise; some key motivational component had left and was watching from a distance, noncontributing, perhaps taking notes. All he could do was to be still, neither limp nor stiff, so to speak (ha ha) but some kind of trance state in between, enfolded by the warm, muscular flesh of this skinhead in playing-card boxer shorts who was carrying him, bearing him, more than cautiously, more than carefully, but (the word popped like a flashbulb) ceremoniously. Neither stiff nor limp (ho ho), but distinctly alert, his being crouching somewhere deep within the body, taking a keen if somewhat academic interest. Maybe it was one of Wendy's little freak shows. Yes. Whatever it was, there was no part of him that he could move, nothing that he could move it *with*, nothing that was capable of wishing it to move.

The skinhead nudged the bathroom door with his knee, and it swung open a few inches more: nonetheless, Daniel's left knee brushed the door as the skinhead twisted him sideways, feet first. When they were fully inside, the skinhead hooked a foot round the door and swung it to: it didn't quite make it, leaving a gap of about eighteen inches.

For the first time it occurred to Daniel to wonder what it was that the skinhead was doing, what he wanted. It was clear that he had something in mind: another bath perhaps? Daniel felt an undeniable jolt of unease at the thought and a spasm for a second animated his legs, one foot kicking weakly.

*(no, no be)*

He couldn't help himself, the part that had fled was creeping back now, peeking through the spread fingers, and it was starting to get the smallest bit jumpy; some kind of awareness was returning, something beyond the simple pressure of the skinhead's warm skin and the steady push of his muscles, the strong, hard grip of his hands and fingers. There was also now the realization that his face was just a few inches away from Daniel's own, that he could feel the cool breeze of the skinhead's breath over his bony chest and sunken belly, that he could smell pickled onions on his breath, that the skinhead was actually there, holding him

Jesus now wait now

carrying him, transporting him, that he had a mouth, eyes, eyes that must presumably be open (unless he was in a fugue state of some sort, some kind of sleepwalking, and even then he would surely have to have his eyes open wouldn't he?) that the skinhead was actually, really, doing this, that Daniel was genuinely, incontrovertibly, physically having this done to him....

oh oh

His leg kicked again, and he could feel his neck trembling with the effort of holding his head in anything like an upright position (neither flaccid nor erect, nudge nudge) and with the strain of not looking up into the skinhead's face where he would inevitably meet those open eyes.

The skinhead, however, showed no signs of trying to put him into the bath, but seemed rather to be heading for the area behind the bath where there was a variety of cleaning utensils, bottles and aerosols and general bathroom stuff: he was quite clearly intent on something in this region. Surely though he would have to put me down, Daniel though, to do anything

anything like what oh Christ oh

*(still)*

His leg kicked again, and the skinhead's grip with his left hand loosened momentarily as he shifted his fingers to change his hold, bracing Daniel's lower back against his forearm for a second. I could get him off balance, Daniel thought, and —what? Unless he was able to confidently put him out of action entirely, at least for a few seconds, then resistance was surely only likely to increase the skinhead's determination: he might find it necessary to do something to restrain him, for instance. The thought flapped ignominiously at him: there might be physical pain. No, wait and see, wait and see,

*(that's right, shhhh)*

and if things got any worse then definitely, definitely he'd have to do something about it, oh yes. (Oh yes?)

The skinhead seemed to have come to a stop now, though he was still adjusting the weight in his arms, trying to get a better grip. Even the big, smoothly bulging muscles were starting to feel the strain now, and Daniel was aware that the skinhead was trying to get a little relief.

He jiggled around for a few more seconds, balancing, adjusting, then took a step forward and (puzzlingly) slightly up, definitely up. Daniel tried not to breathe as the skinhead tilted his head down to look, seemingly, at the floor beneath him, beneath them, and then Daniel got it, a flash of understanding:

he's weighing us

as the skinhead muttered something, and made a small sound of the "humph" variety, a quiet, internal sound: yup, that's what I thought.

He's weighing *me*.

Q: how do you weigh someone without their actually having any motive force themselves, without their knowledge or consent or cooperation?

VIRGINS *and*
MARTYRS

A: pick them up, stand on the scales, subtract your own (known) weight from the total, the remainder is the nonconsenting, noncooperating party's weight. QED.

Yes that's how, all right, so how about—

The skinhead stood a moment longer, and another of the uhuh-I-reckoned-as-much grunts escaped him. Then a step backward and a few inches down again.

—how about "why?"

Daniel chose not to meditate too fully on this latter problem, preferring instead to pretend this was indeed one of Wendy's you've-been-framed video clips, that this half-naked, wide-awake-eyed, muscular skinhead had not carried him to the bathroom and calmly ascertained what his present weight was. No, he thought, as the skinhead maneuvered and twisted and transported him back to his room, no that wasn't happening *at all*, not for any reason. The salt-water and wet-iron smell lingered in his consciousness, but he denied that as well. Easy.


"It is widely recognized that many of the earlier saint cults were simply preexisting local gods grafted, more or less successfully, onto later Christian models...."

Medway was in his orderly home office, sitting at his heavy, compact 1950s insurance-company desk with the large flat drawer handles and the pull-out bakelite stationery tray. He was reading from a stack of photocopied typescripts. The typing was uneven and subject to a great many errors, the spacing was erratic, and the margins were too narrow. It was the typing of someone who was writing quickly, urgently, the pressure of thought coming almost too fast for their fingers to catch it.

"So, at least outside the sophisticated urban centers, in the villages and rural heartlands of late medieval Europe, the saints were in many cases no more than the old gods in new bodies, with new names. The stories and the images, in very many cases, were the same."

So far so unremarkable, Medway thought, and remembered how he had been tempted, when he had first held this particular essay, to skip ahead, to see if anything more substantive, more *meaty*, was coming up. It had been by no means clear to him where the writer was heading. He had been on the verge of picking up his red biro and writing something dry and damning in the (inadequate) margin, something along the lines of "relevance?" or "so you keep saying" or (one of his favorites) "Yawn…"

"But what of course was new was precisely the physical presence of these old/new gods, the fact of their comparatively recent incarnation, in comparatively recent flesh. The old gods existed as names, stories, perhaps pictures crudely painted on the walls of barns. But the new gods, the saints, they had more

VIRGINS and
MARTYRS

than stories and pictures, they had bodies. Relics. Body parts. Limbs, pieces of limbs, fingers, hair, samples of blood, specimens of bone and skin, teeth: (Medway sensed in the density of the type an increasing avidity, a warming to the theme here that raised his hackles) from complete cadavers to the merest scrap of human tissue.

"The preservation of these bits and pieces was of course the best that could be obtained at the time, but fell far short of what we now would consider best practice. Often only the most rudimentary techniques were available, essentially evisceration and tanning. The vitals would be scooped out, often being preserved separately in sealed boxes, and the remainder treated with preparations of herbs and resins, which, when kept from the air, could be very effective. Properly carried out, this treatment could keep a corpse from absolute dissolution for a considerable time, and the stories of saints' tombs being opened up decades, even centuries, after their deaths and being found to contain well-preserved remains are perfectly compatible with the technology of the day. The secret was not in the combination of magical herbs and spices, nor in the extraordinary piety of the subject, but in the skill of the coffin-maker in excluding water and air. The skin would, of course, be subject to some deterioration, becoming the color and consistency of leather."

*simon maginn*

Again, Medway felt a faint draft of unease at the excitement in the tone, and the direction the essay was taking. Again he felt that wisp of revulsion, that one of his students should be pursuing this line. When he'd first read the paper he'd found it shocking, repugnant, insane, but now he discovered that he mostly found it frightening.

"And of course, far from any kind of smell of decay, the saint at death and later exuded an odor, sweet and powerful, often described as like the smell of roses.

"Nevertheless, despite this denial of the full human physicality of the saint, it was precisely their bodies, their relics, their physical human remains, that were of powerful interest. In other circumstances, in any ordinary circumstances we would describe the attitude of the worshipper at a saint's shrine as necrophilic. Relics—remains, by which we mean human body parts—were fondled, kissed, stroked, rhapsodized over, adored.

"The term 'necrophilia' is a recent coining, but it very exactly describes the attitude of the pious at a shrine. For us, human remains" (again the shudder, again the nudge of anxiety, as Medway felt the simultaneous urgency and casualness of the writing, the matter-of-fact use of terms like "body parts" and "human remains," coupled with the intensity of the fascination the writer was obviously feeling) "are an object of superstitious dread, and the only proper end

VIRGINS and
MARTYRS

for them is swift disposal, either burial or cremation. To delay this process is a serious matter and done only for compelling legal reasons such as the need for a post-mortem examination. Such remains are objects of horror and, very quickly, of disgust.

"Within half an hour of death hypostasis will begin, the process whereby blood remaining in the vascular system will be pulled by gravity to the lowest parts of the body, causing a purplish discoloration. Unless arterial embalmment is carried out right away, this staining will be permanent, since the blood will clot. Three or four hours after death rigor begins to set in, first in the eyelids, and in the jaw and neck, having a serious effect on the expression of the face. The rest of the muscles follow, and the limbs become immovable. Care must be taken at this point not to break bones or joints. The process begins to reverse about forty-eight hours after death, after which the first signs of putrefaction begin to appear. Greenish tints can be seen on the lower abdomen, on the right, then over the rest of the abdomen, the chest and the thighs. It is at this point that the body begins to smell: up to now there may well have been only the faintest of odors, a little like damp plaster, unless, of course, bowel or bladder contents have been evacuated, or other fluids have been squeezed out by the rigor mortis.

"By the end of the first week," (Medway flinched, guiltily, as he heard a sudden sound: it was just someone coming in downstairs, and he returned to the papers) "the discoloration will have covered most of the body, and a putrid fluid will begin to emerge from blisters than can be as large as three inches across. The skin begins to come loose, and great care must be taken in handling the body at this stage...."

(Handling?)

"otherwise large sections of skin can become detached. Also, because of the great amount of putrid gas being produced and contained in the organs and cavities, as well as in the fatty tissues, the smell by now is very high and cannot be mistaken by anyone who has ever experienced it."

(*Handling?*)

"By the end of the second week the stomach is bloated, also breasts. Fluid appears from nose and mouth, very strong-smelling, mephitic, foul.

"By the third week the whole body is bloated and swollen. The cavities are beginning to rupture, and the organs also are degrading, becoming slimy, turning to liquid. Also limbs can become separated very easily now, so great care is needed to preserve the whole. The head, also, if not supported somehow will fall of its own weight, breaking the neck. This is the worst stage, when the smell is at its highest, the noxious, penetrating, sweet, nauseating stench of..."

Enough, enough. For God's sake. Medway

VIRGINS and
MARTYRS

evened up the stack of photocopied pages, tapping them into alignment, and dropped them back onto his desk.

This wasn't an academic essay. It started out as one, but it quickly became something more like a rhapsodic meditation on human decay. No, more than a meditation, more than a description, this had the quality almost of

(a journal?)

Medway stood up and reached above his head, to the top bookshelf. He brought down a box file and took out from it a key: he unlocked the bottom drawer of the insurance-office desk and dropped the papers into it, locked the drawer again, returned the key to its hiding place. His fingers felt powdery, sticky, from the paper, and he rubbed them unconsciously on the lapel of his jacket.

Sean stood and screamed, and Terence Outhwaite ran to him, grabbed him by the shoulders and punched him, hard, in the face, then again. Fierce joy flooded him. Sean staggered backward but he was still screaming, and Outhwaite reached for him again; Sean squirmed, trying to wrench himself away, and fell awkwardly under Outhwaite's feet; Outhwaite, disgusted, appalled by the unassuageable, unremitting, inhuman screaming lashed out with his left leg, kicking wildly. He was yelling himself, *shut up you bastard!* and *get the fuck off me you fucking animal!* and he aimed for Sean's mouth, the source of that screaming, he took hold of Sean's hair (something not right, something), holding his head steady, launched a great, hefty, lethal kick at his mouth:

*smack!*

Sean's head partly caved in, but the screaming continued nonetheless, and abruptly shifted to a higher register, becoming broken into a series of short shrill yelps, like the cry of a seagull.

He was sitting in his car: he was waiting for someone he knew, and the seagulls were shrieking and flapping over the chimneypots. He had a special distorting mirror, and he caught a glimpse of someone going into a funny house as he twisted it around. Then he remembered—the person he was waiting for was waiting for *him*, he had to go and meet him. He got out of the car, and walked up the short, gently inclined street. Someone was clearing out the boot of his car, and Outhwaite came up to him and said

Oh there you are

but the person turned his head and shook it, and Outhwaite saw that this person had long black hair. But this was wrong and Outhwaite reached out and took hold of it, saying

This isn't your hair

as it came away in his hand.

No this isn't your hair because

VIRGINS *and* MARTYRS

Outhwaite turned over and opened his eyes and the words emerged from his mouth into the silent blackness of his bedroom:

"It matches the color of your eyebrows, your stubble, but it's obviously been dyed. You can tell quite easily from the sheen, and the purplish tint."

He waited for the thought to complete itself.

"It is therefore not your hair. You are therefore lying to me. So, first of all, why are you lying to me? What else of what you've told me is a lie?"

Karen breathed softly beside him, and he thought he could hear Grant coughing.

"And, finally: whose hair is it?"

He lay for a moment longer, waiting to see if there was any more. To clear his mind (and the remorseless, implacable screaming that had been drilling into him as he slept was still ringing somewhere just out of his range of hearing) he reran the contents of the dream.

Sitting in the car (something before that, but he was unwilling to look at it too closely) and waiting for someone. He had had some kind of trick mirror that made people look different from usual, a special distorting mirror, the kind you get at fun fairs. He had had a glimpse of someone, just for a second, right at the back, or rather at the far end of the street, going into a funny house, but because of the special mirror this person looked different from usual. It had only been a very quick impression, but

Outhwaite tried to freeze the moment. For a start, he was wearing different clothes, and what was interesting there was that they were bigger than his usual clothes. Was that it? Or was it perhaps that he had become smaller, or, more specifically, thinner? Yes that was it. *Much* thinner. But there was something else, and when it came Outhwaite felt the blood dropping flat in his veins:

his hair.

He was out of bed and fumbling for his clothes before he'd had a chance to decide to do it.

The person going into the funny house was Daniel Blennerhassett, and not only was he much thinner than when Outhwaite had interviewed him, but he'd had his hair shaved completely off.

As a disguise? Pretty stupid kind of disguise, wasn't it? (And yet it had worked. Or nearly worked anyway.) Or was he up to something, some kind of ritual that required a shaved head? Was that where the hair on top of his wardrobe had come from, from someone else involved in his game?

Wendy.

So who was going to be next?

Outhwaite cursed as he tripped over the bloody pastel valance, and Karen muttered sleepily. She'd taken something, so she wouldn't wake up yet.

He got his clothes on and left the house, quietly, but *quickly*.

## chapter twenty-five

Daniel woke with that familiar chalky taste in his mouth. The room was dark around him, and there was a blurred quality to it also that distracted him. The space didn't seem to be fixed, it was sliding, shifting, like stew in a pot. He tried to sit up.

His head, he noted, was lying at some kind of odd angle on the bed, and seemed to have been stuffed full of dense material. He lifted it up and it fell again, sideways. He smiled. *Pissed as a fart*, he thought. *Arnchoo?* He moistened his lips, they felt like ancient parchment, dried out. He levered himself into an upright position, and everything cascaded softly around him. He was the showman in the snowstorm paperweight, but the snow was black, a blizzard of black particles flitting over and in front of him, carrying him to the floor, where black bin bags lay chaotically. The order imposed by the skinhead had not lasted.

He sprawled, stunned by this sudden contact: this was surely as far as he could go. You couldn't go any lower than the floor, could you? (You could if you were dead, he thought, and smiled at the thought, a soppy, slippery smile.) Yes, well not dead yet, apparently, so the only way, presumably, is up. Onward and upward, up up and away, he thought, as the Haloperidol that the skinhead had adminis-

tered after the weighing session—two small yellow
pills bought months ago from Keith at £1.50 each—
gave him a giddy rush of sensation.

**(up)**

I really ought to try and stand, he thought. That,
after all, is what people do when they get out of
bed. They don't go rolling round the floor like beer
barrels, they stand up and walk around in a dignified, vertebrate way. Very bad form to be lolling
about down there, it's no wonder you never get invited to the best cocktail parties, Dr. Medway said
from an immense height, what would people think
of you? Look out everyone, here comes that funny
rolling chap?

He lurched to his feet, a desperate and barely
controlled maneuver, and banged sideways into the
table; there was a pain in his hip, but someone had
tied the nerve pathways into neat bows and the
message didn't quite get through.

Now he was standing, no longer swimming
about in the black plastic sea, he felt tremendously
tall: he ducked his head to avoid hitting the ceiling. He moved a foot forward and felt his weight
shifting across, as if he were hollow and full of a
heavy, inert liquid. It seemed to work OK. He
brought his other foot into line. He was holding on
to the wall and dragging his feet without lifting
them. It was the best he could do.

He reached the door, yanking at it until it

VIRGINS *and*
  MARTYRS

opened, cra-*ack*: it swung toward him and threw him off balance. He grabbed hold of the side of the wardrobe which swayed on its heels under his hands. The whole room seemed to be swaying and swinging and carrying on, it was just one damn thing after another, he thought crossly, how was he supposed to be able to move about with all this going on? Say one thing for the floor, he commented to himself, it at least stays still. He lost his grip on the wardrobe and fell again, his head landing against a black bag. *Fuck*.

The wardrobe door swung nearby and he took hold of it, pulling himself upright again. For a moment the wardrobe rocked toward him perilously, threatening to fall and encoffin him, but it held. More solid than it looks, he thought, or else I don't weigh enough to pull it down. One or the other. He was up to the door again now, and tottered on the threshold.

The hall outside was completely dark. There was a window at the far end, above the stairwell; it too was dark, black even. No moon he thought, or it hasn't risen yet. Or it's very cloudy. These numerous possibilities tired him out. There was probably a light switch somewhere, but he was buggered if he knew where.

And anyway, that would just show him the way down, whereas of course as had been agreed earlier on, he needed to go up, which was the only way etc.,

*(up yes)*

though quite *why* this was so eluded him temporarily, but there it was anyway.

He raised his head.

Ah yes. There above him, stuck neatly onto the black ceiling, was a patch of deeper black, a rectangle. No not a patch, he corrected himself, but a hatch. The hatch into the attic, open. That was where he must go. Up into the attic. She had to show him something, and he would be safe up there, he could close the hatch after him and no one would be able to get him.

He stumbled back into the bedroom and thrashed about until he found the chair, then pulled it out into the hallway. He flattened his right hand against the wall, and raised a foot onto the chair: immediately the dizziness, the black snowstorm, was around him again, and he fought against it, head down, as if walking into a strong wind.

I'm going to need two hands for this, he thought dimly. Have I still got two hands? There was an insensate lump down his left side where his arm should have been. He defiantly took hold of it and tried to raise it. It still moved, which was, he thought, a blessing. He took it and jammed it against the wall; it seemed to lock into position, like a brace. Splendid, he thought, *bellissimo*!

He put his other hand higher up the wall and then transferred his weight, that sluggish liquid, onto the foot that was on the chair. The chair rocked, but held. He was making it! He lifted his other leg, and his whole body came up. The braced left arm tilted at a less acute angle now and, balancing hilariously with both feet on the drunken chair, he lifted it and propped it higher up the wall. He was now able to reach with his right hand up to the patch, the hatch on the ceiling.

He lifted a foot onto the back of the chair, and stretched up for the rim of the hatch with his right hand. His fingers closed over the wooden rim and he hung on. He tried to raise himself but, even in his emaciated condition, he was far too heavy to lift himself with one arm. It was no use. There was nothing for it, he would just have to get his left arm to move.

He fastened his eyes on it and, screwing up his face with the concentration, *demanded* that it work. All the filthy words he'd ever heard (and never used) came to his mouth as he stubbornly, ferociously, insisted that the bloody useless bloody stupid bastard arm, the damn fucking lump of a piece-of-shit sodding *arsehole* of a fucking—

It twitched.

Only just, but it definitely twitched. Something was coming back into it, sentience or maybe just the habit of obedience, but it was quite undeniably coming back to life. It tingled horribly, and then as he sweated and cursed and willed it into action, it raised

*simon maginn*

itself, trembling, quivering like a newborn calf's leg, and ascended, up into the hatch. Now for the fingers. Bastard sodding cunting bloody *fingers*. *Move*.

Nothing. His right arm was growing heavy and weary from gripping the hatch above his head. If he could make his left hand, his *sodding* left hand, grip the hatchway as well then he would be able to lock his forearm over the rim of the hatch and lever himself up on his elbow, standing on the back of the chair. He was sure of it. Well perhaps *sure* was putting it a bit strongly, but it was a definite possibility anyway. But first those four-letter-wording bloody fingers had to grip the rim of the hatch, those bloody—

the hand jerked, stiffened, jerked again.

Grip, get a grip, get a fucking—

They gripped, like a mechanical claw, locked into position. He had to do the next part fast, he knew, or he would end up crawling about on the floor again. Not just that, of course, but any moment the skinhead could come creeping up the stairs and along the corridor behind him, could pounce on him and—

He whirled round, could see nothing but the blurred, seething darkness. He felt appallingly vulnerable, stretched out in midair with just the flimsy chair for contact with the ground.

The sequence had to be: weight transferred to foot on back of chair, simultaneously with right arm thrust up into attic, and then bent down, other foot onto back of chair, wobble about a bit, head and neck and hopefully shoulders into hatch, straighten out arm along floor of attic, and pull.

He couldn't do it. There was no bloody way he could possibly do all that, he was overwhelmingly certain of it, it was quite simply—

transfer the weight, wobble wobble

—out of the question, out of the ballpark, was that what the Americans said?—

wobble wobble oh Christ

head up, head *up* now, heave now, that's the way, arm stretched out, quick, he could be anywhere, he could be right behind you, quick quick dammit—

*pull.*

He hung, half in and half out and it could have gone either way, but his good right arm was dragging him up and into the hatch, and finally he was there, exhausted, dripping with sweat, shaking uncontrollably. His left arm had gone to sleep again, but it had done its job.

He was safe. He was up.

He lay for a while on the bare boards of the attic floor, panting, waiting for his limbs to stop shaking and his heart to slow down.

Why was he here?

It was a good question. He'd just damn nearly killed himself trying to get in, and now here he was breathing in the scent of old dust and hot-water pipes, and he had no idea why. Safe, yes he was safe up here, but he could hardly stay here and be safe forever, could he? What was it that Wendy wanted to show him?

He stood up and looked around. It was a low attic, only high enough to stand in for a few yards. It was impenetrably black, and warm. He put out his hand and immediately yanked it back again: he'd touched something hot and dusty, just a pipe, but it had felt shocking and alien, like the internal organ of a sea-monster. There were pipes everywhere, he was beginning to be able to dimly trace them as they wove in and out along the walls and between the beams. Somewhere, he knew, there was the cold-water tank, an item that filled him with a disquiet he didn't care to investigate too fully. A squat metal tub that sat up here throughout the endless days and nights, in complete darkness, deep enough to drown in, perpetually filling and emptying itself, gurgling away in its black isolation. You could drown in it and no one would ever know, you would stay up here forever as the cold water gurgled around you, ducts and valves and pipes filling and emptying, sending streams of water down through its secret arms, the pipes that nestled like parasitic worms in the fabric of the building. Secretive, intent, quiet.

He groped forward stooped low, more from fear than necessity, treading cautiously from beam to beam. You'd put your foot through the ceiling below if you weren't careful. And weren't there electrical wires running about between the beams? He didn't want to start getting tangled up in them.

Something brushed his face; he jolted back, held onto a beam for balance. *Shit.* It was just a loop of a wire. Christ. Get a grip now. His eyes, though enfeebled by the absence of contact lenses and the presence of strong chemicals in his bloodstream, were adjusting to the darkness and he was able to discern certain crude forms. The beam he was holding, for instance, a great sturdy thing of solid timber like the mast of a ship. Solid? He found that one of his fingers was exploring a discontinuity in it, more than a discontinuity, more like a hole really.

A neatly made, somewhat irregular hole, big enough for him to get two fingers into.

Oh really? And what could have made that then, do you think? Woodworms he answered, convincing no one. Woodworm. Uhuh. Have to be quite a size then, these woodworm. Wouldn't they? No, this was a bigger animal altogether, some kind of fat white grub that had survived in the timber and burrowed its way out. Presumably not alone. And had gone where exactly, turned into what?

He tried not to think about it. He had, after all, more important things to think about such as why he was up here at all, for instance, and the fact that while he *was* up here he couldn't hear anything that happened in the house below him, couldn't hear the skinhead as he crept about on his unfathomable business.

He had to duck lower still as the pitch of the roof closed in on him. There was a wall coming up, marking the boundary of the house. As he approached it, he felt a change in the atmosphere, something damper, chillier—fresher. He came nearer and felt rather than saw that there was a large ragged hole in the wall, leading through to God knew what expanse of darkness and dust on the other side. He had a sudden sickening flash of the fact that the house, as well as going up and down, was also continuous from side to side, that the boundary walls were just a temporary addition to the structure, that it was only a piece of a much larger whole, a whole that ran the length of the street, and that attics and cellars were more or less continuous. A person could crawl about for hours up here, could quite easily get lost, confused, stumbling blind through these warm, dusty, dark chambers, moving from one to another, squeezing through these ugly raw holes, calling out to no one—

He froze at the thought, and closed his eyes, breathing deeply. Imagine calm pastures. Meadows. Streams. He opened his eyes, moved on. He was far from calm.

He crept forward, hunched against the air that was coming in through that ghastly dark hole, from those other attic rooms, stretching out, leading him on to confusion, disorientation, madness—

And stopped.

For a very long second his heart stopped, just seized up. The air in his mouth and chest and throat came to a standstill, solidified. The pulse in his groin and ear jolted, shuddered, banged to a halt. He had seen a movement.

Only the faintest, dimmest, palest, subtlest thing. Straight ahead. A few steps away, no more. Something that wasn't the darkness, wasn't the wall or the roof or the floor, wasn't a pipe or a beam or a tank. A face.

He was frozen, no air to scream with, no muscles to move the mouth. He became aware that his eyebrows were raised in a comical stage expression of surprise. He looked with all his eyes at what was in front of him.

Slowly, slowly he discerned that there was an edge to it, an outer limit. A frame.

A mirror. For God's sake, it was a mirror, that was all! He breathed again, and came toward it, as his reflection came toward him. A mirror up here in this hellish blackness, reflecting nothing to no one, showing perhaps the hole in the wall, ready to reflect back the image of anyone who came crawling through it.

Funny place to put a mirror. Particularly considering that the attic was otherwise, as far as he

*simon maginn*

could tell, empty of the household detritus that usually accumulated in such places. Perhaps the space was simply too small to be bothered with, or the hatch too narrow to get anything of any size in.

He picked the mirror up. It was a goodish size, in a stout frame. He noticed that there were several more beside it, of various shapes and sizes, a bathroom cabinet with mirrored doors, hand mirrors, a peculiar circular one with a lethal-looking spiked frame.

*(Look)*

He examined the mirror in his hand: there was something funny about it, a flaw across its surface that split his face, made him appear gaunt, bony, deathly. He peered into it, squinting against the darkness, and just for a moment he thought, he *thought* that he did indeed see someone crawling through the hole in the wall, like a fat white maggot, someone standing behind him, someone dressed all in white and holding something in his hand; a ring. A wedding ring?

Daniel dropped the mirror and stumbled for the hatch.

And didn't find it. He had no idea which direction it was in, no idea as to where he was in space, could make out nothing in the darkness, the blackness that was suddenly forcing itself into his mouth and into his eyes, his ears.

He heard something, a movement coming from behind him, unexpectedly. It sounded like something bumping against the floor below, and he turned slowly; he became aware of a new quality in the air, a warmth or a scent.

"Daniel?"

Oh Christ oh shit oh

"Daniel?" said the skinhead, his head popping up in the hatchway, invisibly smiling. "So this is where you've been hiding. I've been looking for you."

"Shit!"

Outhwaite braked, too hard, as the figure stumbled out into his headlights, quickly followed by another. The two half-fell onto his bonnet and rolled away.

Outhwaite got out and saw them struggling on the wet road. One of them was instantly recognizable as a Catholic priest in dog-collar and cassock. The other was also quite unmistakable, knotted matted hair stained yellow in streaks from incessant smoking, patchy growth of beard, tweed jacket decorated with unidentifiable smears of something or other, and a personal odor that could win wrestling matches and pull trucks with its teeth.

There was a broken bottle nearby and the sweet smell of alcohol.

The two men picked themselves up and the derelict shuffled away, saying something like "Kiss me nurse." It could have been "kiss my arse" equally easily. "Thank you sir, God bless you sir," he called out as he retreated, away from the uncharitable clarity of Outhwaite's headlights. "Fuck 'em all."

"Sorry about that," the priest offered. "I hope your car is not damaged."

"Are you hurt?" Outhwaite asked, guiding the priest out of the road.

"No, no, a bruise maybe." There was more than a hint of Irish in the voice. "How about you? You look a little startled."

"Yes," Outhwaite laughed, an unusual event, he realized. Yes, he was slightly shocked.

"Would you like to come in for a moment? A cup of tea or something?"

Outhwaite noticed the church, an ugly thirties brick affair, resolutely unfussy to the point of baldness.

"I'll just get the car out of the road," he said, accepting the invitation. The priest kicked the broken glass into the gutter as Outhwaite parked the car. Double yellow, but what the hell. Who was going to arrest him?

The priest led him down a dark passage thick with overgrown buddleia and in through a side door.

"Powdered milk, I'm afraid. I don't have a fridge here. Father Blunt," he said, all in one breath. "Austin."

He messed about with cups at a small sink with an equally small boiler above it.

VIRGINS and
MARTYRS

Outhwaite stood in the corridor by the door.

"I don't really have anywhere to sit either."

"Unworldly," Outhwaite said, intending a joke, and the priest gave him a keen, inquiring look, not understanding.

"I don't know if you know, but we have a kind of a night shelter downstairs, in the crypt. For the homeless, obviously. I started it up a few years ago and it's really been quite a success, I have to say. Many nights we have to turn people away. You'd never think it, would you, looking around you? But the unmet need is tremendous. Not all like him either, though it's a good man's fault, drinking; no, youngsters, clean-shaven, well-presented, neat and tidy. And people who've just somehow got caught out by it all, didn't see it coming maybe, or didn't take it seriously enough. It's them I'm sorriest for. They've known better and had it snatched away, not usually through their own fault either. Are you a political man, Mr.—?"

"Outhwaite. Detective Inspector."

"Oh I see."

"Terence."

"How do you do, Terence? I may call you that? Then you'll know all about us, being a policeman?"

Indeed he did. Probably half a dozen calls a month from the shelter would come through to the Comms room, though as often as not the problem was minor.

"It's not often I get to talk to a policeman, except for business," said Father Blunt, and gave Outhwaite a cup with a chip on the handle.

"That one just now, he'd found out that we have wine up here. For the Mass obviously. He knows he can't have it, I have to account for it. We have a very 'hands on' kind of bishop now, I don't know if you know? He'd be very interested if I was ordering more wine every week."

Outhwaite sipped the tea, scalding the roof of his mouth. There was a smear of undissolved milk powder along the rim. He was still shaken from the near accident.

"Shall we sit in the church? No shortage of seating in there," Father Blunt said, and moved away past Outhwaite, through a plain white-painted door.

He flicked on lights and the high-ceilinged church came to somber life, the glass glowing with dim intensity.

"Beautiful," Outhwaite said, surprising both himself and Father Blunt. He hadn't set foot in a church for longer than he could remember.

"Beautiful. Yes." The two men stood by the altar-rail looking up the nave of the church. Outhwaite felt obscurely guilty about the cup of tea in his hand, but if the priest was doing it, it must be all right.

"The glass isn't original of course. There was a fire, just after the war. I wasn't here then. Gloucester.

VIRGINS and
MARTYRS

But the glass didn't survive, sadly. I've seen some photographs, not really my style, but very nice. Arts and Crafts movement. School of William Morris. I'm sure you know the kind of thing. Lilies and so on. Very nice I must admit, and in keeping with the rest of the decor, the tiles and the carvings and so on. Very fresh, very innocent. Perhaps just a little deficient in what you might call awe.

"But this stuff now, beautiful, yes. Came from a derelict church in Belgium, near Brussels. A very nice, high kind of style, you'll agree. Some would say Romish."

Outhwaite gazed up at the windows where tall, stiffly posed figures stood holding things, while under their narrow feet white ribbons bore Latin inscriptions in heavy Gothic letters. Dark, enclosed, shrouded. He walked up the nave.

"It had to be cut to fit, naturally, and there was only a fraction of it that we could use. But it was surprisingly inexpensive. They had no purpose for it over there, and they were just going to scrap it. Incredible isn't it, the things that get discarded in this world? Quite incredible."

Outhwaite came to a halt in front of a window.

"Who's this?" he asked; there was something about it that struck him at once as odd, though he couldn't initially say why.

"Her?" Father Blunt came up behind him, following his gaze. "Truth to say, we're not actually

100 percent certain. The iconography, as they say, is idiosyncratic."

The glass showed a young woman holding out a lily. She was crowned. Behind her were angels and around her ankles, dogs. Outhwaite could make out the word "*Oculis*" on the curving ribbon beneath her feet.

"*Oculis*? Patron saint of opticians?" he suggested, and was again treated to Austin Blunt's polite incomprehension.

"Opticians? No no. Well not exactly. We think, or at least some of us do," he said, hinting delicately at his opinion of the opposing camp in this matter, "that she is the Blessed Alena. She has what is called an Approved Cult around Brussels, so it's quite likely. Approved Cult means that we, that is to say We the Church, haven't really decided yet whether she is truly one of the Blessed Company of Saints. There are many such round the fringes, I don't know if you know. These things are so rarely black and white. She is said to have healed a blind man, and so is invoked for intercession in connection with complaints of the eye. Glaucoma, cataracts and the like I suppose. There is one other she could be, but we think the arm is fairly conclusive. Or most of us do, anyway."

"Arm?" Outhwaite said, as if in a dream. He found that he couldn't take his eyes off the pale pink face hanging there in the glass.

VIRGINS *and*
MARTYRS

"Yes, can't you see? She has only one arm."

### chapter twenty-six

Outhwaite rang the bell, three times in quick succession, then efficiently kicked in the pane of fluted glass nearest to the handle. The sharp fragments crunched under his feet. The dreamlike lethargy that had come over him in the church, presumably some kind of shock reaction, was gone now; he was back in gear. (Perhaps in too high a gear?)

There was a draft blowing down the hallway and out through the broken pane in the front door.

"Hallo?"

The house had the feel he remembered from the last time, long-deserted, abandoned, neglected.

"Mr. Blennerhassett?"

No response. He'd have to go up and look. What he was looking *for* exactly was another matter. It all seemed a bit half-cocked suddenly.

He paused halfway up the stairs to the first floor. His nostrils quivered at a scent coming from above. What *was* the point of looking if he didn't know what he was looking for? How would he know if he'd found it or not? The question foxed him and he stood, perplexed.

No, that was stupid. The whole point of a search was that you never knew what you were going to find. If you already knew then you wouldn't have to search would you?

*(so you don't have to search)*

Now where had that come from? He went up a few more risers, again came to a halt. It was the strangest thing, but he was having the utmost difficulty in persuading himself that this was necessary, or even advisable. (Or even legal.) Leaping out of bed, driving like a maniac, almost knocking down the priest and homeless man, smashing through the front door like some seventies television cop with overgrown sideburns. It was just a bit overstated, wasn't it? Hardly his usual way. He didn't have a search warrant, so any evidence he did find probably wouldn't be admissible anyway. The law is the law, after all. He should really go back to base and start organizing a warrant.

*(yes go back)*

And really, at this time of night he'd be better off leaving it till tomorrow.

*(leave it)*

Sleep on it, perhaps. It seemed increasingly unimportant, just a minor chore. He came back down the stairs, and was standing on the doorstep with the glass under his feet before he realized what had happened. Something had got into his head and changed his mind. He felt a shudder of weirdness pass through him, and doggedly retraced his steps, back up to the first floor.

VIRGINS and
MARTYRS

The kitchen, dry as a bone. Not a plate or a cup out of place. Front room, bare, shabby, empty. Up the stairs with that draft tickling the hairs on his ankles. Second floor, bathroom—the bath was wet, he noted—and along to the front room: double bed, stripped and orderly, desk, shelves. Dust. Nothing. These exhibits are not open to the public today, we apologize for any inconvenience caused during the
  (rehang)

Was that the word he'd wanted? It had appeared to come from somewhere else. He wasn't sure he liked the sound of it.

He started up the stairs to the top floor, Daniel's floor. The draft was stronger up here, and a small scrap of paper lying on the step in front of him stirred in the breeze. He picked it up; it was just a few inches square, covered in a tiny spidery handwriting. He tried to make out the words and thought he read "'heresy." It could have been "hearsay" or even "horsey." He dropped it again and mounted the last few steps; Daniel's room was straight in front of him. But between him and it, in the middle of the hall, was a chair. He saw the hatch above it. I'm going to have to squeeze myself up through there, he thought. The room first, though.

He felt a tingle of apprehension as cool air moved round his feet from under the bedroom door.

He pushed it open, cra-*ack*, and was astonished at what he saw. The bed was stripped, pillows and

*simon maginn*

sheets stacked neatly against the wall. The bin bags were all gone. The smell was gone, eased away presumably by the air from the open window. There was no trace of Daniel Blennerhassett, apart from dozens of little scraps of torn paper which fluttered and danced in the air and across the bare floor.

He picked one up: the same miserable scrawl, the letters tiny as if in an effort to economize on ink and paper, closely written.

"—inflationary boom" something something, "In the decades following the Black Death, with labor costs rising as" something "demand" something. He couldn't make sense of it, but it was clearly the essay that Daniel had spoken of, his Master's thesis.

Shredded.

Alarm bit into him like a cold wind; he checked on top of the wardrobe—no hair.

born in 1322, the brother of

He opened drawers, looked under the bed, nothing. Not a trace. He could have gone anywhere. Torn up the essay he'd spent the last two years researching and writing and disappeared in a rage.

later to become the Bishop of Danzig

And taken the skinhead with him?

He saw something lying under the window, bright yellow, the approximate size and shape of a mobile phone. Hair clippers. He picked them up;

VIRGINS and
MARTYRS

he ran his finger over the jagged pair of blades and saw a line of oil and particles form.

He came back out of the room and looked up at the hatch. It would be quite a squeeze, he thought. He was carrying a few pounds too many these days, it didn't seem to make any difference what he ate or whether he exercised or not (though "not" was, in fact, the only of the two options he'd tried recently, he had to admit). Must lose a bit, he said sternly to himself, or I just won't fit in.

Fit in where?

Up there of course. Through that hatch. He would surely need to get his weight down before he could go up there.

*(fit in nicely)*

He shook his head angrily to clear the thought which seemed to be echoing round him. More bloody nonsense! He had to get *on* with it. The chair creaked under him ominously.


Bobbing about.

Quite a breeze out here, Daniel thought, and not as dry as might be wished for either, cozy otherwise though. He was tightly wrapped in something, it felt like a bandage going from neck to toes, a cocoon. It was a weight off his mind, though, to be relieved of the obligation to move limbs, those difficult, lumbering things. He doubted if he would have been able to even without the bandage (little yellow pills again) but being wrapped up nice and tight disposed of the question once and for all. All the hunger was gone too, staved off; he felt hollow and clean and exquisitely pure. Almost perfect.

Warm too. Except for the cool damp air on his cheeks and over his shaven head, he was snug as a bug. In a rug. Things didn't seem to want to stay still though, that was the only drawback. He seemed to be slipping about all over the place.

Also he couldn't really *see* anything. It was dark, so that didn't help obviously, but on top of that he didn't have his contacts in (he'd put them down somewhere, some time ago, he'd really have to go and look for them. They didn't grow on trees did they?) And he felt woozy. Blurred round the edges, porous, not clearly defined.

There was a nice smell, a damp, rubbery smell. It was all a bit wet, but you couldn't have everything could you? There was someone with him, he was bobbing about as well! It was funny really to think of them both, out here in the dark, bobbing about like apples in a tub. Near his head he could see a little patch, he could just make it out, it was a different color from the rest. It had some kind of marking on it, writing. His eyes moved over it, the habit of reading overcoming the dark and the wooziness. He thought he could make out the words "exceed" and "Dublin," but it was really much too dark to read anything. And anyway, who could be

VIRGINS *and*
        MARTYRS

bothered! Just bob about, like a plastic duck in a plastic bath, all wrapped up like a bug in a rug, with a nice cool breeze. Lovely!

Whoosh! He felt spray tickling his face, a fine, exhilarating spray. Salty. He wondered if it was therapeutic. He could feel each tiny droplet separately; it was as if someone was drawing a picture on his face made out of water, or writing a message. Watch out! maybe. It probably all meant something. He really couldn't say just at the moment.

He seemed to be shifting round in a circle, as well as the up and down business. He found himself looking up at something, bright pink, big glowing letters in the sky, a sign! It was saying something, he couldn't quite make it out, then he shifted round again and it was gone, leaving a confused blur on his retina. Pink reflections fell about on the water around him.

Whoosh! Wheee! Bobbing about, like ping-pong balls in a fountain!

Outhwaite squeezed himself bit by bit through the hatch, heaving himself up with both hands. It was like a difficult, ungainly birth, but finally he was free and clear.

He stood up and banged his head on the ceiling. Shit. He fumbled in his pocket for matches and came up with a clear plastic lighter.

The attic scrambled away from him as he moved

the flame around. Even the bloody attic was clean and tidy, he thought, it just wasn't human. Light glimmered back from the header tank, and then he saw a reflection from the floor. He reached down for it: it was a mirror, broken jaggedly across the middle. There were pieces on the floor, long lethal slivers of silvered glass. Not so neat and tidy after all, perhaps.

He put it down again and noticed something that was nestling along the edge of one of the floor beams, a small brown object that he recognized instantly. Karen had them in the bathroom and in her bedroom cabinet. A plastic pill bottle. He picked it up and held the lighter to it.

Haloperidol. Ugly sod he was but there you go. He used to buy them off me for a pound each. Ooops!

If they were anything like the ones Karen had then they were extremely effective, something between half a bottle of Courvoisier and a good swift kick in the head.

He'd tried one once, against Karen's protests. He wanted to know what she was taking. What if there's a fire, he'd said, how will I know if you're asphyxiated by smoke or just out of it with these? Don't want some big ugly fireman giving you the kiss of life just 'cause you've had a few too many happy pills. Make a change, she'd said, depends on what you mean by "ugly." Give me one, he'd said, and wrestled the bottle out of her hand. Half-joking, half-desperate, as was so much of their life together. I just need to get a proper night's sleep, she'd said, and they're not happy pills. If I've got to grapple with the incredible counting man first thing in the morning I want to make sure I've had proper sleep.

He took just one (she generally had two) and an hour later was having difficulty focusing on *Newsnight*. His mouth had gone dry and when he went to the kitchen for a glass of water he found that he misjudged the doorway and then poured water down his sleeve. And laughed aloud.

"Nice aren't they," she'd said, and he smiled and couldn't disagree. Your own private amusement arcade.

(!)

He jerked up again, banged his head again, said shit again. What had that been? He rubbed his head, water squeezing into his eyes. What had he been thinking about? Those pills. He'd been thinking that two , assuming they were no milder than Karen's, would be as effective as a stun gun, or banging your head good and proper on a beam, and that one alone would put you into a world of your own, insulate you, lag you like a pipe, and somehow the thought had got twisted round to something about an amusement arcade, the kind of place where you'd maybe find—one-armed bandits?

Yes, come to think of it; yes. The draft gathered itself round his feet, and a big cold picture came to him, of a great amusement arcade, huge, but completely deserted, abandoned, neglected, like the house.

Like this house?

Yes, but this was somewhere else, this was another house, the great house.

Something that Daniel had told him in that eerie interview came to him now with the force of clairvoyance: he'd had a hallucination or a dream or *something* about this house, that it was a house over water. He'd opened a hatch, like the hatch Outhwaite had just squeezed his well-cushioned bottom through—and found water.

The house over the water was an amusement arcade, a still, echoing, lonely place, where no one ever went. Dark. And it was an island too. You had to go in a boat. Go up through a hatch. Walk along the bare boards. You could hear dark things all round you, and you could hear seagulls too, screaming and crying, like the ones on the rooftops, and starlings, flocks of them, flying over the domes and turrets and ornamental ironwork, all rising and falling together in clouds, in waves. The whole place was spattered with bird droppings, crackling under your feet. He could smell it. The whole house stank of it. He suddenly wanted to get out. He'd have to leave the same way he came

VIRGINS *and*
MARTYRS

in because there sure as bedamned wasn't any other way. Through the hatch.

He flashed the lighter around and the beams and walls flickered and shifted. He found himself treading glass underfoot, it crackled under his feet, he could hear something pounding underneath him, it sounded for all the world like waves. The smell was getting worse. Was it really bird droppings? It had begun to smell just a bit nastier than that, it was developing a fishy, gassy quality. He was liking it less and less. Oh dear me yes! Maybe it was time we just got our nicely lagged arse the fuck out of here. What do you say?

*(can't)*

He stumbled forward, bang, *shit*. He wriggled through the hatch, onto the inadequate chair, which threatened to topple him at any moment, and out, down the stairs, the smell seeming to pursue him and the draft catching at his legs and feet as if trying to trip him up.

He got to his car and sat for a moment, panting. That smell… He'd never encountered anything like it. It had been worse than the most deteriorated human remains he'd ever been exposed to (the coroner had estimated between fourteen and twenty-one days) it had been like being *inside* the body, it had been as if the house itself was rotting and he was trapped inside as the tissues broke down, liquefied, became putrid— He leaned out of the open door of his car and retched. The smell seemed to be lingering on his clothes. What he really wanted to do was go home and get under the shower.

He sat and collected himself. No good getting rattled. No good to anyone if you're rattled. When he was recovered he radioed for someone to come out to make the house safe, and for a car to keep watch.

He was traveling back home along the seafront when it hit him. He was waiting at a pedestrian crossing, gazing rather blankly out to sea. The light changed and he moved forward; a familiar shape loomed up, an outline that he knew very exactly, albeit unconsciously. His eye traveled over the extravagant lines, the enormous bulk massed against the black sky.

Scandalous, he was thinking vaguely, that it should just be left like that, to corrode, to collapse gently into the sea. There had been a lot of talk over the years about renovation and even rebuilding, but the result had been simply progressive deterioration and the creeping demolition as more and more of it became unsafe. He flicked his windscreen wipers on as a splash of rain came in from the Channel.

First they'd severed it at the land end, so that there was no way onto it apart from climbing up the ironwork. They'd optimistically rebuilt the entrance platform on the prom, rebuilt it completely

VIRGINS and
MARTYRS

with new supports and a smart new deck. It had been this thoroughness, in part, that had been the trouble: one of the major sponsors of the renovation package pulled out because they'd said this was not a renovation at all, but a replacement. Work had stopped. More decay at the far end, submerged dangers to boats and swimmers. Bits coming loose and having to be dragged away, made safe. Then a really rotten piece of luck: what had become known as the Great Gale, a hurricane that had devastated the area, and made perilous another huge chunk of the structure. Further demolitions. The only way on, now, except at exceptionally low tides, was to get yourself wet and swim out to it, then risk life and limb climbing up the treacherous infrastructure. The only progress in recent years had been the erecting of an immense illuminated sign, in pink for no immediately apparent reason, that spelled out the name of this enormous wreck.

(it was an island)

His gaze meandered over the domes and turrets, the ornamental ironwork. It hadn't been so long ago that it had been a fully functioning entity, with a grand ballroom and

(amusements)

yes, but you'd never think it now, its windows shattered and its woodwork disintegrating. It was just a hulk, a crumbling, grandiose slum,

(seagulls and starlings)

empty, as empty as that ghastly house he'd just come away from, except of course that this one was—

He wrenched the wheel round, and the car lurched up onto the pavement, flinging him against the steering column.

This one was over water.

The West Pier.

### chapter twenty-seven

The skinhead tied up under the far end of the structure, navigating the dinghy with some difficulty through the treacherous reefs of jagged iron that came poking up from the sea, where the swell was starting to get up. There was a lot of iron around, tremendous H-section beams and crosspieces and girders, the supports for the outer skirts of the original pier deck, now simply lethal, rusting, serrated fingers jutting up in irregular lines, like a ragged army of spear-carriers.

He found his spot and secured the boat, moving very carefully. The sea had a silky, almost oily character to it, the swell moving gigantically under the surface, flexing its immense muscles. He really didn't fancy the idea of splashing about in *that*.

He checked briefly on his passenger: the pulse in the neck was fairly steady, though he thought the chest felt thready. Maybe three Haloperidols had been too many, particularly since the body weight was now so greatly reduced. Have to keep a weather eye on him.

He stepped out onto a diagonal crosspiece, and began his slow, cautious ascent. There was a ladder at the front and one on the eastern side, not particularly trustworthy, but certainly a good deal less precarious than swinging hand over hand through the grim corroded framework. But he couldn't risk using either one. The only safe way up was at the back, out of sight, the only face of the pier that no one ever saw.

Handholds were one thing, but getting any kind of purchase with your feet, that was quite another. He was wearing canvas boots, so he could to some degree arch his feet and grip with his toes. But the iron was unpleasant climbing, it was wet of course but it had also grown a thick covering of algae and other of the less ambitious plant forms that can live on nothing much except salt water and bird shit. *Bird shit.* Great streaks and lumps of it, build-ups in crevices, snowdrifts against some of the intersections. Gooey, slimy, totally bloody vile in fact. You ended up stinking like some kind of mountain goat. And that was before you even got up there!

He rested halfway. The deck was directly above him, he cold feel it hanging, suspended over his head on its cradle of pitted iron. It was something like one of the great Gothic cathedrals, Chartres or Ely, up in the choir loft or the organist's lonely eyrie. You could get right up into the trembling air and see the pattern of the roof vaults, see how they intersected with the pillars, with the buttresses, the walls. Visual patterns of stresses, rationalized into sweeping arcs of stone and wood, the gargantuan weights and spans held in the most breathtaking balance, so exquisite you had to hold your breath for fear of disturbing the giddy air.

This was just such a structure, where you could see the patterns, *feel* the weight as it passed through the encrusted struts and columns, until the whole thing sank down into the sea. This was a kind of cathedral, for a very secular kind of worship, dedicated to the saints of seaside entertainment and health and bracing air. Designed and built purely to allow gentlemen in blazers and ladies in hats to stroll, taking their serious enjoyment. He was struck, astonished by the idea. To desire a street made of iron and wood to project right out into the sea merely for the purpose of standing on it! And as if that weren't enough, said the planners and engineers, we'll build on top, we'll have a *ballroom*, with opera boxes and stalls and a high, minareted roof in the Exotic style. Grand staircases and balconies, and windows from which you could practically see the perfidious French! The same kind of confidence that had sent up those untried, untested cathedrals, those vast stone enclosures, incredible confidence, never again to be found.

## VIRGINS and MARTYRS

Faith, you might call it, he thought, sitting astride a girder in the dizzy rigging of the pier, cleaning his hands on a rag he'd brought in his bomber-jacket pocket. Maybe that was why he haunted this place, he thought: because it was full of the faith that he himself had been found to be so catastrophically lacking.

How many times had they said that, those simple, innocent men! You must have faith. Have faith, my son. We are not expected to understand, or to question beyond a certain point: all He asks, in His great mercy, is that we love Him and have faith. It's so easy!

Easy, like making a parachute jump. You just get into position, close your eyes, wait for the slap on the shoulder, and jump. If you thought about it you could never do it.

He'd shaved off his hair. That hadn't been easy, it was a denial of something he felt very deeply. But he'd done it. He'd read the texts, he'd studied the sources, Aquinas, Augustine, Paul. At twenty he'd been able to debate the intricacies of Gnosticism and the finest nuances of heresy. He knew an immense amount. Early on in his reading he'd become interested in the saints, and it hadn't taken him very long to find in himself the reason why: because they were the source of miracles.

He was still living at home then, in Exeter. There was an air of unease, of suspicion brewing.

His parents were palpably unhappy that their only son should be so (their word) bookish. Neither of them had had a good experience of formal education, they mistrusted it, they thought it did you no kind of good if you took it too far. As he was doing. His mother (secretly, guiltily) has consulted their doctor, who had suggested counseling, something they'd never heard of. He'd gone along with it, because it upset him to see them tightlipped with disapproval and worry. He'd gone because he wanted to please them, to persuade them that he was fine, he was *happy*, he didn't want to get drunk and go out with girls and smoke. He knew also, without knowing quite how he knew, that they were worried he might be—you know. Queer. He had no close friends, and at twenty was still a virgin. His father had been a rocker, had had a quiff and mechanic boots with chains on and (again, how he knew this he wasn't sure) a lot of girls before he'd settled down.

They just couldn't make any sense of him. He could see the looks they exchanged when he went upstairs after tea; in for the evening again.

His mother was a practical and shrewd woman: she took him into town one Saturday and spent the day with him while he tried on what seemed like hundreds of pairs of jeans to get the right fit. She looked, unabashed, at his crotch and arse and thighs: she certainly had more sense of the importance of the look of things than he did. By the end of the day they had spent a considerable amount of the holiday fund and they had six carrier bags, which between them contained what he thought of, secretly, as a Teenager's Costume. Detailed, authentic, correct. He dutifully wore it, but his mind was elsewhere.

Then he had his head shaved. Right down to the skull, as short as it would go, number zero. It had been a decision that had been building up in him over some months. It was a renunciation, a mark, a discipline.

It was then that his mother had crept away to the doctor.

The counselor recommended by the doctor was a woman not unlike his mother. She differed, however, in that she didn't have that look of thwarted hope and frustrated optimism in her eyes. The counselor had very clear eyes, very direct, she saw him very clearly, he felt. He told her some of the things he was thinking, that it was important to choose a path that would lead you to the truth, that it was necessary to regulate the appetite, that discipline was a habit that you had to learn.

She'd looked at him, her eyes narrowing, becoming, if anything, clearer.

"Truth," she'd said. "Discipline."

He'd elaborated, she'd listened. It was an odd feeling after all this time, to be saying these things out loud, and to have someone listen to them, to you. He'd stopped in midflow, and she'd said to him,

"How do you feel? I mean right now?"

He'd thought about it for a few minutes, and then said:

"Good. I feel good."

He'd continued with his exposition. At the end of the session she'd thanked him for coming and told him that what he'd had to say had been very interesting and perhaps he would like to come back the same time next week and discuss it some more. They would have six discussions and then see how it went from there.

"One other thing, before you go." She'd given him her directest, most unflinching look. "Have you talked to anyone else about any of this?" He'd said no, and she'd said:

"I think you might be well-advised to talk to a priest."

In retrospect, that comment had changed the whole course of his life, he thought, reaching into another pocket for a different rag, this one impregnated with Old Spice aftershave.

It was odd, perhaps the oddest feature of his life to that point, he reflected, that he'd had no exposure to formal religion. Organized religion. He knew no churches, no masses, no sacraments. He had an impressive body of knowledge and absolutely

VIRGINS and
MARTYRS

no experience. Like someone who's memorized a sex manual and never been kissed.

His first priest. You never forget your first priest, he thought, wrapping the rag round his face to cover his mouth and nose. The smell was outrageously strong, but he'd stop noticing it soon, and he'd certainly be needing it. He dug into another pocket and pulled out a little object with an elasticated band, like a pair of swimming goggles.

A decent man, Father Balcome, and of course he'd had the thing that the cool, sophisticated twenty-year-old who knew Pascal and Teilhard de Chardin and Thomas à Kempis had proved to be deficient in.

He smiled at the thought of how he must have seemed to this middle-aged man, in his Teenager's Costume and number zero hair. The priest had agreed to talk to him, and at the end of the meeting had insisted that he take instruction, be baptized, join the Holy and Apostolic Church. It was a scandal, really no less than that, that he should be alone out there in the sinful world, without the Rock of the Church to support him.

The instruction classes were held, appropriately, in a school classroom, one of those open plan breeze-block and carpet-tile places, where everything was some shade of biscuit or mushroom or beige. Three others in the group: the instructor was another priest, a young man. He tried very hard to make it

*simon maginn*

relevant. The skinhead had listened courteously, learned, and six weeks later had had his head sprinkled with water from the font of St. Stephen's in Exeter.

He'd felt nothing. Was that all there was to it then? He'd said his first confession, almost embarrassed at the triviality of his offenses, and been given his first penance, the Joyful Mysteries. Easily enough done. He'd tasted the Body of Christ and it had tasted like damp paper. He'd felt nothing. He was now reading the lives of the saints, and discovering a richer, darker, more exalted tradition: a new kind of sacrament, a penance more tangible than the mouthing of prayers. He discovered the ingenuity of mortification, the hair shirts, the whips and scourges, the hours spent kneeling with arms outstretched, the prolonged exposure to extreme cold. The vows, of silence, of abstinence, of denial. He'd spoken to no one about it.

How did you go about becoming a priest? he'd asked Father Balcome. The priest had hesitated and told him of a retreat that was coming up in a few weeks' time.

Go on the retreat, he'd said, and if you still want to talk about taking training when you come back, then we'll talk about it.

His parents had no idea what a retreat was. To his father, he was sure, it was something dishonorable that badly led foreign troops did. Or nancy boys

VIRGINS and
MARTYRS

when someone threatened them. The skinhead had explained as well as he could, had told them about St. Ignatius Loyola and the Spiritual Exercises. They thought he was talking daft, but they came up with the money. He was still not working, signing on. Drifting. They thought this retreat thing might snap him out of it, give him a kick, get him moving. He couldn't carry on like this forever.

He pulled on the gadget with the elasticated headband. A torch, like miners wore, so they'd have both hands free. He stretched out, making ready to continue climbing. Below him—quite some way below, he noted with a lurch—was the yellow dinghy with Daniel, fast asleep and rolled up in his sheet, being gently rocked by the swell of the tide. He looked very peaceful, and the skinhead envied him. He wished he could just sleep, innocently, like a baby, not have to worry all the time.

Ah well, no peace for the wicked!

He grabbed hold of a piece of iron, wet, slimy with rank green growth, and continued his ascent.

*(wake up)*

Daniel stirred, smacking his lips. His eyes flickered open, then shut again. Everything was going up and down. He didn't feel terribly well.

*(wake up)*

He rolled over onto his back, and his eyes opened again. Verticals and horizontals and diago-

*simon maginn*

nals veered up around him in bewildering profusion. He followed one of the verticals down; it came to rest on the surface of the sea near where he was lying. It seemed to be encrusted with something, shiny black shells. Mussels. If I could move my arm, he thought, maybe I could eat them. Like a shipwrecked sailor on a desert island. Like what's-his-name in that book. Shipwrecked on a funny yellow rubber island, and all the trees made of rusty iron....

*(wake up)*

His eyes jerked open. The iron columns were shaking, rattling. The metal ties between them bounced about, everything was vibrating. Something was going on. The wind blew suddenly hard on his face and the dinghy nodded up and down more violently. There was a hissing coming from somewhere nearby: a few yards away the surface of the sea had become alive with tiny dancing, hissing, spitting snakes. Rain. It wasn't falling on him, though, so he must be protected somehow.

*(nearly too late)*

There must, he thought slowly, be some reason why I'm here. There must be something that I'm supposed to do. These were big questions, important issues. He would really have to start thinking about them. Soon. When he could get his mind working properly again. Maybe he should have a snooze, clear his head. He could feel his eyes drooping. The sound of the rain was so soothing, a gentle, mournful, musical sound. It would be lovely just to lie still and nod off, listening to the sea and the rain. Lovely. Lovely. His heart banged and skidded.

(*wake up*)

Lovely.

The skinhead got to the crawlway below the deck and clambered onto it. It ran the whole length of the pier on both sides and extended underneath the ballroom. It had been put in so maintenance and repair work to the deck could be carried out from below without the need for scaffolding or elaborate safety harnesses. A stout iron grille bolted directly into the girders. There were service hatches at regular intervals.

You couldn't stand, but you could walk stooped: the skinhead liked the feeling of being able to move unobserved all round the pier without risking coming out on deck. Even on the blackest nights you never knew who was watching from the shore, anglers with their nightlights, homosexuals who used the area around the stump of the pier for cruising. He'd been able to observe quite a lot of their activities, had got to know one or two of the faces.

And there were others also, who emerged after everyone else had gone home: dark figures who came and stood in shadows in the silent hours before dawn, patrolled up and down, the smoke from their cigarettes hanging in the air. Three, four, five o'clock in the morning. He had no idea who they were, they were just ghosts, shadows, solidified darkness. He wondered if they too, in their own ways, were waiting for miracles. He liked to watch them, crouched in the iron cage below the deck; he followed their movements and observed their habits.

One in particular interested him, a gangling figure who wore a knitted cap. He would often come at about 4:30 or so and stand below the newly built entrance deck that jutted out from the promenade. He moved very little, and didn't smoke: he did, however, occasionally bark. At first the skinhead had assumed that he had a dog with him, but it had become clear over time that he didn't. He would also jump, quite unpredictably, startlingly, a few feet to his left or right. The skinhead in his own interminable watches had come to enjoy the company of this person, or at least the sound of him, and had spent some time trying to discover if there was a pattern to his behavior, something perhaps to do with the moon or tides. The skinhead, of necessity, was acutely sensitive to these things.

It was far too early yet for any of this tribe to be out. It was just after ten o'clock, which was in many ways an optimum time. The streets were generally quite empty, those who were out for the night had mostly got to where they were going, and it would be an hour and a half before the first wave of drunken activity as the pubs let out. There would be another wave of even drunker carrying-on at around 2:30 when the fights started breaking out outside clubs and in the late-night takeaways up Preston Street and West Street.

But at ten, the only people likely to be around were the homeless, tucked down in their sleeping bags in the doorways. And they never seemed to come as far as the seafront, they preferred the shopping streets, where there was at least the prospect of human interaction, of company.

Also, of course, the police changed shifts at ten, and there was a little window of time, from about 9:50 to 10:15, when you could almost guarantee that they wouldn't be around. If you left it till after the surge of singing and shouting and taxis as people came out of the clubs at 2:30, then you were talking about 3:30 or 4, and any activity at that time would get you noticed. The only thing anyone was supposed to be doing at four in the morning was going home, and it only took one curious policeman to get interested and you were in trouble. Like that Outhwaite, for instance, though he didn't seem up to much.

The higher the tide the better: it reduced the numbers who were likely to be hanging around on the seafront. And of course if you could get a cloudy night and no moon, better still.

He did a quick circuit round the crawlway, more of a ritual observance than a real security check.

Everything was in order as far as he could tell.

He made his way back to the southern tip of the pier, and dropped the rope down. It would be quite a job getting Daniel up here, even light as he was now.

It had been strange about Daniel. It had been as if he were trying to get himself noticed.

With Wendy it had happened almost immediately. He wasn't sure how he'd known: something about her, about her face and the way she moved, an unworldly quality, had attracted him at once. Her near silence, almost muteness, had been fascinating to him. He had seen instantly that some process was under way, and when he had discovered what the process was he had been excited. Very excited. He recalled the occasion: she had just come in and they were sitting together in the kitchen, this was in the first week or so of her short tenancy. He'd been watching her eat something, some kind of a little pie. She sat, not quite straight onto the table, not facing him nor facing away from him, but at a most curious angle. She kept her coat on—indeed he never saw her without it—and what she did was to cut the pie up, smaller and smaller, halving and halving and halving, until it was more mashed than anything. She had appeared completely oblivious to him, intent on this ceremony. She never at any time acknowledged that he was there—often she made him feel invisible. He could

VIRGINS and
MARTYRS

sit in the same room with her for hours and she would be mute and immobile, or engaged in one of her chores, like tearing paper or ironing her innumerable identical black dresses. She had a wardrobe full of them, packed tightly together.

He'd watched her mashing up the pie and understood completely. She was fasting, she was making herself perfect. She was seeking the truth, in her own way. They were alike, twins. He hid the mirrors.

"Looks like you've lost a few pounds there, Wendy, looks good on you," he'd said to her a few days later, and had known that it was as good as a knife between the shoulder blades or a bullet in the mouth. But she wanted it, he was merely assisting a process that she had already decided on. She had barely wavered, she'd had the most astonishing directness of purpose and complete discipline. They had never discussed anything, but they had an almost telepathic understanding, and he knew what to do. She had grown weak, confused. She whispered that she was pregnant. He told her that if she was then it would be a miracle. She nodded, yes, and sat, rocking on her bed. It was true. A miracle. He had said nothing.

The days passed, it was bitter February and she was cold all the time, even in her room with the heating on, in her coat. He brought her up a one-bar electric fire and she sat over it, until her legs became blotchy with the heat. When she became distressed he gave her the little yellow pills, the Haloperidol. He brought her cups of hot water, but she usually left them where he put them down.

Toward the end he brought down a mirror and showed her to herself. See, he said, you're nearly perfect. He wasn't sure that she'd been able to see properly, but she'd struggled as he held her and he'd had to give her more Haloperidol. Probably too much as things turned out. He'd read Thomas à Kempis to her, the section of *The Imitation of Christ* where he says: "Vanity it is to wish to live long, and to be careful to live well," and from the lives of the saints.

He skimmed down the rope and almost misjudged his landing. Nearly got his feet wet. He unwrapped the sheet and passed a loop of rope round under Daniel's arms, then tied the sheet back, more tightly, in a band across his chest so that his arms were pinned in place. He knotted the rope, then climbed back up to the top, hand over hand.

The rope passed over a beam before it fell, and he was able to use it like a pulley. But it was hard going. He was terrified that something would slip and he'd lose him. If he should wake up and start to struggle then they'd be in serious trouble. He chanted mechanically to himself, the old Latin prayers, and after what seemed like an eternity of straining and pulling, until his arms and back and shoulders were burning, until he thought he would simply have to let go, he saw Daniel reach the level of the crawlway. He fastened the rope and pulled him on, then untied him and went on deck, heaving him through the hatch. He sat for a while recovering his breath, and the words fell from his mouth like broken teeth.

*Ostende nobis Domine.*

Show us, O Lord.

They were just words, he knew. He had no faith in magic words, not anymore. Once maybe. But he'd been disappointed so often and so completely that whatever small confidence he'd had in the efficacy of prayer had just dried up and disappeared. He'd sought and found more direct means of expression, and his reward had been those tantalizing glimpses, those flashes of revelation, the arm stretched out to show him what was held in the hand, the cowled figures in the scarlet and gold barge. There had been, as always, a price for these visitations, headaches of such blinding severity that he had been forced to bang his head against the wall until he was dazed and bleeding.

The habit of mumbling prayers, though, was a hard one to break, like the reciting of the Nicene Creed long after he'd stopped waiting for the faith it described to come to him.

*Credo in unum Deum, Patrem omnipotentem.* I believe in one God, the Father almighty.

*simon maginn*

He believed nothing. If he had ever taken vows, he would have adopted the devotional name of Thomas. Brother Thomas. He smiled at the idea of it.

He checked Daniel's pulse again, listened to his chest. Very weak, very thready. Just like Wendy had been at the end. It could be any time now. He would simply have to wait and watch.

He'd thought nothing of Daniel when he'd turned up. He'd had no real intention of letting the room out again after Wendy, but he'd neglected to take down the cards from the university common rooms, and then once they'd met there seemed to be no reason not to let him have the room. He'd come up with the deposit and the month's rent in advance straight-away, which was more than Wendy had done. He was still waiting for her Housing Benefit claim to come through. It was a disgrace, the time they took. But Daniel had had cash, or at least a check that had proved, surprisingly, to be good.

He was spending most of his time on the pier at that stage, and had really only got interested in Daniel after the police visit. After that he'd kept half an eye on him, and had spent a good few hours up in the attic. Not spying, but taking an active interest. And then there had been that strange occasion when Daniel had been involved in some kind of accident. He'd turned up on the doorstep looking more dead than alive. It had been a revelation. It was as if he'd been determined to come to the skinhead's attention one way or another. Trying to get himself noticed. As if he knew.

The oddest thing, though, the thing that had finally commanded his interest, was that Daniel was clearly fasting as well. Quite some coincidence, that, he'd thought. Very interesting.

He had bathed him, and it had almost been like bathing Wendy. Daniel had further to go, naturally, but he'd been astonished at the similarities. Daniel was also highly disciplined in his own way, though his paper sounded, frankly, like a lot of nonsense. But he was working away at it with a kind of dogged thoroughness that the skinhead could only find admirable, if somewhat dull.

He sometimes regretted not finishing his own doctorate. It had been quite an amusing project, initially at least. He'd lost the thread of it somewhere, though, and it had begun to seem rather pointless. The academic approach, he'd come to feel, led nowhere. Something more direct was needed. All that grubbing around in libraries, digging up those tedious old debates and contributing your own little mound to the pile. It was dead, but in the wrong kind of way. For a while he'd withdrawn completely. He'd stopped reading. He'd become a hermit. He'd discovered the pier and it had slowly become a second home.

There was a room here he'd come to think of as his office. It was a little cubbyhole off one of the large halls, presumably a store room. Roughly where the chapterhouse would be if you imagined the pier as a cathedral. There was a table in there and some empty boxes to sit on. He'd brought in a paraffin lamp and some odds and ends, pictures, tried to cheer it up a bit. He had a radio and some books. He had a small metal toy, one of those model roundabouts made of steel rods, matchstick horses and riders with ball-bearing heads; the horses and riders spun round, mounted on a pivot. One twist and they carried on, round and round, for minutes. Very little friction was generated because of the design of the pivot. The light danced off this glittering object, casting intricate shadows round the room.

He left Daniel where he was lying—he seemed OK for now—and went down into the accessway, emerging onto the deck near his office. He lit the lamp and put the radio on, then took the lamp away with him to light the candles and the incense burner in the ballroom. The ambulatory.

He was back in his office a few minutes later.

"Do it the right way, do it the right way—"

He hummed along. He liked a bit of noise around him. It was like company. The rain was drumming on the roof and dripping through in a couple of places. He looked at the pictures stuck up on the walls, mostly pictures taken from magazines and newspapers of people's faces. He preferred it

VIRGINS *and*
MARTYRS

when they were looking straight to camera, looking back at you. There was, he felt, something fascinating about the human face, any face, though it was so much clearer when the face was a thin one. Children and old people, for some reason, were particularly good, they had an integrity to them that seemed to disappear in midlife. He had some of his own photographs as well, just Polaroids, and the lighting wasn't right, but they weren't too bad. Sometimes he missed his videos, though.

He sat on the boxes. He was tired from the exercise and the worry of the past hours. He'd just get Daniel settled and maybe call it a day. He very much doubted that anyone would miss Daniel for a while, so there was no particular hurry. It had been weeks before anyone had come snooping round after Wendy, and then it had only been that funny alcoholic old woman: she hadn't been difficult to shake off. No sign of the boyfriend with the low hairline. No, the melancholy truth was that Daniel wouldn't be missed for months. He wasn't due to deliver his paper until early October, and the skinhead could always do that for him. Do a damn sight better job than he'd been making of it himself, if the truth be known.

The horses had run themselves to a standstill and he suddenly felt much the same. He thought he could hear something banging down at the north end. He debated whether to go and see and decided, reluctantly, that he'd better. He'd crawl round and take a look, though it was probably just the wind, which seemed to be freshening. Check on Daniel first, then go round. Only take a minute.

Daniel woke up and it was as if someone was forcing his eyelids open. Gummy, he thought. I feel gummy, gluey, caulked up like a barrel of something sticky. He lifted his head. It was horrible, like trying to lift an armchair out of deep water. There was something tied round him and he picked at it, trying to get free. Nearly too late, he was thinking, I think it's nearly too late.

Outhwaite was hanging off a ladder that seemed intent on swinging him around in the wind. He was wondering if it had any other tricks in its repertoire, like perhaps throwing him off into the damn sea. It wouldn't entirely surprise him. He was soaked through and had lost his shoes. The short swim to the pier had almost been enough to finish him off and now here was this ladder trying to kill him.

He was making quite a bit of noise as the thing bounced around, and he was silently praying that this should not matter too much, though he was certain it did. It was surely enough to wake the dead. If I could just get my foot back on, he was praying, then I'd be able to stabilize it and I wouldn't need to keep on kicking. Please. Just let me get my foot back on the damn slimy thing. Please let me not fall off. And please let me be not—

*(too late.)*

Daniel struggled to his feet, strange, rubbery things that flapped about in an absurd manner underneath him. He didn't even try to work out where he was or what it was he was meant to be doing. Someone had filled his head with glue and it was taking all his powers just to stay upright and get those ridiculous rubber feet shuffling forward.

He could hear banging coming from somewhere far away. He could also hear a radio somewhere a bit nearer, and he tried to locate the sound. It was inside the building which was rearing up straight ahead of him; it looked for all the world like a theater, at least as far as he could make it out. He kept going forward, the fear of being too late stronger than the strange, uncomprehending fear of this impossible place, this theater, this music—

"—you got to do it right, do it right, do it right—"

And the other thing, the thing that was intruding more and more on him as he progressed, the *smell.*

He came to a door and pushed it open, and the smell was suddenly overpowering, rank, mephitic.

"Daniel."

He stopped, swayed, fought to stay vertical.

*simon maginn*

"Where are you going?"

He peered over to where the voice came from: it seemed to be at the other side of this funny place, with this terrible smell, he'd never smelled anything like it, it was like all the rottenness of the whole rotten world rolled up and sprayed into the air.

The skinhead was carrying his hurricane lamp, and still had the rag tied round his mouth and nose.

Daniel could see a glimmer of light at the far end, coming from a screened-off compartment on the raised platform that must at one time have been used as a stage. It was an unsteady, flickering light. Candles.

"Do you want to see?"

He was coming closer. He seemed to have a light sticking out from the middle of his forehead. Daniel's feet turned from rubber to something looser, less well-defined, jelly perhaps. Oh no, he didn't want to see, no, no, he tried to speak and succeeded in emitting a heavy, furry, slithering sound.

"Do you want to touch her?"

No, he really didn't think so—

"Shall I take you to her?"

Oh Christ oh shit oh. More sounds came out, wet, bubbling liquid sounds. He was rocking backward and forward as if in a strong wind.

Closer. Another smell, the sweet, waxy smell of aftershave.

(*Run*)

VIRGINS *and*
MARTYRS

Sodding bloody bastard fucking shithole *feet*—
*(Run)*
"—don't listen to what your momma say,
you got to love me, love me—"
*(before it's)*
"—love me the right way."

Slurred, toothless, gummy murmuring, rocking backward, forward, backward blessed Mary ever Virgin, blessed Michael the Archangel, blessed John Baptist, the holy apostles Peter and Paul, and all the saints

*(before it's)*

He felt an arm dropping over his shoulder.

### chapter twenty-eight

There were candles on either side of her, tall yellowish tallow candles, and piled round her feet masses of brittle, brown, crumbling flowers. Incense rose up to the great vaulted, gilded ceiling. Flies buzzed around, held at bay by the smoke. This end of the ballroom was sheltered from any wind and the smoke went straight up. The sound of the rain was strong, gusting against the rotten wood and cracked glass, the wind rattling the frames and singing through the holes in the ceiling and floor. The waves boomed underneath, and the structure shivered and moaned.

Wendy was inside a kind of alcove to one side of the stage, screened off by a projecting part of the wings. The original plush and gilt was still largely intact, the boxes and galleries emerging from the surrounding gloom, the great dome of the ceiling poised overhead like a vast black cloud.

She wore a crown made of twisted metal strips, and in her right hand she held a withered, long-stemmed flower. She was spread out in an attitude that he knew well, had seen before in the library. Crucified. Her hand had been nailed to the plaster of the wall, the wrist had also been tied with wire. She wore an ankle-length white dress. Her head was shaved, and there was a veil pushed back over it. She was hanging forward asymmetrically, because, he saw, one arm had come away, was missing. He could see the nail still in the wall and the loop of wire. Her dress was torn at the shoulder.

"If this was a cathedral, then we would be standing in the ambulatory. Historically—I know this is of interest to you, Daniel—the ambulatory started out merely as a kind of porch at the rear of the altar where the side aisles met, and gradually grew until it had become a fully fledged semicircular arena, lined with niches and chapels. It was intended to take the relics of saints, to allow the pious to come and look at them, touch them."

I don't want to see, I don't—

"If the fragment—and they were rarely more

VIRGINS *and*
MARTYRS

than that—was of a bone of the foot, then the reliquary would be in the shape of a boot, jeweled, enameled, inlaid with gold. If of a hand, then the form would be a glove; if of a bone of the skull, a head. There would be a glass window at the top to display the sacred tissue. The smaller ones would be kept—"

Daniel found that his head was being held, that he couldn't move his *head*.

"—in a movable box, a feretory. Also inlaid and highly decorated. People came, would come from hundreds of miles away in the most difficult conditions, risking illness and injury and robbery, and not infrequently murder, on the dangerous roads, spending huge sums of money, just to see these things."

The grip on his head increased, he was being pushed toward her.

"To touch them."

Her face loomed into view, a hideous leather mask, teeth protruding from the withered lips, blackened tongue jutting obscenely from the teeth. Some of the teeth appeared to be missing. The eyes had sunk down into their sockets, and the nose was horribly wrong, broken.

"There ought to be a book called *Handy Hints for Home Embalmers*, but I'm afraid there isn't. I found out what I could but it's not a professional job, as you can see. The jaw's starting to come away, do you see? What you need to do is to get a thread between the inside of the lip and the gums and up through the nose, the septum. You have to get the needle out through one of the nostrils, through the septum, then out the other nostril, you see? Like this."

don't, don't show me

"...then back down behind the lip. Problem is though that if you puncture the skin you'll get burns from the embalming fluid, so I didn't risk it. Too late now really. And I should have padded behind the eyes, stop them sinking down so far. As for the rest of her—"

don't tell me

"—I did the best job I could, but I left it a bit too late. You need to get the blood out before it starts to clot, otherwise you never get the color right. I was trying for a two-point job, just axillary vein and artery. In the armpit. But she needed much more than that by the time I got started. I should really have given her a full six-point, axillary, carotid and femoral *and* I needed better drainage. Should have used more fluid, less concentrated. And of course you need to puncture the internal cavities and drain the contents *before* you try to introduce the fluid. I can do a much better job now, don't you worry. But that explains the smell, I'm afraid. Live and learn."

The skinhead's voice was fading, coming from a long way away.

"The biggest mistake though is all too obvious I'm afraid. You'll have noticed already that she has

VIRGINS and
    MARTYRS

only one arm remaining. There's a leak in the ceiling overhead, do you see? and water got into the joint and it just came away. I was adjusting her position and it just came clean away. Nothing to be done about it."

the flesh cool and closely packed

"Never quite perfect. Maybe that's why nothing ever happened. Never quite perfect." He seemed to be talking more to himself than to Daniel, who could feel himself falling, feel strong arms around him.

"OK feller."

The voice snapped back, businesslike again.

"Let's get you lying down. Open wide."

gaa-ah-ah, nice little yellow pills

"Now swallow. Come on now." He felt his throat being massaged, gagged.

"Daniel we haven't got all night."

He swallowed. He was sat down on the floor against the wall. Too late

*(too late yes)*

too late. He could have wept.

The skinhead was putting his yellow rubber gloves on. No real risk of infection, but better to be safe.

He hadn't expected much. He hadn't imagined there would be great beams of light in the sky or visions of the Virgin Mary or anything of that sort. When it came, he thought, it would be subtle and

*simon maginn*

beautiful, and completely unmistakable. Something would happen, there would be something that he could see: that was all he wanted. It wasn't so much to ask was it? *Ostende nobis Domine.* Show us, Lord. Something clearer than that fuzzy hand holding out that unidentifiable glowing thing anyway.

He had spent hundreds of hours here, watching, waiting. He had witnessed every event in her history, every stage of decay. The changes after death, that universal performance, usually given in secret, had played out for him here, on this stage, in this ruined theater. He'd sat, listening to the waves and the wind, ready for the miracle to happen.

Waiting in vain. She must have been imperfect in some way. He must have been wrong about her. She too must have been lacking in faith.

Anyway, no use dwelling on it. He would just have to try again.

He mounted the platform. There was a steady hissing now as the rain pelted down onto the rotten surface of the building, and a leak started up overhead, dropping down from the towering ceiling onto the mossy floor with explosive, reverberant splats that echoed round the deserted galleries and passages. The wind was tearing at the loose timber and rattling the boards, sending huge billowing drafts up from the floor.

And was there another sound as well? The rustling of dry paper?

VIRGINS *and*
MARTYRS

He listened intently, his eyes fastened on that crowned, leathery mask in front of him, the mask with eyes that were, surely, sunk less deeply now, which were regarding him with an expression like—

He stood on the platform—she was no more than a foot away from him. And he was suddenly sure that her position had changed. The light was very uncertain, candles and the periodic throbbing of the hurricane lamp, plus the beam of his own headlamp, but wasn't her head tilted slightly toward him now? He felt a sudden, sick thrill in the pit of his stomach.

He was certain. He could hear her voice, she was telling him something: he put his ear to her mouth, trying to catch the faint, whispering voice. He touched her hand.

Could it be?

He untied the rope at her wrist and she slumped forward, the nail in her right hand slipping out effortlessly. He held her up and backed down off the platform; the crown and veil fell sideways and rolled away out of sight into the darkness. He stumbled, the hurricane lamp toppled over, the glass shattering over the floor. He held her under her arm and behind her back.

*(look look)*

He carried her out, shoving the doors open, and the wind hit him in the face. Her white dress was surging and billowing and in the sudden darkness

*simon maginn*

outside he was more certain than before that there was some kind of expression in her eyes. Exaltation, rapture.

*(Look!)*

He looked out to sea. The deck was potholed and uneven, sloping crazily in places. The sea was a heaving black swell underneath, pulling and sucking at the iron columns. The rail was sagging badly all over the place. He carried her to the edge of the deck.

*(Do you see?)*

There, out at sea. Was there something? It grew quickly, becoming clearer, he could make out some of the details already. He could even see the colors, beautiful, vivid, against the black sea and sky. Scarlet, saffron, deep ochres and blues, all edged and decorated with flashes of gold. A fleet of barges. They came closer, they swept past, the wind from their passage stroking his face with savage blows. He leaned further out. A procession: and in the last boat a throne covered in scarlet silk, and round the throne was a rainbow that looked like an emerald. A figure sat in the throne, he appeared like jasper and carnelian. His arm was outstretched. The skinhead took a step further and the wood groaned and twisted under him. Wendy was at his side, her eyes flashing out a message, was it some kind of fierce joy? The flames were getting stronger behind him, the rotten timbers of

VIRGINS *and*
MARTYRS

the ballroom effortlessly catching light from the spilled kerosene of the hurricane lamp.

The figure wore a monk's cowl; and as the boat swept by, propelled by the regular beating of the oarsman, he took off the hood.

*(Yes! Look!)*

The skinhead looked and a scream tore itself from his mouth as the exquisite vision crumbled, came apart, the face behind the hood leering wolfishly with a mad, ferocious hate in its eyes. The outstretched hand grabbed him, pulled him forward; he stumbled again, held onto the rail.

Exaltation? More like triumph.

He was flung forward and for a moment he was in balance, with Wendy ragefully, triumphantly beside him, then they were falling, and he was received onto one of the rusting foundation poles, speared. He screamed and the blood bubbled into his mouth. He reached for Wendy—she was a few feet away, floating in the furious sea. Her eyes were blank again, dead, all expression gone. His arm reached for her, and his mouth moved. Almost. Almost perfect. A great black wave took him, covering him, filling him, burying him, as the barges swept away, out into the hissing blackness.

The fire was spreading quickly, taking the floorboards and the sagging windows, licking round the holes in the glass. Smoke rose up through the ceiling, mingling with the incense, swirling in the draft from the roof.

Daniel was lying still, and the flames danced in front of his eyes, beautiful, living, audacious forms, colors swarming and fusing and spinning, and the tremendous hissing from outside was challenged now from within, a hungry, thrilling roar.

Then someone was with him, holding him, *kissing* him for God's sake! He lay motionless as the arms supported him and the warm, wet mouth moved over him, sweet drafts of air blowing through him like breezes through a forest. Lovely!

Outhwaite satisfied himself that Daniel was breathing and picked him up, appalled that it should be so easy, that he should weigh so little.

He carried him out onto the deck and ran round to the other side, away from the flames which were threatening to engulf the entire structure, in spite of the pelting rain. The wind was fanning the flames, spreading them around like a grinning arsonist. He found the hatch and the rope and, hoisting Daniel over his shoulder in a fireman's lift, began the dangerous descent. His priority was just to get out of the reach of the fire and smoke, and it was a surprise when he saw the yellow dinghy tied obediently to a post.

He laid Daniel down into it and cast off, pulling as hard as he could away from the pier, the flames

VIRGINS *and*
MARTYRS

breaking through now from windows and doorways, glass shattering as the heat grew, pieces of burning timber falling into the sea, great jagged colorful reflections spattering the waves.

He rowed steadily but fast, and Daniel lay quiet as the world spat and flickered and roared around him.

### chapter twenty-nine

"They did a study. In Finland," said the Dowager.

"Oh yes?"

They were sitting outside the hospital on the step by the bins in the sunshine, smoking like chimneys. The Dowager alternately smoked and drank from a quarter of Three Barrels brandy. The Dowager's friend alternately smoked and coughed, shaking and convulsed, until she was exhausted and red-eyed.

"The people who smoked lived till they were a hundred."

The woman looked at her as steadily as her condition allowed.

"Are you sure?"

"Oh yes," the Dowager said, having a little cough herself.

"I never heard that before," said her friend, and regarded her suspiciously. She was beginning to think the old woman was drinking too much.

"My lollipop likes a little smoke. I blow it at her and she breathes in. You can see her little ears flapping."

"Oh yes?" Maybe it was more than just the alcohol, the other woman was thinking. Maybe she's mad. The smoke hung around them, a warm fragrant fog.

The launderette was quiet as the three by the door slept, the cans scattered round their feet. Someone came in, laden with carrier bags of washing and box of powder, and one of the three stirred and said "Kiss me nurse." Up at the university library someone was scratching a message into the wood of his enclosure: "Life's a bleach and then you dye." There were other messages dotted around, faded and half obliterated with newer ones scrawled on top. One of them seemed to involve the word "decomposing," and he leaned forward to read it. He looked up suddenly, startled by a small sound from a nearby stack. Nothing. He went back to work.

"Mr. Steadman?"

The taxi driver looked blankly at her. The ward was quiet and dark; he was standing in the middle of the four-bed bay.

"Back to bed now Mr. Steadman. Much too late for all this."

VIRGINS and
MARTYRS

He looked inquiringly at the nurse, peered round the side of her to check that she had both arms. He'd got up to move something out of the way, it had been lying on the floor. He'd gone to it, his face twisted with disgust and horror, and picked it up. What was a thing like that doing in the middle of the floor? What kind of place was this?

"It's all right Mr. Steadman. That's the way."

He cried out, in awful raw terror, and then again, louder.

"Shhhh, now, back to bed now."

### chapter thirty

There were more people at her funeral than Outhwaite had imagined, and more flowers, bright bunches wrapped in cellophane. One particularly sugary confection spelled out the name Wendy in pink carnations. Must have cost a bomb, Outhwaite thought. It was from the Dowager, who was wearing a peculiar navy suit from the 1950s, and an enormous amount of jewelry. She wasn't entirely steady. Her three dogs were in black collars and leads, bought specially for the occasion.

There was a quiet, smiling young man with a low hair line whom Outhwaite didn't recognize; he kept his hands resolutely in the pockets of his black denim jacket throughout the interment and winked when Outhwaite met his eye. Daniel was also in only a very approximate version of mourning, and his trousers and shoes looked distinctly seedy. He was well enough to stand and walk now, and was eating again, though he still refused to handle money. His face was horribly gaunt, and there was a quality to his eyes that Outhwaite didn't care to dwell on. He was starting to use his left hand again, though with considerable reluctance.

Outhwaite had visited him in hospital a few times, and had accompanied him home when they discharged him. The door had been boarded up and the glass cleared away. There had been a pile of junk mail, catalogues and special offers, addressed to Julie Park and Denise T. Montgomery. They'd gone up to his room. A peculiar, delicate smell was lingering on the stairs, and Outhwaite stiffened, ready for anything. He opened the door, and the smell was stronger. Daniel had peered around and seemed to be looking for something. Outhwaite finally saw a small plastic case under the table and Daniel took it thankfully. His contact lenses.

On the table he'd found the cause of the smell: Wendy's plant had flowered, small, sweet-smelling blossoms. He'd held it as he and Outhwaite stood in the clean, empty room and Daniel had said: "It wasn't anything to do with me. It was just between the two of them. She was just trying to draw atten-

tion to herself, so she'd be found so you'd find *him*.
You don't believe any of this do you?"

Outhwaite shrugged. Belief, disbelief, what did
it matter? The case was closed, and he'd been wrong,
disastrously wrong.

"I thought it was you," he said to Daniel, "I
thought you'd killed her." Daniel accepted it as a
confession, said nothing. The skinhead's cause of
death was massive internal bleeding and trauma
caused by impalement. Wendy's death certificate
said primary cause of death unknown, but second-
ary cause was severe malnutrition. The coroner was
happy that no further investigation was needed.

Outhwaite was given compassionate leave. He
took Sean out for rides in the car, held his hand,
talked to him. He and Karen were to have a week
in the Algarve, just the two of them.

Daniel applied for and was given a further extension on his dissertation: the slip of paper was
signed by Calvin Medway and spoke of "exceptional
personal circumstances." He thought that sounded
about right.

The coffin containing the corpse of Wendy
Bishop, including her arm, though in a condition
that an undertaker would describe as "bad remains,"
was lowered into the raw earth. Daniel threw down
a flower, and Loulie, nearly at term and almost mad
with the strain on her little kidneys, leaped snarl-
ing into the hole and set up a mighty growl.

*simon maginn*

"Lollipop!"

The old woman giggled and reached unsteadily down for the dog, who bared her teeth and howled, completely out of control.

"Loulie! Come here this minute."

She looked round at the shocked faces and giggled.

"Sorry everyone. *Bad* girl."

After the funeral, Outhwaite brought Daniel home to No. 8. Daniel had rung his mother and told her, without saying exactly why, that now would be a good time for that visit. She'd understood that he had been in some kind of trouble and was coming down straight-away. He was expecting her later that evening.

He and Outhwaite sat in the kitchen and Daniel offered tea, which Outhwaite declined.

"Will you be OK?" Outhwaite asked and Daniel said yes, of course, he was fine. Never felt better. And it was true. He felt intensely alive and excited, somehow; the drugs were out of his blood now, leaving him wired and energetic and purposeful. He wanted to get on.

Outhwaite shook his hand and patted his shoulder and muttered something about taking it easy son, and left.

Daniel went upstairs. The light in the house seemed clearer and stronger than previously. He shut

VIRGINS *and*
MARTYRS

his bedroom door behind him and sat on the bed. The scraps of his dissertation lay in a pile on the table, waiting to be cleared away. He went over and picked up a handful.

A surge of excitement hit him as he realized that now he could start again, from scratch. A completely fresh start, a rebirth. It would be marvelous.

A flash of memory came to him, a fragment of something about the pier, then fell away again. Outhwaite had explained to him what had happened, had done his best to describe it: the pier, then the hospital, the stomach pump, the thirty-six hours asleep. Daniel took his word for it; his throat was raw from the tubes and his belly felt bruised and pulverized. He had no reason to doubt it, but he couldn't actually remember. The reality of it was only now beginning to filter through the drug-induced amnesia, like flashes of light reflected from a mirror ball. For now, all he could recall was a picture, a woman standing on a stage, and smoke. It would all come back eventually. He would wait.

On one of the scraps in his hand were the words "sword-blow to the depths of my breast," and Daniel recalled the passage it came from, a section of Prudentius' *Crowns of Martyrdom*. He knew it by heart:

"This lover, this one at last, I confess it, pleases me. I shall meet his eager steps halfway and not put off his hot desires. I shall welcome the whole length of his blade into my bosom, drawing the sword-blow to the depths of my breast; and so as Christ's bride I shall overleap all the darkness of the sky and rise higher than the ether. O Eternal Ruler, open the gates of heaven which formerly were barred against the children of earth, and call, O Christ, a soul that follows Thee, a virgin's soul and a sacrifice to the Father!"

Could that be right? These were supposed to be the final words of St. Agnes, faced by her executioner after a torture so violent and prolonged that it became absurd. She seemed rhapsodic, exultant, ecstatic! Was that how it felt, to be a martyr?

He recalled the thin, high, dizzy winds that had swept through him when he was starving; he could almost remember the rush as the Haloperidol had hit, and again the delirious clarity after the purging of the stomach pump. Ecstasy.

He glanced down at his hands: he was clutching scraps of the dissertation so hard that his sweat was leaching the ink out of the paper, staining his fingers. He shook the pieces away.

He was finished with reading, for good.

He had been approached earlier in the day by a keen-eyed youth who had pressed an amateurish-looking leaflet into his hands.

"Do *you* want to discover the Real purpose you aren't even yet AWARE of, the forces that shape the world and DIRECT IT! Politics, science and

VIRGINS *and*
MARTYRS

the satan-directed so-called RELIGIONS try to conceal the forces. When you become conscious you will acknowledge that these are Real and True, and UNIVERSAL!"

There was an address at the bottom, and a date and a time, and a badly drawn flower with little symbols in each of the petals, and an eye in the center.

The youth held Daniel's eye, and Daniel had felt between them a commonality, a sense that they were alike because they were so different from all the others swarming around them. The youth, Daniel felt, recognized this. They were both looking for something beyond books, beyond patient scholarship and humble reason. Daniel watched the fever flickering in the youth's eyes and said yes, he would come, and the youth had touched him lightly on the left shoulder.

A new purpose. A new method. He picked up the pile of torn paper and stuffed it into a big bag.

A few weeks later a car pulled up at the cemetery and two men got out. They walked in bright sunshine to the grave of Wendy Bishop, where the soil was still fresh and brown and the flowers were drying and wilting. One of the men held a bunch of freesias and pinks tightly.

They reached the grave and the flowers were placed carefully near the headstone by the younger of the men, who was stiffly dressed and held himself awkwardly, his head ducking down repeatedly.

The older man took the younger man's hand and gently placed it on the headstone, holding it there for a few seconds. His eyes were closed and his lips were moving. They stayed a few minutes longer, then walked back to the Rover.

By the car the younger man broke the silence, speaking in a harsh, curiously modulated voice.

"How many graves are there here? Do you think there are more than a hundred? Do you think there are more than two hundred?"

Outhwaite ignored the question and climbed into the car, whistling "Moon River." It was not the first time he'd brought Sean here, and it would not be the last. Nor were they the only visitors: On their last visit they had seen an old woman pushing a young girl in a wheelchair. The old woman wore the grim, ingrained optimism of the true believer. Outhwaite had nodded "hello" to her as they passed.

Sean fastened his seat belt, and Outhwaite patted his arm, staring out at the well-tended grass and neat paths. He would come again.

### chapter thirty-one

The beach was a furnace. Everywhere you looked you were confronted with oiled, baking flesh. Self-basting, seemingly. The reek of coconut oil fought with the smell of pheromones, as muscled young men lusted inside their Speedos and glossy, leathery-skinned women insouciantly, unselfconsciously bared their breasts and shouted at their children. This late in the year, after the August Bank Holiday, people were either deep chestnut brown or defiantly, unrepentantly bone white. Lone wolves hung about by the promenade railings and along the groynes, in brightly colored shorts. One wore a baseball cap which bore the words "Just Do It," contributing his own strand to the lubricous, libidinous atmosphere.

The pier lurked even more malevolently since the fire. There had been little real damage, except to a section of the ballroom facing east, but there was a great deal of smoke discoloration, and there were now more broken windows, more Danger! signs, more ruination.

Two little girls were splashing in the sea at a safe distance: they were in bright pink and bright yellow respectively, and their hair was in bobbles. They were daring each other to go nearer and nearer. There was a monster on the pier. He was three feet tall and hunchbacked and he hobbled around with a stick. He lived there all the time. Sometimes at night he came off and rowed ashore in a boat. Then he took people back to the pier and kept them there. Sometimes he ate them alive,

*simon maginn*

sometimes he just kept them. You could see them staring out of the windows.

Debbie splashed Louisa, and she screamed. The sound echoed back from the blackened hulk, a dead, flat, booming ghost of sound, and Louisa screamed again when she heard it.

"That's him. He listens to what you do and then he does it straight back again," said Debbie, and Louisa fiddled with her bobble and wondered whether to believe her.

"Let's do it again," she said, and they counted three and screamed together, as loud and long as they could, until their mothers came to drag them away and feed them ice cream and Coke. The pier screamed and laughed back. Soon it would be dark.

*the end.*

VIRGINS and
MARTYRS

## biography.

SIMON MAGINN was born in Liverpool in 1961, and is the youngest of five children. He studied music at the University of Sussex and still teaches music when he isn't writing. Maginn finished his first book, *Sheep*, in 1993, and his unique voice and ability to appeal to the horror market made him an immediate success. Following *Virgins and Martyrs*, Maginn has completed a third novel, entitled *A Sickness of the Soul*.

# SHEEP

"He's given the
horror genre
novel a badly
needed blood
transfusion."
— Campbell
Armstrong

James and Adele arrive in west Wales,
hoping to heal from the trauma of their
daughter's death. Together with their
son Sam, they settle into a deteriorating
farmhouse, with intentions of rebuilding
and renovating it. They are shocked to
find that the former occupants ended
their lives in a vicious cycle of drugs,
madness, and murder.

Horror
Paperback
ISBN 1-56504-910-1
WW10001
October 1996
$5.99 US/$7.99 CAN

As the renovations proceed, strange
events and behaviors are linked to the
family, raising questions. James digs up
some odd-looking bones. Sam has a fall
and sees something incredibly disturbing,
while Adele's behavior is inexplicably
linked to the increasingly bizarre content
of her paintings.

BOREALIS

Meanwhile, the mysterious contents of
the freezer wait to be discovered....

WHITE WOLF
PUBLISHING

Written by Simon Maginn